A CORNISH WINTER'S KISS

JO BARTLETT

Boldwood

First published in Great Britain in 2025 by Boldwood Books Ltd.

Copyright © Jo Bartlett, 2025

Cover Design by Head Design Ltd

Cover Illustration: Adobe Stock, Shutterstock and iStock

The moral right of Jo Bartlett to be identified as the author of this work has been asserted in accordance with the Copyright, Designs and Patents Act 1988.

All rights reserved. No part of this book may be reproduced in any form or by any electronic or mechanical means, including information storage and retrieval systems, without written permission from the author, except for the use of brief quotations in a book review. This book is a work of fiction and, except in the case of historical fact, any resemblance to actual persons, living or dead, is purely coincidental.

Every effort has been made to obtain the necessary permissions with reference to copyright material, both illustrative and quoted. We apologise for any omissions in this respect and will be pleased to make the appropriate acknowledgements in any future edition.

A CIP catalogue record for this book is available from the British Library.

Paperback ISBN 978-1-83678-128-8

Large Print ISBN 978-1-83678-127-1

Hardback ISBN 978-1-83678-126-4

Ebook ISBN 978-1-83678-129-5

Kindle ISBN 978-1-80483-999-7

Audio CD ISBN 978-1-83678-121-9

MP3 CD ISBN 978-1-83678-122-6

Digital audio download ISBN 978-1-83678-125-7

This book is printed on certified sustainable paper. Boldwood Books is dedicated to putting sustainability at the heart of our business. For more information please visit https://www.boldwoodbooks.com/about-us/sustainability/

Boldwood Books Ltd, 23 Bowerdean Street, London, SW6 3TN

www.boldwoodbooks.com

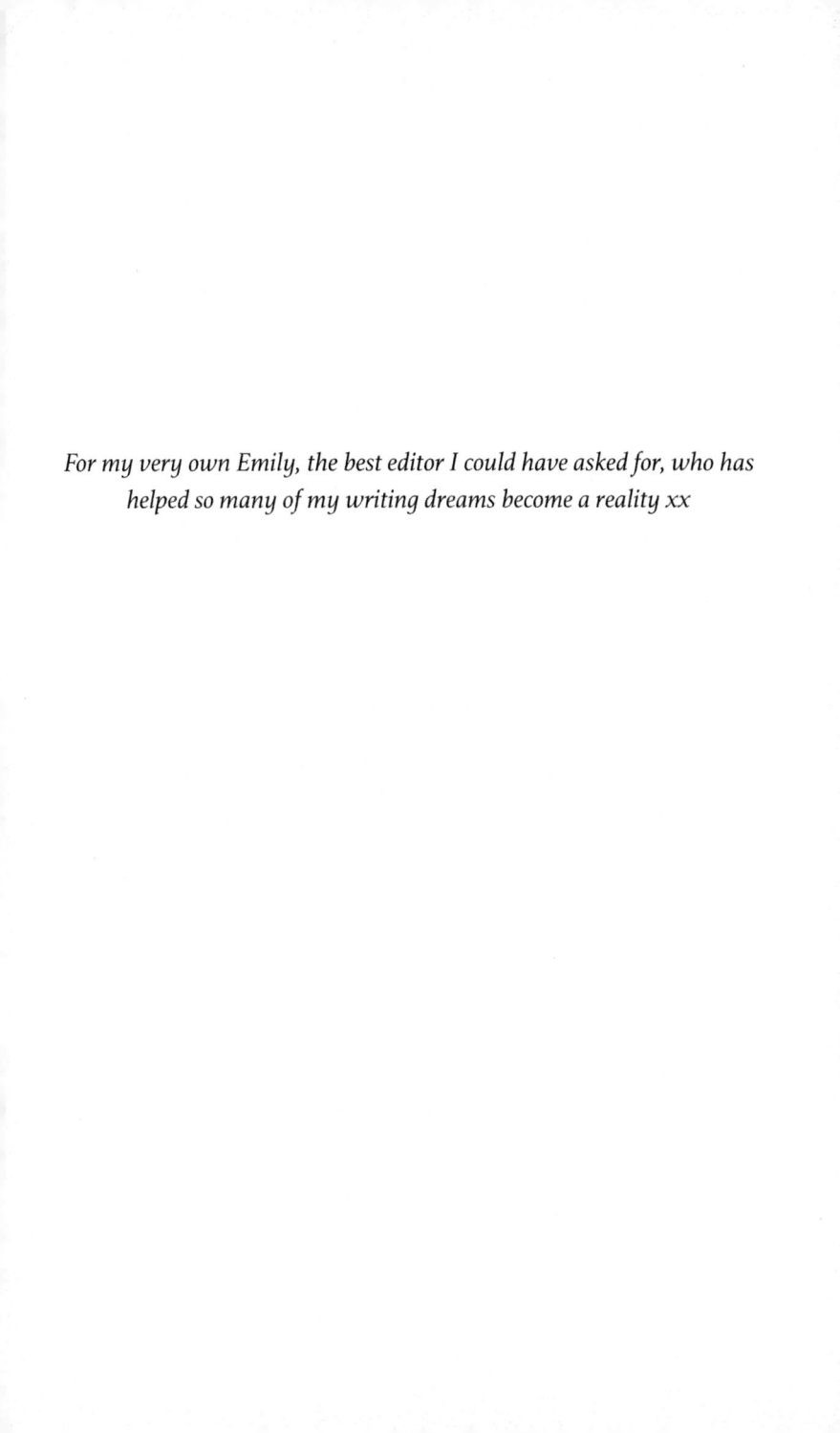

For my very own Emily, the best editor I could have asked for, who has helped so many of my writing dreams become a reality xx

1

Ever since she was a child, Emily had been certain that one day a magical moment would change everything. She'd meet the person capable of altering the entire path of her life and, when their eyes met, she'd know that this was it. Okay, so she was still waiting, and her certainty might have wavered a long time ago if she hadn't watched almost every romcom ever made and devoured romance novels like her life depended on it. They were her escape whenever things got tough and they'd saved her during the most difficult time of her life.

Emily had been fifteen when her mother, Patsy, had been involved in a car accident that had threatened to tear her whole family apart. Patsy had been in a coma for five days, and the road to recovery was gruelling, painful and terrifying. Emily's father had been forced to keep working full time to pay the bills, and her older sister had just left home to start university. So it was Emily who sat by Patsy's bedside for days on end, not knowing if or when the mother she adored would ever fully come back to her. The doctors had warned them that the head injury she'd sustained might change her forever, but Emily couldn't bear for that to happen, and she'd promised herself she'd do whatever it took to get the mum she knew back.

Emily had been there to help with physio and all the practical support her mother needed. She didn't mind that her entire life consisted of going to school and coming straight home to care for her mum, or that she never got to see her friends. Prior to the accident, Patsy's two main passions had been reading and listening to music. Before Emily left for school, she'd put the radio on for her mum, but as soon as she got home, she'd turn it off and sit down to read to her instead. Patsy had always been obsessed with the Brontë sisters and Emily had reread the classic novels to her first, but then they'd moved on to paperbacks that she'd picked up from a charity shop in the next road to her school. She'd always pick cheerful stories, with colourful covers, that promised both her and her mother an escape from the harsh realities of what they were going through. Family holidays were on hold indefinitely and, for the best part of a year, Emily was almost as housebound as her mother. But it was those romance novels that had transported them both to another world. Emily could lose herself in the stories, living a completely different life through the characters' eyes. She'd travelled the world without ever leaving home and had worked her way through countless careers, when in reality she didn't even have time for a paper round. Best of all, the stories guaranteed the kind of happy ending she'd so desperately needed to believe in back then.

Even after her mother eventually made an almost complete recovery, and Emily had managed to put the whole experience behind her, that love affair with a happy ever after had never waned. She didn't care if some people thought she should be reading Tolstoy or Virgina Woolf for it to be worthwhile. Reading was all about joy for Emily, and there was nothing more joyful than a good romance, even if her best friend in the world still didn't understand why she loved those novels so much.

'This is why you're still single.' Jasmine jabbed a finger at the book Emily had just put down on the kitchen worktop. If she could have found a way of reading and chopping vegetables for the stir fry at the same time, she'd have done it. Her inability to put down a book when she was really into it had got her into trouble in the past. She'd stopped borrowing books from the library after dropping one into the bath, and she'd even walked into a lamppost trying to read and walk at the same time.

'Reading is why I'm still single?' Emily ran a hand through her honey-blonde hair and gave her friend a quizzical look. 'If I have to choose between books and a boyfriend, I'll take the books.'

'Hmm, exactly, but it's not even that.' Jasmine's voice was muffled as she reached inside the fridge for some milk. 'It's giving you unrealistic expectations. Real life isn't like a romance novel.'

'More's the pity.' Emily laughed at the look of exasperation on her friend's face as she turned back towards her, milk in hand. 'And there's nothing wrong with not wanting to settle.'

'I'm not talking about settling. I'm talking about expecting some kind of love-at-first-sight encounter where fireworks start exploding in the sky the moment you lock eyes.' Jasmine wrinkled her nose. She was a data analyst, and if something couldn't be explained logically, she wasn't interested. There was nothing she liked better than an algorithm, and the fact that one had matched Jasmine and her now fiancé, Sam, via a dating app made her an even bigger fan.

'It doesn't have to be fireworks, I just don't want to swipe right on an app, that's all. We could just be in a shop, reaching for the same thing, at the same time and...'

'Serendipity.' Jasmine shook her head. 'Seen it. They reach for the same pair of cashmere gloves and then pow, fireworks, and a connection they can't deny. Like I keep saying, Em, life isn't a romance novel, or even a romcom.'

'Okay then, maybe I'll be somewhere, doing something really ordinary, like queuing for the loo, and he'll step aside and let me go ahead. What better way could there be to show who he is?'

'Yeah, but Matthew Perry already did that to Salma Hayek.' Jasmine's voice was monotone. 'Your Mr Right is going to have to be more original than that.'

'For someone who thinks romance novels and romcoms are ridiculous, you certainly seem to know a lot about them.'

'Years of living with you will do that to someone, Em.' Jasmine's face softened. 'I love you, but it's your film choices that have got me addicted to the serial killer documentaries that freak Sam out so much. It's just an antidote to all that saccharine sweetness, but I think he's starting to worry about what he's getting himself into.'

'He just has no idea how lucky he is.' Emily couldn't resist giving her friend a hug, and she smiled to herself when Jasmine squeezed her back. It had taken a while for her friend to be able to be that demonstrative. They'd met at university and clicked immediately because of a shared sense of humour, although they'd already had very different reputations by then. Jasmine was the 'ice queen' according to those not lucky enough to know what good fun she was just below the surface, and Emily was the daydreamer; when her head wasn't in a book, it was in the clouds. They'd shared a student house from year two onwards, and then a flat when they'd both moved to London after graduation for work. Six years on, they were still as different as ever, but they knew and understood one another's quirks.

'He should know how fortunate he is, because I remind him

every day how lucky he is that I swiped right instead of left. It was a close-run thing.'

'You try to pretend it was all algorithms and technology, but we only set up your profile the night you matched with Sam because the open-air concert we were going to was rained off. The same concert where he was supposed to be meeting up with someone else from the app. Then the two of you matched in the meantime and that was it. He never rearranged a date to see her because he'd found you. See, Jas, even with the apps serendipity plays a part.'

'Only inside the mind of a hopeless romantic like you.' Jasmine shook her head again, but she was still smiling. 'At least I'll get to watch as many murder documentaries as I like while you're away.'

'You know you'll miss me really.' Emily nudged her in the side. 'And just in case it gets too much, I've loaded up the planner with a romcom for every mood, from *Fifty First Dates* to *The Proposal*.'

'I'm not going to watch any of them.' Jasmine gave her a pointed look.

'We both know you are.' Emily stuck out her tongue, and Jasmine mirrored the action.

'Just get yourself on that train back to Port Agnes and leave me to my Netflix serial killers.' Jasmine's face was suddenly serious. 'Although I do need you to promise me that you won't fall for a stranger who's waiting to have a documentary like that made about him.'

'I promise.' Emily gave her another hug. She really needed to get going if she was going to make it to Waterloo in time for her train home. She might not have found the love of her life yet, but Port Agnes came pretty damn close.

* * *

Emily defied anyone not to find Waterloo station romantic. It had its fair share of stressed commuters, admittedly, as well as crying children and their frazzled parents, who were desperate to be almost anywhere else, but that could never tell the full story. Waterloo also had trains bound for the southwest coast, the most beautiful part of the country in Emily's opinion. She could have gone from Paddington station and got the train direct to Cornwall, but there were two reasons she always went from Waterloo. The first was that changing at Exeter gave her a chance to meet up with her sister, Charlotte, and the second was the huge station clock. It was something that couldn't be missed, and it had become the perfect meeting point as a result. Sometimes Emily would get to the station early, just so that she could sit on a bench with a view of the clock to observe some of those 'meet me under the clock' moments. She'd seen couples meet for the first time on blind dates, greeting each other with 'It's nice to meet you in person at last' and sometimes even going straight in for a kiss. She'd watched reunions she wasn't ashamed had brought tears to her eyes, and had even witnessed a couple of proposals.

The clock had been there for over a hundred years, and who knew how many couples had experienced their own life-changing moment beneath it. It was no coincidence that its hands were shaped like Cupid's arrows. There was no time to hang around today though. She needed to be in Exeter by one o'clock to meet Charlotte, before heading on to Port Agnes to spend a week with her family. A whole week where she wouldn't have to wonder what the hell she'd done agreeing to take a job at the same firm where Jasmine worked. Spending all day doing things with data that she still didn't fully understand and which had never been part of the plan for her life. It paid far better than her previous job had, although she'd never have taken it for that reason alone.

Emily had loved working in the city library where she'd got her first job after university, surrounded by books and kindred spirits who loved them as much as she did. The library had hosted a wide range of regular events too, from book clubs to parenting groups, aimed at encouraging people to read to their children and build a foundation for a lifelong love of books. It had made Emily feel like part of a real community, even in the midst of a city where she sometimes felt lost. When the local authority had announced it needed to make cutbacks in order to fill a ten-million-pound hole in its budget, Emily had feared that the library might close, and sadly she'd been right. It had happened to so many libraries across the city and she'd known that finding another job like that would be hard, but it had proved to be impossible. When Jasmine had urged her to apply for a post at her firm, just as a stop gap, Emily had decided to go for it, not intending to stay more than six months. Now here she was, eighteen months into a job that was slowly sucking the life from her soul, one data entry at a time. She'd thought about moving back to Port Agnes, but she'd been so certain that she'd find her purpose in London, and it would have felt like admitting defeat to move back home, no matter how much she sometimes wanted to.

'Do you need a hand?' The woman standing in front of Emily on the station platform looked seriously harassed. She had a baby and a toddler in a two-seater pushchair, with a large suitcase wedged underneath, half of it overhanging at the back and bashing her legs every time she tried to walk.

'Thank you so much.' The woman seemed to sag with relief.

'My husband was supposed to be here, but he's got the flu and I promised I'd go back home with the kids for my dad's seventieth birthday. I thought it would be okay, but I've got no idea how I'm going to get these two and our luggage on the train by myself.'

'I can put your case and mine in the luggage rack, and then come back and help you with one of the children, if you like?' Emily smiled, but when she sensed a tiny bit of hesitation from the woman in front of her, she said the first thing that came into her head. 'It's okay, you can trust me. I've got a DBS check and I used to run a parent and toddler group at one of the libraries.'

Emily flushed bright red. Why the hell was she talking about DBS checks? It made her sound as if she was a dodgy character trying to cover something up. The woman held her gaze for a moment and then started to laugh, lifting the last of the tension from her face.

'Well, how can I say no to that? Thank you so much. My name's Bella, the baby is Max and this little madam' – she gestured towards the toddler, who at that moment was attempting to chew her way through the straps of the buggy – 'is Maple. She's three but acts like she's thirteen most of the time. I've never been bossed about so much in my life as I have since she learned to talk.'

'Great to meet you all. I'm Emily. Shall I get the luggage loaded on the train? We've still got fifteen minutes until it's due to leave, so there's plenty of time to get settled.'

In the end it took less than ten minutes for them to all get onboard and settled. Bella's little family were seated at a table on one side of the carriage, and Emily took a seat on the opposite side, not wanting to sit down with them and seem like the weirdo she'd painted herself to be, with her earnest assurances about DBS checks.

'Thanks so much again, Emily, I don't know what I'd have

done without you.' Bella let go of a long breath, the baby held against her chest as Maple sat in the seat next to her, busily colouring. 'If I wasn't already married, I might have had to propose!'

Bella had a contagious laugh, and Emily couldn't help joining in. If this had been the plot of one of the books she loved so much, Emily would have offered to help Bella when she got off the train, and her handsome, single brother would have been waiting to pick her and the children up. He and Bella would invite Emily to join them at their father's birthday celebration, and it would be the start of her very own happily ever after. But this chance meeting with Bella and her family wasn't going to be the moment that changed her life. It was just one of those moments that helped solidify what she already knew – that brightening someone else's day invariably brightened hers too. When she eventually worked out what she wanted to do with her life, that was an aspect it needed to contain. She just had no idea how to make it happen yet.

Emily had always quite enjoyed train journeys, at least when she wasn't wedged on to a packed carriage with no available seats, desperately trying to avoid nestling her face into someone else's armpit. That was what came of being five feet one and a half; when you could still shop in the children's department, that half an inch definitely counted. Thankfully, on this occasion, the train was relatively quiet and it wasn't until they reached Salisbury that someone sat in one of the spare seats close to Emily. The woman who sat across the table from her was beautiful, in a way that could only be achieved by winning the genetic lottery. She was probably in her late fifties, or early sixties, although it was hard to tell, with thick, silver-grey hair cut into an immaculate bob and blue eyes that sparkled when she greeted Emily.

'Good morning, is anyone sitting here or is it okay if I take the seat?'

'Please do.' Emily returned her smile and held up the book she'd been reading. 'This book is the only company I've got today.'

Emily regretted the words the moment they were out of her mouth. The woman seemed very nice, and Emily had a feeling she'd be an interesting person if they sparked up a conversation, but you could never tell. She'd given this stranger an open invitation to talk to her, and it would be almost impossible to cut her off even if she turned out to be an over-sharer with no sense of personal space, who wanted to spend the entire journey to Exeter discussing the problems she was having finding the right wormer for her cat. It might seem unlikely, but it was a conversation Emily had been caught in with a man called Graham, on the way back from her last visit home, which had lasted all the way from Exeter to Basingstoke.

'Good book, is it?' The woman raised her eyebrows as she took her seat, and Emily braced herself for a lecture about wasting her time reading stuff like that. She'd had that from strangers before too, and she deliberately kept her expression neutral, despite the fact that she was loving the book and could have waxed lyrical about it for the entire journey if she was given the chance.

'It's great, but I love everything by Sophia Wainwright.'

'Really? Me too.'

'She's brilliant, isn't she?' Emily leant forward in her seat, instantly forgetting her fears about getting embroiled in a boring conversation, delighted to have found a fellow fan. 'I buy every book she writes, as soon as it comes out, and my friend, who works in a bookshop, says she's writing a series set in Cornwall next. I'm so excited that my favourite author is going to be writing a series about my favourite place. I can't wait.'

'I should imagine Cornwall inspires lots of writers, so it's probably no surprise that—'

'Mummy! I wanna story now please, please, please, please.' Maple's plea cut the woman's response off, and Emily turned to see the little girl tugging at her mother's sleeve, while Bella tried to give the baby a bottle.

'Two more minutes and I'll read it to you, sweetheart, okay? Max just needs to finish his bottle.'

'But I want it now!' Maple was clearly desperate for a story, and Emily understood that feeling only too well. She was considering offering to help out, but she didn't want to interfere and make it seem in any way as if she thought Bella couldn't handle the situation, because she was doing an admirable job of managing two children on her own. Then there was a development she couldn't ignore.

'Oh no, not now, Max, please.' Bella's words swiftly followed a sound emanating from Max that could only mean one thing. He'd filled his nappy in no small way.

'Do you want me to sit with Maple and read her story to her while you go and change the baby's nappy?' This time when Emily made the offer, Bella didn't hesitate. The help she'd given them to get on the train was clearly much stronger evidence of her trustworthiness than the mention of a DBS check.

'Oh my God, yes please. Although are you sure you don't want to do a swap?' Bella grinned, holding Max out towards her for a moment, before wrinkling her nose. A smell like overcooked cabbage wafted up as she did. 'This is going to be fun.'

'Thanks for the offer, but I think I'll stick to the reading.'

Emily stood up, returning her smile, and slid into a seat opposite Maple as Bella got up.

'Right, darling, Emily is very kindly going to read you a story while Mummy goes and changes Max's bottom.'

'Max has done a poo poo, Max has done a poo poo.' Maple sang the words and then turned towards Emily to give her an appraising stare. 'Mummy does funny voices when she reads to me. Can you do funny voices?'

'How about this one.' Emily said the words in her best robot voice and Maple burst into peals of laughter even more infectious than her mother's laugh.

'Yes, yes! What else can you do?'

Emily slipped easily into a much heavier version of the Cornish accent than she usually possessed. 'Where I grew up some people have an accent like this. What do you think?'

Maple giggled again and Emily caught the eye of the lady who shared her passion for Sophia Wainwright books, and she was smiling too.

'Shall we read this book then? I'll see how many voices I can do, and you can try some too.'

'I know how to sound like Mummy when she's cross.'

'Do you now?' Emily couldn't help smiling again.

'Pick up some of your toys, young lady.' The little girl affected a serious tone and wagged her finger at Emily.

'Very good. If there's a part for a cross mummy in this story, you'll definitely have to do the voice. Although it really does help Mummy if you can put your toys away sometimes, and it's lovely to be helpful, isn't it?'

Maple gave her a sage nod. 'Yes, but not Max. He only cries and does poo poos.'

It was hard for Emily to read with a smile tugging at the corners of her mouth, but very soon both she and Maple were completely lost in the story. Every so often, Emily would stop and allow the little girl to repeat a line, so that it felt as if she was reading it too. It was a technique Emily had perfected in the readalong sessions at the library, and it was a big hit with most children. Maple was definitely among that number, and when her mother returned with Max, she begged Emily to read the story again on the basis that her little brother hadn't heard it yet and that it wouldn't be fair if he didn't.

'Thank you so much. She loved that.' The gratitude would have been written all over Bella's face, even if her words hadn't spelled it out.

'So did I. Maple's such a character.'

'Tell me about it.' Bella rolled her eyes. 'Although I wouldn't dampen that spirit of hers for the world.'

'She's absolutely perfect. They both are.' It was moments like this when Emily wondered if she should consider a career as an English teacher, but the pondering never lasted long before she decided against it. She wanted to connect to people through the power of books, but not as a teacher. When she fell in love with a story, it was because it brought her joy, and having to stick to a curriculum would have been too restrictive. 'I'll leave you to it then, but you know where I am if you need another nappy change.'

'We're getting off in three stops, thankfully, so we shouldn't have to bother you again, but I really would have been lost without you. You're an angel.'

'It was my pleasure.' Emily's cheek flushed with heat. She always found compliments hard to accept and for that reason alone, it was a relief to be able to move back to her original seat on the other side of the carriage and disappear into the pages of the latest Sophia Wainwright book. She didn't look up again until Bella and Maple called out goodbye, and she got up quickly to help Bella unload her bags and the pushchair from the train.

'You're very kind.' The elegant lady who'd been sitting opposite her since Salisbury nodded, as if to add emphasis to her words, and Emily felt her cheeks flush again.

'Not really.' She always brushed off compliments, but in this case the denial that she'd done anything special was justified. 'I probably enjoyed reading the story to Maple more than she did. I used to work at a library, and we hosted all sorts of community events, but the ones that involved story time were always my favourite.'

'You're very good at it. What made you leave?'

'Redundancy.' Emily sighed. 'I drifted into a job in data entry, because my best friend works at the same company and she got me an interview. It pays the bills, but it's also killing my spirit and I know I need to find something else.'

'You should always attempt to follow your dreams, even if it doesn't work out. That way no one can ever say you haven't tried.' The older woman gave her a thoughtful look. 'So, tell me, if you could do anything for a job, what would you choose?'

'I'm not sure, seeing as no one is going to pay me to read all day.' Emily had to suppress the urge to laugh at the thought. 'I suppose I could train as a proofreader, or even an editor, but I'm not sure I'd have the skills. And looking for mistakes, or things to alter, would ruin the enjoyment for me.'

'There is another way you could get paid for reading, one I might be able to help you out with.' The woman leant forward conspiratorially in her seat. 'I think you'd make an excellent voice actress, reading audio books.'

This time Emily couldn't help laughing, and it was a few seconds before she was able to respond. 'I'd love that, but I can't see anyone wanting to employ me.'

'I would for one.' The expression on the other woman's face was completely deadpan. 'I've recently completed a novel and I'm not happy with any of the samples my publisher sent me of voice artists to record the audio version. None of them have the passion I heard in your voice when you were reading, or the hint of an authentic Cornish accent I can hear when we're talking now. I'd love to put you in touch with the studio my publisher works with, to see what we can set up.'

'Oh my God, really?' Emily was having to hold on to the seat to stop herself from bouncing up and down with excitement as the woman nodded. 'Please tell me this isn't some kind of elaborate prank, because I don't think my heart can take it.'

'No joke, I promise. Have you got a card you can give me, or your name and email address if not?'

'My name's Emily, Emily Anderson, and I'm sure I can find something to write my email address on. I suppose I could always tear off the back cover of this book and write my details on the inside.' She looked at the novel in front of her, contemplating the decision for a moment, before shaking her head and madly rooting through her handbag for something else instead. 'Sorry, I just can't do it, but I must have something else in here.'

'I'm very glad to hear you don't want to sacrifice the cover of your book, and don't worry, I can put your details straight into my phone.' The other woman gave her an amused look and Emily's face flushed red yet again, her words coming out in a rush.

'Sorry, you must think I'm so stupid, not thinking of that, but I'm just so excited, and I still haven't even asked your name or what kind of books you write.'

'I'm Sophia Wainwright and what I write is that.' Sophia laid her hand on top of Emily's book and this time there was no denying the amusement in her eyes.

'You're Sophia Wainwright?' Emily's mouth dropped open as

Sophia nodded, but she was still struggling to believe it. She'd read a lot about Sophia Wainwright and all the photographs Emily had seen of her were shot in an artsy kind of way, with sunlight streaming through a window while Sophia scribbled words into a notebook, or an image of her walking by the sea taken from a distance. There were never any close-up portrait-style ones which would give away her age, or reveal what she looked like in enough detail to identify her clearly, which was why Emily hadn't had any idea she was sitting opposite her favourite author.

'I am indeed, and if you need any evidence that I'm not some kind of mad crackpot, I've got the proof pages of the first book in the Goodwill Cove series right here, ready for one final read through before I confirm that I'm happy for them to go to print.' Sophia pulled the proof pages out of her handbag and Emily caught her breath. She hadn't needed any evidence that Sophia was who she said she was, but now her next novel was right in front of her and it was all Emily could do not to grab hold of it and start reading.

'I can't believe I've met you in person, and I can't tell you how much your novels have helped me at difficult times in my life.' Emily's addiction to Sophia's novels had begun years ago as she'd sat and read to her mother, but she didn't want to gush about how much of a fan she was even more than she had already. She needed to at least act like she was cool enough to be able to narrate one of her novels without letting enthusiasm get the better of her.

'That's really lovely to hear, thank you.' Sophia touched her hand briefly. 'So what do you think? Would you be willing to talk to someone about being involved in recording the first book in the new series?'

'If I could get off this train while it was still moving to get to the studio, I would.' Emily still couldn't believe this was happening, and she was terrified she might wake up any minute and discover it was all a dream.

'It's a deal then.' As Sophia held out her hand and they shook on it, the feeling Emily had always known she would experience one day washed over her. This was it, the moment that was going to change everything and alter the entire path of her life.

2

THREE YEARS LATER

There was something incredibly disconcerting about seeing a life-size cardboard cutout of yourself staring back at you. Jude had never got used to having to walk past his in the foyer of his publisher's offices, his blue eyes staring back at him and his thick, brown hair looking far more carefully styled than it did these days. It was one of five cardboard cut outs, a rogue's gallery of Foster and Friedmann's bestselling authors. There was something so creepy about them, and they made Jude cringe every time, except today the breath caught in his throat for another reason.

His cardboard cutout wasn't there. It had been replaced by one of a woman he knew wrote romantasy, whatever the hell that was, and whose debut novel had only been out for two months. She was standing in his spot, right next to Sophia Wainwright, whose cardboard cutout was sporting a large straw hat, obscuring most of her face, but he'd still recognise her anywhere. For the last four years, he and Sophia had jostled for top spot as their publisher's overall bestselling author. Now it looked suspiciously like he wasn't even in the top five any more, and he was almost certain he knew why his editor had asked him to come in for a meeting. He wanted to address the downward trajectory of sales, and Jude had a horrible feeling he was about to be given some advice he didn't want to take.

'Jude, great to see you!' Marty Daniels had been Jude's editor for almost eight years, and over time they'd become pretty good friends. Whatever disagreements they might have had about his books, and they sometimes did, he'd always felt they were on the same wavelength.

'Good to see you too, Marty.' He shook the other man's hand before taking the seat opposite him. 'What have you done with my cardboard cutout?'

'Ah, you noticed.' Marty's smile didn't quite reach his eyes. 'I thought you always hated that thing.'

'I do, but I know what it means; that I'm selling less than a debut author who writes books about having sex with dragons.'

'That's not what romantasy is.' Marty shook his head. 'And you know how it goes with debuts sometimes. They can be huge, but it doesn't always guarantee ongoing success.'

'Neither does writing fifteen bestselling crime novels apparently.' Jude was well aware that he was being a bit of a dick, but he couldn't seem to help it.

'You said it yourself, your novels are still bestsellers, but I'm not going to lie. The sales are slipping and so are the reviews.' Marty clearly wasn't going to pull any punches. 'And I think we need to look at the plans for the next book in the DCI McGuigan series.'

'What do you mean, *plans* for the book?' Jude was almost at the end of the third book in his new series, and it had been years since he'd had to pitch a novel, or even run the idea past his editor before he started. Marty trusted him to produce the goods, or at least he had done. 'Do I need to speak to Adele?'

Adele James was the marketing manager for Jude's books, and

the three of them met at least once a quarter to review how things were going, but when he thought about it now, they hadn't met for almost six months.

'I've already spoken to her.'

'You had a meeting without me?' Jude's scalp prickled. It had always felt as if Adele and Marty had his back and that they were a team, in it together to make his career a success. He'd been offered his first publishing deal with Foster and Friedmann despite being taken on by an agent who'd turned out to be a fraud. Jude had never felt the need to get another agent as a result. It meant Marty and Adele were his entire support system, and if they were talking about him behind his back, that couldn't be good.

'No, nothing like that. We were at a launch party together, for one of the authors Adele looks after, and we just talked about what we thought might be going wrong.'

'Going wrong?' Jude couldn't seem to stop parroting back what Marty was saying.

'Look, we're all on the same side here, we all want Jude Cavendish and the Cole McGuigan series back there in the number one spot, but you have to acknowledge that the series is losing readers, and the reviews give a clear indication of why. They're not investing in McGuigan's story because the character arc has flatlined. Grizzled cops with a divorce behind them and whose only meaningful relationship is with alcohol are a bit of a cliché. This is your second series and I think readers expect more of DCI McGuigan than to be a replica of the lead character in your first series. When you wrote the first book in the new series it looked like they were going to get something different, but his story has stalled. Readers need to feel invested in his life, not just the murder cases he's working on. The feeling is the stories have become what some readers are calling "unrelentingly downbeat".

We need something to balance all the murders out, and to achieve that I really think McGuigan needs a personal life people care about.'

'Let me guess, you want him to fall in love.'

'The readers do. It's what most people want in life, Jude, and they want it for the characters they're invested in too. They want to see McGuigan finding something to keep him going when everything around him has gone dark, otherwise they'll lose interest. It's just one disturbing murder after another.' Marty sighed. 'You're a brilliant writer, Jude, it shouldn't be too difficult for you to add that aspect in.'

'And what if I don't want to?' There was no *what if* about it; Jude definitely didn't want to do it.

'Then I think this will have to be the last book in the series. We could move on to something fresh instead, to see if that re-engages the readers we've lost, but...' Marty didn't finish the sentence; he didn't have to. There were no guarantees in the world of publishing, and an author was only ever as good as their last book. Jude was signed to one of the biggest publishers in the UK – it had been a dream come true when they'd offered him his first contract – and yet here he was, seriously considering walking away from them because he wouldn't, or couldn't, write his character a meaningful relationship.

'I'm already most of the way through the story.' Jude crossed his arms over his chest, defensiveness creeping into his body language as well as his tone.

'I can look at that with you, see where we could add in this aspect of McGuigan's storyline. It doesn't all need to play out in this novel, but there needs to be enough promise of a relationship to keep the readers coming back for more.'

'No.'

'Look, Jude, I really think you should—'

He cut Marty off before he could finish. 'I mean I want to do this on my terms. If I've got to give McGuigan some kind of love interest, I at least need to feel I've done it my way. I'll go back over what I've done and see where I can weave it in.'

'Okay, if that's the way you want to play it, but it needs to feel authentic, and you could do worse than look at the work of some of our authors whose books focus on relationships.' Marty pushed his glasses up his nose, an earnest look in his eyes as he slid a book across the table towards Jude. 'This is Sophia Wainwright's latest. The most recent book in her Goodwill Cove series has been our number one best seller this year.'

'I don't read romance.' Jude couldn't stop his lip from curling slightly as said the word, and he didn't move to pick up the book Marty had slid towards him. He only had to see the covers of those kinds of books to feel irritated. They brought back too many memories of sharing his flat, and his life, with a woman who'd claimed to believe that anyone could live happily ever after if they wanted to. The trouble was, the characters in those books were never ordinary people; they sold a dangerous fantasy that real people, living real lives, could never live up to. Jude certainly hadn't been able to, not in Mia's eyes anyway. Now, when he saw someone reading books like that on the Tube, he couldn't help wondering if they really believed in all that sickly-sweet happy ever after stuff, where love conquered all. Somehow, he doubted it, and he knew first-hand what a load of crap it was. Love didn't conquer all, and it was never unconditional either; there were always caveats. Lots of them.

'Well, maybe it's time to try.' Marty shrugged. 'Switching up the genres you read might help freshen up your writing. It can't do any harm, and what's the worst that could happen?'

'I could end up splashed across the papers for murdering my

editor in cold blood.' Jude raised his eyebrows, and for the first time Marty's smile reached his eyes.

'Oh, and what would your weapon of choice be? We must have seen nearly all of them across your books.'

'I don't think I've ever had a murder where the victim was beaten to death with a romance novel.' Jude's tone was deadpan and he tried not to question what it was about him that made the idea of that storyline so much more appealing than giving his lead character a successful relationship.

'I don't think we have seen that yet.' Marty was still smiling, but then he fixed Jude with another of his 'this-is-no-joke' looks. 'Are you confident you can you still deliver the first draft by January?'

'Once I've read this it should be a piece of cake.' Jude picked up the Sophia Wainwright novel gingerly, as if it might suddenly grow teeth and bite him. 'After all, how hard can romance writing be? The plot's the same in every single one of these things.'

'Hmm. Lots of people seem to think writing romance is easy, but you don't see any of them on the bestseller lists with Sophia, do you?' Marty gave him a wry smile. 'But you're a talented author, Jude, and I really hope you're right about how easy this is going to be. Either way, I'm sure you can pull it off and get your cardboard cutout back on display where it belongs.'

'What better motivation could I ask for than that?' Jude shook his head, not willing to acknowledge the tiny part of him that wanted to see his cardboard cutout the next time he walked into the offices. He might hate the sight of it, but it signalled success and when success was all you had, the thought of losing it was terrifying.

* * *

If Jude's life had been a Hollywood movie, he'd have been surrounded by lots of balls of screwed-up paper; abandoned attempts to revise the story, discarded in a fit of rage each time he realised just how terrible they were. Highlighting and deleting great swathes of text on his laptop wasn't nearly so poetic, but that was what he seemed to have spent most of his time doing lately, and DCI McGuigan wasn't the only one taking comfort in the arms of an old friend called alcohol.

The conversation with Marty hadn't been a complete surprise; his editor had mentioned before the start of the new series that readers would need to be invested in DCI McGuigan's personal life for it to have longevity and to feel different to his first series. He'd tried to provide that in his lead character's flirtation with Dr Imogen Matthews, the icily cool pathologist who Cole was thrown into close contact with, but even he could see how wooden their interaction was. He'd spent the best part of the last twenty-four hours trying to escalate the 'romance', if you could call it that, and it was a disaster. Jude could describe the grisliest of murders without missing a beat – the arterial spurt, the puddle of scarlet blood pooling around the victim's body, even the unmistakeable stench of death – but when it came to trying to describe a kiss, he was floundering. Reading back what he'd written, attempt number twenty-seven no less, it all sounded so clinical; more like two robots exchanging data than two people taking their relationship to the next level.

'Jesus Christ!' Jude highlighted the last two paragraphs he'd typed and hit the delete button so hard that his laptop jumped on his desk. He took off the dark-rimmed glasses he was wearing for a moment and rubbed the right-hand side of his temple. This was proving even more of a headache than he'd imagined.

'Maybe I could just get him a dog.' He said the words out loud, despite the fact he was the only person in the room. Getting a dog was something that might humanise Cole McGuigan for readers, and it was something Jude could get on board with too, because his fox red Labrador, Rufus, was undeniably the most important thing in his life. Part of the reason he was finding the whole romance thing impossible to write was because he didn't believe in the forever kind of love that those stories perpetuated. It was a fantasy, a chemical reaction that people tried to build into a lifelong commitment, which more often than not failed.

If someone had asked Jude to explain what he thought about the concept of love, they'd probably assume he was cynical because of what had happened with Mia, but there was more to it than that. He'd been incredibly sceptical long before he met her. He should have listened to his head back then, instead of allowing a chemical reaction to make him forget everything he knew to be true.

They'd met as interns, both of them fresh out of university and trying to take their first steps in a journalism career. Mia had ambitions of working for *Vogue*, and Jude just wanted to write as a way of making sense of the world. They'd moved into a tiny studio flat together, taking on bar work at night to make ends meet and still barely having enough money for food. At first, their situation could have come straight out of one of the romcoms Mia loved so much, and they hadn't needed anything apart from each other.

Sundays, when neither of them worked, had been the highlight of the week. They'd wake up and make love, before going out for a walk and grabbing lunch together. Fancy restaurants were way out of their league, but sharing a portion of chips down by the river had seemed about as good as life got. Afterwards they'd go home again, curl up in front of a movie and just enjoy being together. Mia had been the one to start talking as if their relationship might be 'forever', and she'd also been the first one to say she loved him. Jude had surprised himself when he'd told her that he loved her too, and had realised he meant it. There'd even been a moment when he'd thought that maybe he'd been wrong all these years and that those kind of feelings really could last forever, but then Mia had met Bexter.

Bexter was an internationally renowned fashion photographer, twenty years her senior, who went by his surname, because his first name was the far more mundane-sounding Colin. The first day they met, he invited Mia out to lunch; *in Manhattan*. She'd laughed when she told Jude about it, at just how ridiculous the idea was, and how she'd never have said yes 'in a million years'. Pretty soon, Bexter's name began creeping into the conversation more and more, and that 'million years' Mia had promised became a little over a fortnight. That was when she'd agreed to have dinner, and a whole lot more, with the brand new 'love of her life'. Mia had tried to spin it with those exact words when she'd told Jude she was leaving.

'I didn't mean to fall in love with Bexter, but it was something neither of us could control. Almost as soon as I met him, I knew I'd found the love of my life.' She'd sat doe-eyed and tearful, on the edge of the bed she'd shared with Jude for over a year, and he'd wanted to laugh. What she'd said had been such a cliché, and he'd thought of asking exactly what it was about Bexter that she'd fallen in love with so incredibly quickly. But he already knew. Mia's new love could help make all her career ambitions a reality; he could take her to any restaurant, anywhere in the world, and give her the kind of lifestyle most people didn't even dream of. How could Jude possibly have expected her to say no to that? Only a fool would have turned down that chance, unless it had been for love. Except Mia hadn't really loved Jude; at least nowhere near enough. She'd spelled that out to him, in the midst of what had seemed like a very well-rehearsed goodbye speech.

'I'm so sorry, Jude, but a part of me will always love you.' He hadn't been able to stop himself from laughing at that bit, and a few minutes later Mia had walked out of the door to start a new life with Bexter. Jude had almost wanted to be heartbroken. If he'd been heartbroken, it would have meant he'd loved Mia enough for forever to have been a possibility, but he hadn't. He was hurt, but not heartbroken; not even close. All it had done was reinforce his belief that no one had ever truly loved him, not from the moment he was born. That was the part of his story that could really have broken his heart if he thought about it for too long, but he didn't allow himself that kind of indulgence. Instead, he buried himself in writing his first book and, by the time it was finished, Bexter had moved on to someone even younger than Mia. She'd got in contact, telling Jude it had all been a big mistake and that she wished they could go back to when it had been just the two of them in their cramped little studio flat.

In some ways, Jude had felt sorry for Mia, but he couldn't even pretend that was what he wanted. Not with her, and not with anyone, because love – such as it was – only ever lasted until something better came along, and he didn't want to live his life like that. It wasn't just the romantic kind of love that Jude had serious doubts about. He wasn't sure that anyone could really love another person unconditionally. There was always some kind of transaction involved. He'd learned that lesson as a child, but he couldn't let himself think about that too much either; it wouldn't do any good, and he had work to do.

Jude started typing again.

McGuigan had seen the dog before. The mangy-looking mongrel had taken to hanging out around the bins behind the station, searching for scraps, but he was out of luck. DC Thomson polished up whatever leftovers there might have been long before the trash was taken out. McGuigan kept his voice low as he approached the dog, whose luck was about to change. There was a packet of ham in Cole's pocket, bought with the sole intention of trying to win the dog over. It wasn't the first bribe he'd ever tried to employ, but this time the stakes were far higher than with an informer. The outcome of this particular exchange could change the whole direction of McGuigan's life.

Jude stared at the screen for a moment, before highlighting the text again and pressing the delete button even harder this time. He was never going to pull this off, and it could finish his career if he didn't; Marty had hinted as much. Sloshing another double measure of whisky into his glass, Jude sighed. What the hell was he supposed to do now? Gripping the glass and desperately hoping for some kind of flash of inspiration, he suddenly caught sight of the copy of Sophia Wainwright's novel that Marty had given him.

'For God's sake.' Even the thought of reading it made irritation prickle his scalp, and he took a long slug of his drink, which burned his throat. Forcing himself to reach out, he picked up the book, the cartoon-like cover of two figures intertwined with one another on a deserted beach irritating him even further. Flipping open the front cover, he flicked past the dedication to a letter from Sophia that he could only bear to read the first few lines of:

To my dear readers, thank you from the bottom of my heart for choosing another Goodwill Cove novel. It feels like home to me now and I know it does to so many of you too. I can't wait for you to discover Abigail and Saul's story. It really is the perfect romance!

'Eurgh.' Jude slapped the palm of his hand against his forehead and took another slug of whisky, flicking forward to the first chapter. He got halfway down the second page before he threw the book across the room, just as his phone started to ring.

'Jude, I was just calling to see how the meeting with Marty went.' Adele had been in charge of marketing his books from the very first one he'd written, and he knew her well enough to pick up on the tension in her voice, despite the singsong tone. Jude had neither the time nor the patience for beating around the bush.

'I think you know exactly how it went. He wants me to give McGuigan a romance.' The word felt so unnatural when he said it.

'He doesn't want a romance, he wants a relationship.'

'Same shit different semantics.' Jude sighed.

'So you're not willing to give it a go?' There was a note of caution in Adele's voice now, which spelled out how stupid he'd be to come to that decision without her having to say it out loud.

'I've been trying.'

'Really?' She sounded doubtful, and Jude tightened his grip on the phone.

'Yeah, you might not believe me, but I have. I've been working on a chapter to build the relationship between McGuigan and his pathologist, but it feels so forced.'

'Did Marty have any advice? I could suggest some good examples of—'

Jude cut her off before she could continue. 'He gave me a copy of Sophia Wainwright's latest novel.' He tried to keep his tone even, but the muscles in his jaw had tightened and Adele had clearly picked up on his distaste, despite the fact she couldn't see him.

'I know it's not your thing, but she's at the top of her game, and no one writes relationships better than she does.'

'Really?' Jude switched the phone to speaker mode, setting it down on his desk, before grabbing the book, flicking it open to a random page and starting to read. '"Saul stood on the shoreline, scanning the horizon. No one had heard from Abigail for six long hours, not since she'd launched her boat from the jetty to the west of the harbour at Goodwill Cove. The argument they'd had the night before had felt like the final nail in the coffin for their relationship, but now he knew how wrong he'd been. All he wanted was to hold her and tell her how much he loved her, but he was terrified he might have left it too late."'

Jude shook his head, dropping the book back down onto the desk. 'Is that really a book you'd want to read?' It wasn't the writing itself, it was the fact that anyone could get invested in stories where the happy ever after was guaranteed, when real life almost never worked out that way. He couldn't believe Adele was one of those people.

'It would help if you didn't read it with so much sarcasm. Of course it sounds ridiculous if you say "how much he lurved her" like that.' Adele mimicked the tone Jude had employed and he had to admit she had it spot on, but he couldn't have read the words with a serious tone if his life had depended on it. The trouble was, his career just might.

'That's the way it sounds in my head.'

'Why don't you listen to the audio book instead? Maybe if you hear Sophia's words the way they were intended to be read, you might actually take something from it.'

'Do you really think that's going to make any difference?' Jude could imagine it already. Listening to the sickly-sweet narration of an already saccharine story would almost certainly make it worse rather than better. His stories might be works of fiction too, but he did a lot of research to make them as realistic as possible, spending time interviewing police officers and other professionals involved in murder cases. Although realism probably wasn't what Sophia's readers were after; her novels were pure fantasy in Jude's opinion. Either way, they were never going to be his sort of thing and he couldn't imagine listening to an audio book would do anything to change that.

'Just give it a go. What have you got to lose?' There was that intonation in Adele's words again, the none-too-subtle hint that he stood to lose a hell of a lot more if he *didn't* give it a go.

'Okay, but I think we should get a meeting in the diary to discuss a Plan B if I can't make it work.'

'You need to find a way to make it work, Jude, because we both know a Plan B is always going to be inferior to a Plan A.' Her tone left no room for argument, and it was crystal clear she wasn't prepared to listen to one. 'I want the best for your career just as much as you do, and I'd hate to see you throw away any opportunities you have to get things back on track. I think Marty is planning a group video call for the three of us sometime next week.'

'Right.' Jude nodded, despite the fact she couldn't see him. 'I'll speak to you then.'

'I look forward to it.'

'That makes one of us.' Jude's parting shot made him feel better for all of about five seconds after he ended the call, but none of this was Adele's fault, or even Marty's. They were just asking him to produce what the market demanded, and they couldn't help it if Jude's past experiences made it so hard for him to write about love in any kind of believable way. Adele and Marty were on his side and they just wanted him to succeed, so lashing out at them was stupid. His anger should have been directed somewhere totally different, but raking up old hurt like that wouldn't do him any good either. It wasn't like it could rewind time to when he was a child and set up the kind of life where being loved felt like a certainty. It was better just to bury those feelings, the way he always had done.

When Jude glanced at the laptop, his heart sank. He still wasn't sure he could pull this off, but he'd never been a quitter, otherwise he wouldn't have got this far. He was going to give it his best shot and if Adele really thought that listening to Sophia Wainwright's novel had a cat in hell's chance of helping, he was prepared to give it a go. Clicking on the Audible app on his phone, Jude typed in the title of the latest Goodwill Cove book, desperately trying to keep an open mind as he waited for the book to load. He didn't even get to the end of the first chapter before he realised Adele had been right. It still wasn't the sort of book he'd ever want to read, but the woman narrating the story had a beautiful voice that somehow captured emotions in a way he could make a connection with. He'd found himself having to swallow hard against a lump that had threatened to form in his throat during part of it, and he knew he'd never have felt that way if he'd been reading it himself; his inner dialogue would have been reminding him just how far-fetched it all was, but somehow he forgot about that when he was listening to her. The story sounded completely different when it was being read by someone who clearly had a genuine love for it. If there was a chance, even a small one, that he could find a way of harnessing that kind of connection with the emotion, it might just help him write a believable relationship for DCI McGuigan. Suddenly, he had a whole new determination to try.

3

Emily pulled at the stretchy fabric that was clinging to all the right places, as well as all the wrong ones.

'Maybe if I wore a jacket over it?' She wrinkled her nose as she looked at her reflection again, with Jasmine standing behind her, but her best friend was shaking her head.

'You don't need a jacket, you look fabulous in it, but it's no good unless you feel confident.' Jasmine looked her up and down. 'I'd kill to look that good in a dress like that, but sadly I'm a fully paid-up member of the no-arse club. So it wouldn't work for me.'

'You're gorgeous, and I could always donate some of my bum to you. There's plenty going spare! I don't know why I'm worrying so much, anyway. I don't suppose anyone will notice what I'm wearing. They'll only be interested in hearing what I'm saying.' It was a statement Emily could make confidently, because the words she'd be saying would come straight from the pages of Sophia's new book, *Christmas at Goodwill Cove*. There'd be an army of her fans at the event in Waterstones Piccadilly, and the novel was being marketed as the most romantic novel yet, from the queen of love stories. It was something Emily could attest to, having recorded the audio book back in the summer. She recorded books for lots of authors now, but Sophia's would always have a special place in her heart, not least because meeting her favourite author had led to her dream job.

'Of course they're going to notice what you're wearing. You'll be up there at the front and they might well be hanging on your every word, but that doesn't mean they won't be looking at you too.'

'Well, thanks, that really takes the edge off my nerves.' Emily gave her friend a playful nudge.

'You've got nothing to be nervous about. Sophia's fans love the way you read her books, and you're starting to get a few fans of your own.' Jasmine grinned. 'It's just a shame they're blurring the lines between fan and deranged stalker.'

'I think it's nice that they want to send me messages telling me they enjoy the way I read Sophia's books.'

'That bit is sweet, but some of the gifts that have been sent in…' Jasmine shuddered. 'I thought the industrial-sized box of out-of-date chocolate was bad enough, but that teddy bear with a recording of your voice was something else, and you can bet your life that Christian from Slough got himself one too, and that he tucks it up in bed with him at night.'

'Well, the bear might as well have some romance in its life, because the real me definitely hasn't.' When Sophia's publisher had forwarded on the gift, she hadn't known whether to be as freaked out as Jasmine seemed to think she should be, or whether to just laugh. It had been the accompanying note that had given her the most reassurance.

Dear Emily

I hope you don't mind me getting in touch with this gift, but I wanted you to know how much comfort I get from listening to you read audio books. I lost my mother last year. We were very close and when I was a child, she used to read to me all the time. In the last stages of her illness, which lasted almost two years, I returned the favour. After she died, I had no one to read to, and no one to read to me, but listening to audio books helped me feel less alone, especially the ones you read. I am sure someone like you never feels lonely, but in case you ever do, I wanted to send you this little friend, to thank you for being a friend to me, despite the fact we've never met. Wishing you all the best with your career and many more wonderful narrations. Best wishes, Christian.

The note had resonated with Emily, because of the echoes of her own experience of reading to her mother. There was nothing sinister about it, no request for personal details or an expectation of anything in return for his kind gesture. It wasn't the only gift she'd received, but it was certainly the most unique, and she was secretly touched. The truth was that there were times when she was lonely. Since Jasmine had moved out of the flat they'd shared and got married, life in London had begun to lose some of its appeal. The draw to be back home in Port Agnes with her family was growing stronger and, despite the fact it was only the first week of November, the countdown to Christmas and a longer visit home was well and truly on.

The Christmas lights in Regent Street would be turned on the day before the reading of Sophia's new book, which was a big part of the reason why the publisher had timed the event the way they had. Everyone would be starting to feel festive, and it was a time of year Emily loved, when twinkling lights gave the whole world a more magical feel. It was the perfect season to set a romance novel in, and who didn't want to be cosying up with someone special beneath the mistletoe? It was no wonder so many of her favourite films were set at Christmas too. Fictional romance was the only kind she had in her life, but she was trying not to obsess any more about the idea of meeting someone to share forever with. She'd found a different kind of happy ever after that she was incredibly grateful for. Emily wasn't giving up on love, she just didn't want to make the search for it her sole focus any more. Unfortunately, her newly married best friend didn't seem to understand.

'Why don't you give that speed-dating event I sent you a go? Or stop living in the last millennium and get on the apps.'

'I've told you before, that's not for me. Anyway, I'm already in love.' She kept her face as deadpan as her tone, but Jasmine still grabbed Emily by the shoulders, her eyes wide.

'Why didn't you tell me? Who is it? When did you meet him? I need to know everything!' Her words came out in a rush and Emily laughed, despite a twinge of guilt that she was about to disappoint her friend.

'It's not a he.'

'Well, that's okay, of course it is.' A flicker of shock had crossed Jasmine's face, but she was still smiling. 'Maybe that's been the answer all along; you just needed to embrace other possibilities, and I could see you with a woman, I really could. We all just want you to be happy, Em, and it's brilliant if you've found that, whoever it's with.'

'Well, that's good then, because the woman I've fallen in love with is me.' Emily shrugged and Jasmine's face fell in response, her mouth moving silently for a moment or two before any words came out.

'Oh God, please tell me you're not going to do one of those weird-arse things where you marry yourself.'

'No, nothing like that. I just mean I've fallen in love with the life I've made for myself. I'm doing a job I can't believe I get paid for, I've got the best friends I could ask for, and a fantastic family back in Port Agnes.' There was a wistful tone to her voice that she couldn't stop from creeping in, because the truth was she was torn between two loves just lately. But that was a problem for another day.

'I'm so happy that you're happy, and I'm incredibly proud of what you've achieved in your career.' Jasmine gave her a hug. 'But I still want you to meet someone. I don't want to become old, boring and settled all by myself.'

'You could never be boring, Jas, you like leopard print too much.' Emily nudged her again, looking down at the ridiculously impractical killer heels in Jasmine's favourite print that she'd decided to wear for their shopping trip. 'And if I meet someone, I meet someone, but if I don't that's okay too, because I really am happier than I've ever been.'

'Just make sure those fictional heroes you spend all day reading about don't put you off the real thing. A real man might not be anywhere near as perfect, and you might feel an almost overwhelming desire to hold a pillow over his face when his snoring wakes you up at 3 a.m., but it does give you something to warm your feet on. You can give Sophia that line for one of her books next time you see her, if you like.' Jasmine grinned.

'I'll bear it in mind. But weren't you the one telling me last time we met not to get involved with another man after Ed?'

'No, what I actually said was not to get involved with another man *like* Ed. You don't need another emotionally unavailable man-child.' Jasmine shook her head, her sheet of shiny black hair swinging back and forth. 'You need to find yourself a nice, normal guy. Not one like a character from the books you read, who gives off the air of being mysterious and aloof but who's really a complete knob. You need someone who realises how amazing you are, Em, that's all, and who loves you more than they love themselves.' Jasmine made it all sound so simple.

'And where exactly do I find this nice, normal guy, who worships the ground I walk on?'

'Not on the pages of a Sophia Wainwright novel, that's for sure.'

'I know you find it hard to believe, but I'm quite content with my fictional heroes for now. As for finding someone in real life, I'll leave it to fate, because I really am happy.'

'Okay, I believe you.' Jasmine held up her hands. 'But if you change your mind, just promise me you won't let anyone mess you around again and keep you dangling. If this really is Emily Anderson's independent woman era, you need to fully commit to it.'

'I promise.' Emily held up the hanger in front of her. 'Now the question is, do I buy this ridiculously expensive dress for less than ten minutes in the spotlight or what?'

'If you don't buy it for yourself, I'll buy it for you as an early Christmas present. I'll even lend you these shoes if you want them, despite the fact I'm almost more in love with them than I am with Sam. And who knows where ten minutes in the spotlight will get you? You'd never have thought that a train journey back to Port Agnes would have led where it did.'

'That's true. Right, I'm doing it.' Emily headed back into the changing room. She knew exactly where she wanted her ten minutes in the spotlight to lead her – to more work doing the job she loved. A job that was still providing regularly pinch-me moments three years after it had begun. There was nothing else she was expecting from the event, and nothing she could imagine it leading to. But as Jasmine had already reminded her, sometimes life had its own surprises in store.

4

Jude could feel the irritation building up inside him for the entire journey from Paddington to Piccadilly. He didn't want to be crammed inside a Tube carriage, face to face with a man who stank of stale alcohol and cigarette smoke, just to be introduced to a bunch of people he'd usually have absolutely no interest in meeting. He wanted to be at home on his sofa, with just his Labrador, Rufus, for company, but somehow his editor had railroaded him into attending Sophia Wainwright's book launch.

'How are the revisions going?' Jude had known Marty's question was coming when he'd asked if they could set up another call, just two weeks after the Zoom meeting with him and Adele.

'I'm still mulling it over.' Jude had done his best to sound casual, as if the whole thing would be easy once he put his mind to it, but he'd already put his mind to it and the revisions had stalled completely. Deep down he was terrified that nothing he did would make any difference and that his career was over, but he hadn't been anywhere near ready to admit that. Despite his attempts to play it cool, the tightness of his tone had clearly given him away, because Marty had realised he needed all the help he could get.

'What don't you come and meet Sophia in person? If you're struggling, she might be able to give you some useful advice.'

'I don't think that—'

'We need those revisions, Jude. It's not up for debate.' Marty had sighed deeply and for a moment neither of them had spoken, but then his editor's usual upbeat demeanour made a swift reappearance. 'Look, come along and have a chat. What's the worst that can happen? There's a private reception at the 5th View bar after the meet and greet with Sophia's fans. There'll be champagne and some of those fancy canapes I know you've got a taste for.'

'Why don't I just come for that bit?' Even that had felt like a compromise that Jude didn't want to make.

'Because I think you'll get more out of it if you have some interaction with Sophia's readers. I think it might help you get over this snobbery you have about romance writers, which could help you embrace the changes you need to make too.'

Jude had been about to argue that it wasn't snobbery that made him dislike romance, more a matter of taste, but he could hardly say that when more than half of his publisher's revenue came from those kinds of books. He'd had his share of people looking down their noses at the kind of popular fiction he wrote too, as if it was somehow a less worthwhile way for him or his readers to spend their time. But he knew his stories had helped people escape into another world during difficult times; he'd had lots of messages telling him so, and he had no doubt Sophia's books did the same. He realised he'd probably come across as a bit of a dick about it all and in the end it had been easier to agree and get the phone call over with.

It also meant Marty couldn't question him further, probing

just why he found it so hard to write about love. Jude didn't want any speculation about why he was so convinced it didn't exist. Now here he was, heading to an event he didn't want to go to, which he suspected was going to serve no purpose other than to waste time he could have spent writing. If only he could remember how to do that.

His irritation grew more intense the closer he'd got to the venue. He'd got off the Tube at Oxford Circus, just to get away from the guy with the bad breath who'd pressed even closer to him as the carriage had become more and more crowded. It had been a relief to get outside at first, but he'd ended up jostling with tourists who stopped dead in front of him to take photographs of the Christmas lights high above Regent Street. Some people were already wearing Christmas jumpers, and it was still only early November, for Christ's sake. Why the hell they needed to start celebrating Christmas so early he'd never know. The logical part of Jude could accept those people weren't hurting anyone, but he could happily have written a murder plot for the group of women who'd walked in front of him, blocking any attempt to overtake them, who'd shrieked with delight every time they so much as spotted a fairy light. A red double-decker bus could so easily have careered out of control, driven by the vengeful ex-partner of one of the women. The words flowed in his head as he followed them down the road, how their squeals of delight had suddenly turned to screams of terror, before a horrific bang finally gave way to an eerie silence, amongst the mangled bodies left on the pavement. Those were the sorts of scenes he could write without hesitation, but he still couldn't get DCI McGuigan and his pathologist to exchange more than a few words of flirty banter.

'Glad you made it, Jude.' Marty slapped Jude on the back the moment he spotted him, scuppering his plans to turn around and pretend he'd never made it. The venue was packed with a crowd of Sophia Wainwright's hardcore fans. Quite a few of them were wearing sweatshirts with pictures of her book covers on them, and in some cases 'I love Sophia Wainwright' was emblazoned across the front instead. Jude had his fair share of diehard fans, but they mostly stuck to online discussion forums that lobbied for his books to be made into a TV series. He'd never seen anything like this before and he wasn't sure how it made him feel. Part of him wanted to believe that the kind of people who enjoyed books like Sophia's were bound to be drawn to over-the-top displays of love for their favourite author. But there was a tiny part of him that wondered what it was like to have that kind of adoration, and whether that helped Sophia on the days she was struggling to get words on the page or if it just piled on more pressure. Not that he was ever likely to find out; crime readers weren't usually quite so adoring.

'You didn't really give me much choice about coming, Marty.'

'Now don't be like that. You know it's only because I want the best for you.' Marty waggled his eyebrows, and Jude's shoulders relaxed slightly, because he knew it was true. Jude had been very lucky that he'd been partnered with an editor like Marty so early on, and he knew not every author was as fortunate. Forcing a smile, he nodded.

'I know you do.'

'Good man.' Marty slapped him on the shoulder again. 'Right then, let's get you and Sophia together before she speaks to this lot, because you won't get near her after that.' Marty gestured towards the crowd, and Jude did his best to keep the smile on his face, despite it getting tighter by the moment. It took them a few minutes to make it through the throng and, even after that, they'd had to wait until Sophia could extricate herself from the conversation she'd been having when they reached her.

'Jude Cavendish, I never thought I'd see you at one of my

readings.' Sophia's mouth twitched as she looked at him, and it took everything he had not to tell her the truth – that he'd rather be almost anywhere else – but his smile never wavered as he held out his hand. They didn't really need an introduction, despite the fact they'd never met in person. Their profiles were both plastered all over any kind of online presence Foster and Friedmann had, even if Sophia's face was often partly obscured, like it was on the image used for her cardboard cutout. He had a feeling that despite her huge fanbase, she tried to keep a reasonably low profile, although it was probably next to impossible these days. He'd passed advertising hoardings for both their latest releases when he'd taken the Tube. They were at the top of their game, but Sophia was ever so slightly higher, and the look on her face told him she knew that.

'Always happy to support a fellow F&F author.' Jude knew he was making it sound as though he was doing her a favour, and her mouth twitched again.

'Well, thank you, I'm honoured.' Sophia sounded as though she genuinely meant it, but the icy look in her eyes said otherwise, and she turned towards Marty. 'Have you met Emily Anderson, my brilliant narrator? She's the best I've ever worked with, and I absolutely refuse to have anyone else narrate my books now.'

'Great to meet you, Emily.' Marty shook the hand of the woman standing next to Sophia, who had long, wavy blonde hair, making her look like she should have been stepping out of the surf on a beach somewhere rather than standing in the middle of a crowded bookstore. She had the most amazing blue-grey eyes, like the sea on a stormy day, and they were regarding him with interest as Marty gestured towards him. 'This is Jude Cavendish, and he's here to discover just how powerful a love story can be as a storytelling device.'

'Nice to meet you both.' Emily shook Jude's hand. 'You've come to the right place to learn about love stories. Sophia is the best in the business.'

'So I've heard.' For some unfathomable reason, he was finding it hard to drag his eyes away from her face, but then Sophia interjected.

'I had you pegged as the sort of person who looks down their nose at romance novels, Jude. Don't tell me you're thinking of switching genres?'

'God no.' He hadn't meant to be quite so blunt, but the words were out before he could stop them, and Sophia didn't give him a chance to try and rescue the situation.

'Good, because it's a lot harder than it looks.'

'I don't doubt it.' Jude met her gaze.

'Ah, but you do, don't you?' He had to hand it to Sophia – she was unrelenting, her gaze never wavering from his, and he could tell that Marty and Emily were hanging on their every word.

'I'm not saying it's easy, it's just…' There was no real way to get out of this now that she'd put him on the spot, so he may as well tell the truth. Jude always found it easier to defend his position if he was being honest about how he felt, so he might as well tell it how he saw it. 'I'm not suggesting they're easy to write, but they are predictable. They follow a formula and the reader knows what's going to happen right from the start.'

The look Sophia gave him could have frozen water, and even Emily, who up until now had appeared to never stop smiling, regarded him with something close to disdain. It was Emily who responded first.

'You could say the same about a murder novel, though, couldn't you? You know someone is going to get killed, and that someone else is going to solve the crime. There's a formula of sorts to that too.'

'It's not quite the same, though, is it? You don't know who the murderer is from the start, at least not if the author has done a half decent job.' His smile this time was genuine, but it wasn't reciprocated by either of the women standing in front of him.

'I'm sure you've heard the expression, haven't you, Mr Cavendish, that only two things in life are certain? Death and taxes?' In that moment, Sophia looked as though she could happily hasten the first outcome for Jude, and he nodded. 'In that case, by your reasoning, life itself is predictable, because we're all going to suffer the same fate in the end. What makes life exciting isn't the outcome, it's the journey we go on to get there, and I would argue it's the same with a romance novel. It doesn't matter if the reader already knows the outcome; in fact, in an uncertain world there's a joy in that certainty. The real pleasure comes from losing themselves in the story that unfolds along the way.'

'It's an argument you've won as far as I'm concerned.' Marty shot Jude a look that needed no words, but even if he'd wanted to continue the debate, he didn't think he could have done a convincing job. He already knew from bitter experience that writing romance was far from easy. Sophia had made a good point about the joy of predictability in an uncertain world too, knowing that at least one thing was going to end well. In Jude's novels it happened when justice was served; that was what made the ending satisfactory for readers. Maybe McGuigan having something going well in his personal life was an extension of that. Jude had never thought about it that way before, but perhaps that was what his readers needed in order to feel they could identify with the character; something they could rely on in every new story that would make them want to come back for more. If he'd underestimated Sophia's insight, he wouldn't make the same mistake again, but she'd clearly given him all the time she was willing to spare.

'Right, gentlemen, if you'll excuse us, Emily and I have work to do.' With a slight nod of her head, Sophia turned away and Emily followed suit, catching Jude's eye for just a moment before she did. She didn't like him any more than Sophia did, that much was obvious. It shouldn't have mattered one bit what Emily Anderson thought of him, but somehow it did. It bothered him even more when she started to read aloud to the crowd in that melodic voice of hers that could make him picture the scene she was describing with absolute clarity. Given that the scene featured two characters falling in love, that in itself was nothing short of a miracle. He didn't want to believe in the story she was telling and yet somehow he couldn't help it. Jude could have told himself it was just the tricks of her trade, an ability all audio artists had to get the listener to connect with the story in a deeper way, but he knew that wasn't true. He'd listened to audio books before and he'd never felt quite so immersed in the character's world, even when it had been a genre he enjoyed. Whatever Emily had that made her different, it was something special.

'She's great, isn't she?' a woman standing next to Jude whispered in his ear, and he nodded. He had no idea if she was talking about Sophia or Emily, but he knew which of the women he'd have described that way. Emily fitted the kind of description he imagined Sophia had put into lots of her stories. It might have been another cliché, but when Emily was reading it really did feel like a light had come on in the room. She had an energy and a joy that could only come from doing something you were truly passionate about. He envied her that. Writing had always been his passion, and a way of making sense of the difficult things in life, but he seemed to have lost his love even for that just lately. His writing had started to feel forced and yet, when he watched Emily, it was almost as if he could feel the embers of his love for storytelling reigniting. Despite all his misgivings, it might have been worth coming after all, because if he could find a way to harness that and picture DCI McGuigan in a scene like the one Emily had just described, then maybe, just maybe, he could transfer it to the page.

* * *

The champagne fizzed on Emily's tongue and she let out a long, slow breath of relief now that she could finally relax. Performing public readings had become easier since the first time Sophia had asked her to do one, but she'd have been lying if she didn't admit that nerves still bubbled up inside her every time she did one. It was nice to be up in the 5th View restaurant, with no responsibility other than drinking champagne and mingling. In the early days, the mingling had been easier the more champagne she'd had. It made her less self-conscious about introducing herself to people she didn't believe had much interest in talking to her. She'd been to enough writing events to know that there were certain people who made it their job to work the room, often authors looking for representation or a new publishing deal. They'd take one look at Emily and decide she wasn't worth their time. That used to bother her far more than it did now, because she knew that the people who really mattered – Sophia and the other authors who made her their first choice to record their audio books – valued her.

Nowadays, she let the fact that some people couldn't see her value wash over her, but tonight was different. Every time she looked up, even during the reading, her gaze seemed to rest on Jude Cavendish, and a burning desire had built up inside her to tell him all the reasons he was wrong about Sophia's books. It had nothing to do with her abilities as a narrator and everything to do with the way he'd disrespected not only Sophia's work, but an entire genre that so many people enjoyed, including Emily. It had felt like he was just holding back from openly mocking her, and everyone like her, for their love of something he clearly believed had no worth.

There was an air of arrogance about him that undeniably irked her, but it was mixed with a hint of vulnerability too. She'd caught a glimpse of it in his expression when Sophia had put him in his place about the predictability of romance novels and why people might find that comforting in difficult times. It was almost as if he didn't believe his own argument, but somehow he couldn't admit that, because admitting it would have forced him to confront something else he wasn't willing to accept. Emily had no idea what that was, but if he'd been a character in one of Sophia's books, he'd undoubtedly have been a damaged soul, the kind of man who'd been through some kind of trauma that had left an indelible mark on his soul. The right woman would be able to help him heal, though, and Sophia would have written just the right kind of woman for him. But this wasn't a novel, and whatever it was that had made a troubled expression cross Jude's face, she very much doubted he'd experienced any real trauma. That hint of vulnerability had been just enough to stop her loathing him completely, but the reality was he'd still come across as an arrogant knob for 90 per cent of their interaction. As her grandmother had always said, if it quacks like a duck and walks like a duck, it probably is one. Either way, Jude would have a long way to go to prove her wrong.

He was impossibly good looking, especially for someone who must have spent most of his time hunched over a laptop. His jawline was razor sharp, despite the fact that his Wikipedia profile – which she'd googled in the ladies' loo – gave his age as thirty-six. He had dark brown lashes the same colour as his hair, framing bright blue eyes which were somehow made even more striking by the fact he wore trendy heavy-framed glasses. He really could have stepped out of the pages of one of Sophia's books, except for the fact that he was clearly a total arse. Yet she still couldn't stop watching him. He wasn't working the room, but still people gravitated towards him. He spoke to everyone who approached him, and part of her wanted to admit that maybe he wasn't quite so arrogant after all, but she couldn't do that. Not after the way he'd spoken to Sophia. Eventually, Emily had sought out a conversation with Sophia's proofreader, and they'd chatted easily about what it was like to be on the periphery of such a phenomenal author. It meant that Emily hadn't found herself gazing in Jude's direction for at least ten minutes. So when she looked up to find him standing right in front of her, she caught her breath.

'God, you made me jump.' Emily put her hand over her heart, trying to convince herself that the quickening thud, thud, thud was purely down to surprise at seeing him standing there.

'Sorry.' Jude looked genuinely contrite, but there was just a hint of amusement in his eyes, enough to make her keep her guard up. If he found her amusing, she wasn't going to let him know it bothered her.

'No problem. When you live in London, you get used to all sorts.' Emily turned towards Sophia's proofreader. 'Della, this is Jude Cavendish, he also writes for—'

'Oh, I know exactly who you are.' Della gave the kind of simpering laugh that made Emily feel embarrassed on her behalf, and which probably fed straight into Jude's already inflated ego. 'I haven't had the chance to proofread for you yet, but I keep hoping it's going to happen.'

'Maybe I can make a request.' When Jude smiled, Della blushed and Emily's second-hand embarrassment went up another level. 'Can I get either of you another drink?'

He looked from Emily to Della and back again, and she'd been about to decline his offer when Della's phone buzzed.

'Shit, my Uber's here. I knew I should have made it half an hour later.' Della looked crestfallen, only perking up a little bit when Jude kissed her on both cheeks as she said her goodbyes.

'Don't forget to put in that request!' Her parting words might have sounded light-hearted, but her tone had been quite insistent.

'I think you've got yourself a fan there.' Emily hoped her intonation made it clear to Jude that she wasn't in that particular club and never would be.

'She seems sweet, and she's certainly enthusiastic.' Jude sounded as if he was describing an over-excited and slightly annoying puppy dog, and he wasn't far wrong. If he had any interest in Della, he was doing a good job of hiding it.

'She's lovely and very good at her job.' Emily tried not to acknowledge the feeling of relief at Della's departure. There was no reason why she would be pleased to be left on her own with Jude Cavendish, none at all.

'As are you. Very good.' He adjusted his glasses as he spoke, and suddenly all Emily could picture was his namesake, Jude Law, in *The Holiday*, in a scene that had sent millions of pulses racing. But even she knew that movies were nothing like real life.

'Thank you. I love my job and I count my blessings every day to be doing what I do. I honestly couldn't think of anything better.'

'I used to feel that way about writing.'

'But not any more?' She couldn't keep the note of surprise out of her voice. Partly because he was being so honest, and partly because she couldn't imagine anyone who'd achieved the dream of becoming a published author wishing they were doing something else. Not when so many people were still chasing that dream.

'Just lately no, but I think that's something you might be able to help me with.' Jude held her gaze until she was forced to look away. 'I wondered if you'd be willing to go for a drink with me some time.'

'No.' Her response was emphatic. 'I don't think that would be a good idea.'

It wasn't a lie. She knew without a shadow of a doubt that it would be the worst possible idea, because Jude was clearly bad news. It was written all over him, and she'd had enough of bad boys and commitment-phobes to last her a lifetime. In Sophia's novels, guys like that always changed for the better when they met the right person. But that was just one more example of real life being nowhere near as good as fiction, and she wasn't about to put herself through that again.

'I'll happily pay you for your time.' He was still looking at her when her head shot up again. Who the hell did he think he was? He might assume everyone had a price but he was wrong, and a wave of nausea washed over her.

'I don't know what sort of person you think I am, but it wouldn't matter how much you paid me to spend time with you, it wouldn't be enough!'

He laughed then, actually laughed, and she felt the hairs on the back of her neck stand up. How dare he! Emily took a step forward, ready to slap him across the cheek, like she was the wronged woman in an old black and white movie, but then he held up his hands.

'This is strictly a business proposition. What I'm offering is a payment for you to be a consultant on my novel. My editor suggested I speak to someone who understands what readers want from a romance in a way that I clearly don't and, having listened to you read, I really think that might be you. I need to give my lead character a believable love interest, and I need someone who can help me work out whether what I've written will translate to my readers.'

'So why not just ask a romance writer?' Part of Emily was flattered that he thought she could be the person for the job, but she was in no way qualified to offer what he was looking for.

'Because whatever I write, it still needs to have my voice. If I work with another author, it would just muddy the waters and become their voice in the middle of my story. I've tried doing it myself, but every time I read through what I've put down on the page, it sounds ridiculous to me. The trouble is, when I read Sophia's book, that sounded ridiculous too.' Emily had been about to protest again, but he shook his head. 'That changed when I heard you reading the story. Suddenly that same sentiment seemed much more believable, and I think I need to see my character's relationship through that filter. I'm too close to him and the story to be objective, and I want to be confident that it's authentic before I send it to my editor, because I think he'll just be so relieved I've written anything along those lines that he'll accept more or less whatever I write. So my plan is to write what I think will work and edit that on the basis of how it feels when you're reading it. If you can't make it sound like a believable romance, I'll know I've failed.'

'So you just want me to read what you've written out loud to you?' Emily furrowed her brow, not sure if this sounded like the world's easiest way to earn some extra money, or if she would be getting herself into a nightmare situation.

'Not just that. I'm sure you can give me some pointers about how I should approach it. What makes a good connection between characters in a relationship and the kind of dialogue they might use, that sort of thing. As a connoisseur of romance.'

Jude paused for a moment. He was clearly trying not to allow his expression to give him away, but he didn't quite pull it off. 'Put it this way. I'm sure you've read a lot more romances than I ever will. So you can tell me what the story feels like from that expert perspective and suggest some ways I could improve it, to make it less wooden and forced than it feels right now.'

Emily hesitated for a moment, still wondering whether she was about to commit herself to something she was going to regret, but there was another voice inside her head, telling her that if she pulled this off, it could be amazing. If she could get Jude Cavendish to admit that there was a place for love in all kinds of storytelling, it would be a victory for the authors whose work she loved and who people like Jude looked down upon. It was too tempting an opportunity to pass up, but she wasn't going to make it easy for him.

'How much are you paying?' Emily was amazed at how matter-of-fact she sounded, and when she looked at him pointedly, he laughed again.

'Whatever your hourly rate for the audio narration works out to be, I'll double it.'

'Treble it and you've got yourself a deal.' She held his gaze again, and he hesitated for just a moment before nodding and reaching out to shake her hand.

'It's a deal, but I would have paid you four times what you get for narration.'

'And I would have accepted the same rate.' She couldn't help smiling, but she was surprised when he mirrored her expression.

'I think I might have met my match.'

'You better hope so if I'm going to have any useful input into your book.' Reaching into her bag, she passed him a card. 'Send me some dates and times and we can set up an initial meeting. I'll see you then.'

Turning on her heel, she strode away from him, as if she did this sort of thing all the time. He wasn't to know just how excited she was that Jude Cavendish wanted her to be a consultant on his next book. She'd played it cool for all of ten minutes; she just had to hope she could continue to pull that off. Even more than that, she hoped she could actually be of some use, because it wasn't just her own reputation she needed to uphold. She was doing this for everyone who believed that romance novels were just as worthy as any other kind of book, and she couldn't let them down.

5

Jude looked at the text from his stepmother and sighed. This was all he needed – an enquiry about his plans for Christmas. Worst of all, she'd sent it via WhatsApp, which meant Viv would be able to see that he'd read it and expect a reply he wasn't ready to give.

> Hey Jude! Sorry, you know I can never resist doing that! Your dad and I were just wondering if you've given Christmas any thought yet? It would be brilliant if you came here. Fi and James are coming with the family and we'd all love to see you!!! V xx

It was times like this he wished his stepmother didn't even have his number. It wasn't that he didn't like Viv; he did. She was a warm, welcoming type of woman, with a ready smile and a hearty embrace, whether you wanted one or not. Viv was so nice, he could even forgive her tendency to end most of her sentences with at least one exclamation mark. She was also at least six million times more likeable than his first stepmother, Sandra, who had gone out of her way to make Jude feel unwelcome and unwanted. She'd remind him whenever the opportunity arose that he was adopted and on more than one occasion exclaimed loudly that he was 'not Charles's real son anyway' as a result. Her words had cut Jude every bit as deeply as she'd intended them to, and they'd left scars long after her short-lived marriage to his father had come to an abrupt end, for reasons he'd never been party to, although he suspected she'd just met someone else she preferred.

Jude had been ten years old when his adoptive mother, Ros, had died in a skiing accident that had ripped their little family of three to shreds. All his memories of Ros were good ones; she'd had the same kind of warmth as Viv. Over the years, the sharpness of those memories had blurred around the edges. There'd been many times when he'd wanted to ask his father whether his recollections of his mother were accurate or the result of a combination of the passage time and rose-coloured glasses. But his father had seemed to shut down following Ros's death, at least when it came to communicating with his son. Just six months after she'd died, Charles had met Sandra, and Jude had been shipped off to boarding school when he'd turned eleven. He'd been certain that his father's new girlfriend had influenced the decision, but he doubted Charles had put up much of a fight. By the end of his second year at Membory Grange, two months after his thirteenth birthday, his father had married the woman who Jude was convinced had been the inspiration for every wicked stepmother to ever feature in a fairytale. He'd hated boarding school at first, grieving the loss of both his parents in different ways, but once Sandra was a permanent fixture in his family home, school had become Jude's salvation, and he'd dreaded going back home for the holidays each year, especially the Christmas one, when his old friends would be busy with their families and not allowed to come out, meaning he was stuck with his father and stepmother.

Sometimes when Sandra was being particularly venomous, Jude would crave one of his mother's hugs so much that he'd spray some of her perfume, from a bottle he'd taken from her dressing table after she'd died, on to a pillow. It allowed him to pretend just for a moment that he was resting his head on his mother's shoulder again. In those moments, he'd confide to his mother what was going on, talking to a woman who was no longer there about how tough life had become without her. The idea of anyone ever finding out what he did was mortifying. He was a teenager, for God's sake, not a baby, something Sandra reminded him of every time he tried to seek out his father's attention for anything. She couldn't bear Charles going to watch his son's rugby or cricket games, and there was no way she'd step back to allow them any one-to-one time together. She resented Jude's existence and she didn't even try to hide it.

From time to time Jude had thought about finding his 'other mother', the one who'd given birth to him, but he'd always decided against it. It was a decision he'd made to protect himself from further hurt, having already been faced with what felt like a lifetime of rejection. Why set himself up for more? Especially when Sandra had taken such delight in reminding him, when his father was out of earshot, that even the woman who'd given birth to Jude hadn't wanted him. Weirdly, he'd never even considered trying to find his 'other father', the one whose DNA he shared. Perhaps it was because Charles was still around and he had a father, albeit a very definitely flawed one.

School had become even more of a refuge after Viv's arrival. She'd joined the team of staff as a house parent, essentially taking on the role of stand-in mother to the boys in Jude's boarding house. He'd liked her from the start, but had never dreamt she'd end up being his second stepmother, not least because she'd still been married to Mr Hemmersley at the time, the very jolly new head of maths who'd also joined the school, along with their daughter Fiona. It wasn't until almost ten years later that his father and Viv had got together, in a support group for people who'd been widowed, two years after Nigel Hemmersley had suffered a massive stroke and died. Viv had recognised Charles immediately from their interactions during Jude's time at the school, and the rest had been history. Sandra had been long gone by then, her marriage to Jude's father having lasted less than four years but leaving a legacy that had endured for the eighteen years since their marriage had ended. Nothing had changed between him and his father, despite the fact that Charles had been married to Viv for more than seven years now and she'd never once made Jude feel anything other than welcome.

It made his inability to answer her text difficult to explain. He was very fond of her, his stepsister Fiona, and her family, but Christmas had never been the same since Ros had died. He'd found different ways of celebrating over the years. The run-up to Christmas with friends was usually about get-togethers over a meal and a few drinks, and having a laugh. There'd been the uni years too, and one occasion when Jude and his flatmates had attempted to cook an early Christmas dinner, in mid-December, with only a hob and a microwave. It had been a miracle they hadn't all died, but they were still exchanging photographs of the world's most unappetising Christmas dinner all these years later and laughing at the memory. There'd been some good times over Christmas in the years since his mother had died, but it had never been that same special family occasion without her.

They'd all been in such good spirits setting off for the family ski trip to Val-d'Isère the day after Boxing Day, with plans to stay through New Year. Except Ros hadn't even made it until New Year's Eve. She'd had a terrible accident on the second day and had clung to life for forty-eight hours before the medics had told Charles there was no hope of recovery. The Christmas decorations had still been up when they'd flown home with her body, and something had broken inside both Jude and his father that even Viv hadn't been able to fix. Although he could celebrate the run-up with friends, Christmas Day itself was different, and it still felt wrong without his mum.

Even now, it was easier to do Christmas alone, just him, Rufus, and a bottle of single malt. The sort of festivities DCI McGuigan would be proud of. It had been that way for as long as he could remember, and he told himself there was no reason to change it. Maybe, deep down, he wanted more, but he hadn't felt like a part of his father's family in years. The rejection he'd experienced after his mother's death was what had convinced him that people weren't really capable of loving anyone else, unless it fitted neatly into the plans they had for their own life. It wasn't selfless or unconditional, not in Jude's experience since the death of his mother anyway.

The only time he'd let his guard down and thought he might have found a new life for himself, Mia had reminded him that trusting in anyone else was like building a house on sand. He'd spent time with her family in the year they'd been together, and it had almost felt like a vision of his future, with a family of his own one day. Except all the love Mia had professed to have for him hadn't meant anything when someone else had come along. Whatever she'd convinced herself she felt, it wasn't real, and he didn't want his happiness to ever rely on someone loving him. He'd been let down too many times to be certain that was possible. Rufus was the only one he'd loved who'd never let him down, and that made the thought of spending Christmas with just his dog far more appealing than the alternative. The trouble was not everyone understood.

Closing the WhatsApp message, Jude sighed. He'd think about what to say in reply later, but for now he had somewhere he really needed to be.

* * *

'Right, let me just get this straight in my head, so I don't forget.' Jasmine sounded deadly serious, almost as if she was about to start taking notes at her end of the call. 'Who was it you said you wanted to play you in the Netflix miniseries about your murder?'

Emily laughed. 'He *writes* about murders, he doesn't *do* them. At least I hope his research doesn't go that far.'

'But you've arranged to go out with this man, a man you barely know, and the only info you can give me is that you're meeting him in Covent Garden.'

'It's a very public place.' Emily was already halfway to the Tube station, with her phone clamped to her ear, trying not to get jostled off the pavement into the path of an oncoming double-decker. She was far more likely to meet her end that way than at the hands of Jude Cavendish. She was sure of it. Well, almost sure. There was an undercurrent of brooding darkness about him that she had to admit did feel a tiny bit dangerous.

'Just keep me up to date with where you are and how it's going, and do not turn your location services off. I need to track where you are so they can find your body more quickly.' Jasmine gave a snort of laughter this time, and Emily couldn't help joining in.

'You're a horrible best friend. You know that, Jas, don't you?'

'And you know you love me as much as I love you, which is

why I'm going to lobby as hard as I can for Scarlett Johansson to play you in the miniseries.'

'As long as they cast Miriam Margolyes in your role, my ghost will be very happy!' Emily was still laughing to herself when she ended the call and said her goodbyes to Jasmine as she reached the Tube station. She might not really have any concerns about Jude doing away with her, but she was still nervous about meeting up with him. And like anything that scared her, the sooner she got it over and done with the better.

* * *

Emerging from the Tube station at Covent Garden less than twenty minutes later, Emily scanned the crowd. She'd arranged to meet Jude outside the market hall, where the Christmas decorations had gone up just the day before, and now throngs of people were desperately trying to get photographs of themselves, without hordes of strangers making guest appearances on the edge of their shots. It didn't take long to spot him; he was wearing a dark blue woollen coat and grey jumper, and even among the crowds he stood out. There was no way he could get away with murder; he was far too good-looking to go unnoticed. When he turned towards her, catching her eye, the nerves that had been bubbling up inside her turned into full-blown somersaults.

'Thanks for coming. Shall we get a coffee?' There was no effusiveness in his greeting, no mention of how nice it was to see her. Most people exchanged those kinds of pleasantries, even if it was just a business meeting. But Emily had a feeling Jude wasn't the sort of person who did anything just for the sake of it.

'Coffee sounds good, any preference about where?'

'As long as it hasn't got a cinnamon stick or a candy cane

poking out of the top of it, I don't care.' The expression on Jude's face could have given the Grinch a run for his money.

'I take it you're not a massive fan of Christmas.'

'It's one day, which now feels like it lasts at least two months, and that's not just because of how slowly time passes when you're cooped up with your relatives. Although to be fair, if I have to celebrate Christmas, I've always preferred doing it in the run-up that doesn't involve them.'

'Oh.' It was the only response Emily could come up with. There was clearly a lot to unpack from Jude's words, but launching straight in with questions about his personal life almost certainly wasn't the way to go. She wasn't about to admit that she adored Christmas, and that as far as she was concerned it could last six months and she'd still love every moment.

'Right, let's go and get that coffee, shall we? And work out how we're going to do this.' As Jude looked at her again, Emily dropped her gaze towards the floor. There was an intensity in his blue eyes that was unsettling.

'Sounds good.' He didn't say anything else, and she followed his lead away from the bustling centre of Covent Garden to a quieter side street, where they found a coffee shop that wasn't spilling over with tourists. Jude insisted on paying for the coffees, and she didn't put up an argument. She was trying to act as if she understood his willingness to pay her to advise him on his book, and that she was confident of the value of her contributions. It wasn't that she didn't want to help, she just wasn't sure she could. A few glasses of champagne had left her feeling far more confident when they'd first discussed the idea, but now she was sitting face to face with him, she had no idea where to start. Despite what he'd said about wanting the story to be told in his way and not anyone else's, she still thought he'd have been better off asking for input from someone like Sophia, or any number of authors who knew far more about writing love stories than she ever would. She felt like a massive fraud who was just seconds away from getting found out, but she couldn't stand the silence that was still hanging between them, thirty seconds after he'd set down the coffees, so she decided to make a start.

'I take it there'll be no mention of Christmas in the novel you're writing, given how much you dislike it?' There was a thick red candle flickering in a glass between them, giving off the scent of cinnamon and orange, and the coffee shop had silver snowflakes hanging in its windows. It might have only been the thirteenth of November, but Christmas was all around whether Jude liked it or not.

'The book spans November to February. It's a metaphor for the fact that DCI McGuigan, the lead character, is going through the darkest time in his life.' The expression on Jude's face suggested he knew what that felt like. 'There are a series of grisly murders, with a link to his past. One of which happens on Christmas Day.'

'Sounds festive.' Emily couldn't help laughing, but Jude didn't join in.

'It's not supposed to be festive, it's supposed to show that all the bright lights and decorations are just an illusion; a pretence that Christmas is somehow a special time of year when everything is wonderful. The truth is terrible things can happen at Christmas, just like any other time. The problem is, according to my editor, the DCI McGuigan series is becoming unrelentingly dark, and that's turning readers off.'

'So you need some light and shade?' Emily furrowed her brow as he nodded. 'I think Christmas could provide that perfectly. After all, what's more of a contrast to the darkness than all the light it brings?'

'Oh God, you really do love Christmas, don't you?' He pulled a face. 'I just can't see how all of that forced jollity can fit in one of my novels.'

'I take it there's a lot of blood and gore in your stories?' Emily paused as he nodded. 'Okay, well if you don't want to focus on the jolly side of Christmas, maybe it would help if you thought about the origin of some of the traditions.'

'Such as?'

'The Roman invaders were the first to have Christmas trees, and they certainly didn't shy away from a bit of blood and gore. They had candlelit trees to welcome the end of winter, bringing in the light after months of darkness. Even if they'd spent months in bloody battles as they fought to seize control, they still needed hope that there were better times ahead. If your editor thinks you need some of that hopefulness in your story, then giving your hero a family Christmas that contrasts with the terrible things he sees in his job could make him feel much more relatable.'

'McGuigan is a flawed protagonist, not a hero.' Jude didn't actually roll his eyes, but the implication was in his words. 'And they're not the sort of stories where people have Christmas celebrations straight out of a Disney movie.'

'But if McGuigan did experience something lighter, it could make the point really effectively that no matter how much the rest of the world is celebrating, terrible things can still happen. It doesn't have to be a Disney Christmas, as you put it. You can just show that your hero – sorry, *protagonist* – has more than one side to his personality. The fact that he's capable of enjoying life and seeing good in the world makes the murders all the more harrowing for him. It will increase his motivation to solve them and it will make readers like him more.'

'So you want me to have him fall in love and celebrate Christmas?' Jude was looking at her as if she'd suggested that he give DCI McGuigan a tail.

'Why not? You could link the two things. If he's falling in love, then maybe he's spending it in a different way than he would have done before, with this new person in his life. Maybe that makes him more willing to see the joy of Christmas, rather than viewing it as... what was it you said? One day that goes on for about two months too long?'

'We're not talking about me; we're talking about Cole McGuigan.' For a moment Jude almost looked as if he was about to smile, but then he shook his head. 'God, it pains me even to say this out loud, but McGuigan falling in love and Christmas? I just don't see them going hand in hand and it still being the kind of book I want to write. It'll feel like I'm selling out and losing all my integrity by suddenly writing McGuigan the kind of happy ever after I just don't think he'd ever get. If someone was going to get past the wall he's built up around himself, it wouldn't be with mistletoe and mulled wine in Winter bloody Wonderland.'

'Who said anything about Winter Wonderland?' Emily couldn't help smiling. There was one part of Christmas in London she could admit to hating and Jude had zeroed in on it. 'I still think Christmas is the perfect time to write about love, but it can be a great way to relive the magic from when you were a kid too. Why not reintroduce McGuigan to an old flame, someone he can share the memories of past Christmases with, before his career made him so jaded? You said the murders were linked to his past, didn't you? Why not link the love story to his past too. That way those moments of light your editor wants can be intertwined with the rest of the story, and you won't feel like you're selling out.'

Jude looked at her without saying anything for what felt like forever. She'd been about to apologise and tell him that he should just ignore her, as he clearly thought the idea was stupid, but then he suddenly smiled in a way that changed his whole face. 'You're a genius.'

'I wouldn't go that far, but—'

He cut her off before she could make any more self-depreciating comments, looking more animated than she'd ever seen him before. 'No, that's it. I've been trying to think of a way of not making his relationship feel as if it'd been shoe-horned in there because I've been forced to write it, which is exactly what has happened. I was trying to find a way of him building a relationship with a pathologist he works alongside, but it just felt so false. Doing it your way, his relationship can actually raise the stakes when it comes to solving the crime. As McGuigan realises the murders have a link to his past, and in turn to his rekindled relationship with a former girlfriend, his angst about the risk of getting close to someone can deepen too. Especially if he has to consider compromising himself professionally to protect her. It's brilliant, although I'm still not sure about the tie in with Christmas.'

'There's nothing more romantic than spending Christmas with the person you love. It's why there are people out there already.' Emily gestured towards the window. 'Hunting around to find the perfect gift for the person they'll wake up with on Christmas Day.'

'Sounds like you're speaking from experience I don't have.' Jude shrugged, but there was an expression in his eyes that she couldn't quantify. Emily was tempted to tell him it wasn't personal experience she was speaking from, just the lives she'd lived through the books she'd read and a hope that one day she would get to experience it for herself. She might have told Jasmine she wasn't looking for love, but she still wanted it to find her. *One day*. She couldn't admit any of that to Jude; he needed to believe she was an expert in love and romance, otherwise she'd be no good to him. He'd probably think it was pathetic anyway, that even with a career she loved and so much else to be thankful for, she still wanted to find someone to love.

'Look, even if you don't believe Christmas is romantic, and you don't want to build McGuigan's relationship around it, all you have to do is watch couples spending time together at this time of year to understand what love looks like.'

'But not in Winter Wonderland?' He gave her a slightly crooked smile this time, which somehow made him even more handsome.

'No, and not in crowded department stores either, or stressed out and jostling with the crowds on Oxford Street. I could take you to any number of places at this time of year that will help you see what romance looks like, whether or not you decide to make Christmas a feature of your characters' relationship.'

'I want you to show me what love looks like.' He held her gaze, and she couldn't answer him, because in that moment she could barely remember her own name. But suddenly the crooked smile was back. 'You've already given me a way of creating a relationship for McGuigan that doesn't seem like a total sellout, and if you can find a way for me to mention family and Christmas without it feeling totally false, my editor is going to love you even more than I will. When can you start?'

Emily hesitated, suddenly even less certain than before whether any of this was a good idea. It might just be a business arrangement, but there was a fizz of something between her and Jude, and a line it felt might be dangerously easy to cross. Except Emily would jump in with her heart on a platter the way she always did, and Jude had already made it clear he didn't have a heart. At least not the kind that believed in romantic love. They were a match made in hell, but it was Emily who'd get burnt, and she'd promised Jasmine she wouldn't get involved with someone like him. 'I don't know, it would mean evenings and weekends, and I'd have to charge considerably more than the rate we initially agreed.'

'Name your price.' He was regarding her now with a hint of amusement in his eyes, making her all the more determined to walk away. But the last thing she wanted was for him to know the real reason why.

'Three hundred pounds an hour.' Just saying the amount out loud made Emily's face go hot, and not just because it made her sound like a high-class escort.

'Great.' He held out his hand and she found herself shaking it, because she had no idea how to get out of this without telling him why she'd changed her mind. She just had to keep things businesslike and remind herself why crossing a line with Jude would be such bad news. It shouldn't be that hard; she'd only be spending all her spare time with a man she found incredibly attractive, teaching him about love and romance. What could possibly go wrong?

6

Jude ruffled the fur on Rufus's head. 'Don't look at me like that, I know I've been out a lot this week, but today you get to come, too.'

Jude didn't think the dog really understood what he said to him, but the enthusiasm with which Rufus's tail was thudding against the sofa cushion suggested otherwise. The dog had looked bereft the day before when Jude had gone out with Emily for the second of their 'research trips' aimed at convincing him that Christmas was the perfect time of year for him to have DCI McGuigan reconnecting and falling in love with his ex. Emily was still insisting that all the romance and nostalgia of Christmas could open the most hardened heart. Jude begged to differ, but he had a book to deliver so he had no choice but to try.

Trip one had involved watching couples stumbling around an open-air ice rink, desperately trying to stay upright and almost as desperately trying to pretend they were enjoying themselves. In Jude's opinion, it was crowded and clichéd, and the sort of thing people did when they were trying to force a romantic moment where none existed. To him it was like proposing at the top of the

Eiffel Tower, or with a ring hidden in the bottom of a glass of champagne. Those things were deemed romantic simply by virtue of the fact that someone, somewhere, had once said they were. In Jude's view, that didn't make them so.

'I'm not feeling it.' Jude shrugged when Emily had asked him what he thought of her first attempt to show him just how romantic the festive season could be. 'I still don't see what's romantic about a giant Christmas tree in the middle of an ice rink.'

'Look at those two.' Emily had pointed out a couple who were doubled over with laughter as one of them tried to help the other get up, without much success. When they eventually managed to get to the edge of the rink together, they were still laughing, but then he leant forward and kissed her.

'How did you know they were going to do that?' Jude had narrowed his eyes.

'Because laughter is an aphrodisiac, but so is Christmas. They're having fun and feeling festive, so a kiss was inevitable.' It had been Emily's turn to shrug.

'Okay, but I'm hardly going to have McGuigan dancing on ice. He's a cynical detective whose closest relationship is with a bottle of whisky. The only ice he's interested in comes in cubes.'

'Even if you don't think Christmas is romantic and you don't think McGuigan would do any of the things we're going to see, I still think observing people at this time of year will help. You can watch them going on dates and maybe even falling in love, and emotions are heightened because no one wants to be on their own at Christmas. That could help you identify the ingredients of a believable love story and maybe work out what McGuigan's motivations are for finally getting out from behind his whisky bottle and letting himself feel something else.'

'Okay, so in your vast experience, what are these ingredients?'

Jude had wanted to ask whether it was something Emily had found for herself, but he'd held back. He had no right to ask her to divulge anything personal, just as he had no intention of spilling his guts about the details of his personal life. Anything she chose to reveal would have to come from her.

'I think the list of ingredients can be varied, but for lots of people it's the ability to laugh at the same things, knowing how to have a good time together, and allowing themselves to be a bit vulnerable around one another. What could be a better example of that than going ice-skating together, when you have no idea how to do it? That's how I knew that couple were going to kiss.'

Jude had nodded then. He still thought that Emily's idea of love and romance belonged in the fictional world Sophia Wainwright created, but he could see her point. If he could work out what it was that would make McGuigan buy into that illusion, he might just be able to write him a believable relationship that didn't compromise everything else he'd built his lead character up to be. It was why he didn't just pay Emily what he owed her after that first trip out and call it a day. It was also why he'd agreed to their second trip, to a rooftop bar, illuminated only by rows and rows of golden Christmas lights, where they'd watched an open-air showing of *The Holiday*. Emily had shushed him every time he tried to point out a plot hole in the movie, and by God there'd been plenty of them, mostly around how insanely quickly both romances play out.

'That timeline is all over the place. My editor would think I'd lost it altogether if I presented him with something like that.' Jude hadn't been able to help repeating his objections when he and Emily had been finishing their drinks after the movie had ended.

'No one cares about the timeline, they just care about the happily ever after.' Emily had given him an exasperated look, and he'd suddenly wanted to say something to make her smile again. She was beautiful when she smiled, dimples appearing on either side of her generous mouth as her eyes lit up. But she hadn't given him a chance to respond. 'That's what your editor wants you to present him with. A story where your readers can feel satisfied about the place McGuigan's relationship has taken him to. Maybe not a happy ever after, but at least a happy for now. They might want your character to remain flawed and troubled, but they want to believe he's at least capable of redemption and happiness. We all need to believe that about a character if we're going to engage with them, because it's what we need to believe about ourselves. Even at the worst times of our lives, otherwise what's the point?'

Jude hadn't responded straight away, her words catching him off guard. He hadn't had the certainty of knowing there was someone he could go to about anything, and that they'd be there for him, since before his mother's death. There'd been times when he'd wished he had a partner, someone to love and share the good times with, and to have one another's backs in the worst times. Except all of that was just an illusion; 'love' only lasted as long as it suited. He'd risked it once with Mia, and he wasn't going to be fooled twice. But he'd wanted to understand what it was that made Emily believe in the things she'd said, so that he could try to convince his readers of it too. 'Do you really think the only point of life is love?'

'Yes, but not just the romantic kind.' Emily had taken a sip of her drink before continuing. 'I think it's important and it's what most people want, but I can accept not everyone does. What I can't believe is that there are people who are okay with the idea of not being loved by anyone. One of my favourite authors said that you're no one if you're not loved, and I think that's true.'

'Well, God help McGuigan then.' *And God help me.* Somehow

Jude had kept that last part to himself, but the words had echoed in his head. Maybe that was why he was as attached to his dog as he was, because he had a very strong suspicion that Rufus was the only one who truly loved Jude. Either way, he had to acknowledge that Emily was right again. Even if he didn't believe in the kind of love that she and Sophia peddled, he knew the majority of people did, which by default meant the majority of readers did too, and Marty had already told him what would happen if he didn't start catering to them. It was why he and Rufus were about to set out on a third field trip with Emily, and why he was still confident that the three hundred pounds an hour he was paying her would end up being money well spent.

* * *

Jude knew that keeping a car when he lived in Central London was probably a stupid and unnecessary expense, but on days like today, when he needed to get to Richmond Park, it came into its own. He could have taken Rufus by public transport. The Labrador was laidback, and he'd probably have coped fine with the Tube part of the journey, but now that they were into the second half of November, the long run-up to Christmas was getting busier and busier, and Jude didn't want to put him through that.

He'd offered to meet Emily in town and give her a lift out to Richmond, but she'd told him it was probably easier to meet there. He suspected it was because she found the idea of being in such close quarters with him, for what could end up being a long car journey, disconcerting. He had a brusque side that he was well aware of, and he'd seen her face change when he'd dismissed the things she was passionate about, but he couldn't just pretend to agree with her. Since leaving home, he seemed to have lost the ability to pretend he believed in something he didn't just to appease someone else. Maybe it was because Jude had been forced to maintain a pretence for years, when his father was married to Sandra, trying not to reveal how much he loathed her in front of his dad, and trying harder still not to let Sandra see how much her vitriol got to him.

Still, he didn't like the fact that his inability to agree with Emily made her feel awkward. She'd proved to have invaluable insight and given him ideas to redirect his novel that he'd probably never have thought of without her. She was also what his second stepmother, Viv, would have called a 'lovely young woman'. Viv said that a lot, about the daughters of her friends who were single and who she thought Jude might like to meet. She'd even arranged for two of them to just happen to drop in when Jude was making a duty visit to see his father. They'd been just as Viv had described – lovely – but he wasn't interested. He didn't want to get involved with the daughters of his stepmother's friends, because it would get far too messy when things inevitably didn't work out. Jude wasn't looking for commitment; he'd tried it once and that was enough. If he told anyone that was the reason, they'd probably think Mia had broken his heart so badly that he didn't want to risk it happening again, but they'd have been wrong.

Jude wasn't crushed by the breakup with Mia, just jaded by the fact that people seemed so willing to lie to each other, and themselves, about the relationships they were in, just because they'd rather be with anyone than be on their own. Jude had seen it with his father. He found it impossible to believe that Charles had ever really been happy with Sandra, after having been married to someone as lovely as Ros. Sandra was barely any nicer to Charles than she'd been to his son, but his father had been desperately lonely after Ros's death, and he'd needed someone to fill the void. He'd spent years trying to convince himself that someone was Sandra, but despite never vocalising it, his relief had been palpable when she'd eventually left him.

It was different with his father and Viv, Jude could see that, and maybe they really did love each other. They certainly believed they did, but Jude never wanted that kind of dependence on someone. That was where the real heartbreak was waiting to happen, because one day one of them would be left on their own, all over again. In some ways it would be easy and far less risky for Jude to embark on a relationship, because of the way he felt. There'd always be a big piece of himself he was holding back, but that was just one more reason why he didn't want Viv setting him up with anyone. The likelihood was that these women wanted far more than he had to offer; all he could provide was a kind of parallel existence, where he never let his guard down enough to be heartbroken. He didn't ever want to feel the way he'd felt in the wake of his mother's death again.

If he allowed himself to buy into the idea of love, it meant he'd get hurt eventually, one way or the other, because everyone left in the end. If he'd been honest with the women Viv had tried to fix him up with, they'd have run a mile. Most people seemed to be looking for commitment once they reached a certain age, and women like Emily, who believed whole-heartedly in living happily ever after, would never really understand why he didn't. Maybe they'd been luckier than he had, or maybe he was just a realist, in a world where most people preferred the fantasy. It didn't really matter, because whatever the reason, he'd didn't want to be the one to let someone else down, and that was bound to happen in the end, if he tried to pretend.

Jude had done his best to rein in his responses to the activities they'd gone to so far, but he had a feeling his face was going to give him away today, no matter how hard he tried. They were going to be witnessing a Christmas-themed carriage ride in Richmond Park and he hadn't been able to stop himself from pulling a face when Emily had suggested they check it out.

'We're not actually going to have to ride in the carriage, are we?' The thought was mortifying, but thankfully Emily had shaken her head.

'Not at five hundred pounds, no. After all, that could buy you almost two hours of my time.' Emily had smiled, her eyes shining as she teased him and the dimples reappearing. It had stirred something inside him that he'd immediately pushed down. Being attracted to Emily was no surprise; she was beautiful, but they were complete opposites and the last thing he wanted to do was mess up an arrangement that was working well.

'So we're just going to watch other people taking carriage rides?'

'It's a special event, before they open to the public at the end of the month. This one is being filmed for a TV show, and my friend who works for the production company said they're expecting a proposal.'

'Sounds tacky.' Jude hadn't been able to stop himself from grimacing again. 'Surely the TV crew aren't going to want to have random members of the public in the background.'

'India said they're filming certain parts of the ride, but they can't close off the park altogether. Look, it's pretty clear you don't think this is going to help.' Emily had given him a look that suggested her patience might be running out. 'But Richmond Park is so lovely and there'll be lots of opportunities for people-watching that might give you some insight. We could go for a walk and you could bring Rufus.'

It was that last suggestion that had swung it. He'd mentioned the dog to Emily on the trip to the ice rink, and she'd told him how much she missed having a dog now she was living in

London and it wasn't practical for her to have one. Jude would have thought the same if he didn't have a garden or work from home. He took Rufus out at least once a day, often walking the mile to Hyde Park so that the dog had a bit more green space to enjoy. But Richmond Park would be a whole new adventure, and he was confident that even if the idea of watching people riding around on a horse and carriage for a reality TV show didn't thrill him that Emily would somehow come up with another useful angle to apply to his story. She hadn't failed so far.

'I can't believe how quickly November is flying past, although you can feel the drop in the temperature, can't you?' Emily was waiting outside the Roehampton Café, next to where Jude had parked, as arranged. She was wearing a long padded coat and a bright red bobble hat and matching scarf that would make her stand out in a crowd, even if she hadn't been capable of doing that all by herself. 'Hello, gorgeous!'

For a split second, Jude thought Emily was talking to him, but then she leant down and made a huge fuss of Rufus, who almost curled himself into a ball with excitement. Jude might not believe in love at first sight when it came to humans, but he knew for a fact that it existed with dogs, because he'd just witnessed Rufus's instant adoration of Emily.

'It's definitely colder.' Jude answered her original question, but he might as well have stayed silent for all the notice she and Rufus were taking of him. 'Shall we get a drink before we go?'

'I've brought us a flask and a bit of a picnic.' Emily gestured towards a rucksack sitting on the ground a couple of feet away. 'We might have to find a bench to watch the carriage go past, and I thought bringing lunch was the least I could do, seeing as you're spending so much money on my fee.'

The playful smile was back and it was just as well that Emily's words had been a timely reminder that this was strictly business.

'Great, well, in that case, shall we get going? I think Rufus is dying to stretch his legs and find his own picnic if he gets the chance, probably consisting of deer droppings knowing him.'

'I think we can do better than that, and I might just have packed him a treat or two.' Emily picked up the rucksack.

'I can carry that.'

She brushed his hand away as he attempted to reach for it. 'I'm perfectly capable, thank you.'

'I don't doubt it.' He liked the flashes of feistiness he'd witnessed in Emily even more than the softer side of her personality. 'Right, where are we headed?'

'Holly Lodge, where the carriage rides start, is a mile and a half in that direction.' Emily gestured across the park. 'India suggested we find a spot between here and there as the camera crew will be at Holly Lodge and then towards the end of the route, where they've been told to expect the proposal.'

'I'm still not sure what I'm supposed to be learning from this. For DCI McGuigan to go on a carriage ride, he'd have to suspect the driver of being a murderer. Either that or he's had a frontal lobotomy.'

'Is that what they're called, carriage drivers?' She was getting good at not rising to the bait, and she didn't wait for him to answer as she headed towards the path. 'As for what you can learn from this, I'm not expecting you to put a carriage ride in your books, but what you might witness is the way someone looks when the person they love has planned something incredibly special just for them. Or how someone looks when they're about to take the huge step of asking another person to spend the rest of their lives together.'

'And what gives you the impression I don't already know what those things look like?' He might never have gone all out quite like this, but he'd done silly things for Mia when they'd had no money, like making her heart-shaped toast on Valentine's Day and scouring what felt like every second-hand shop in London to find vintage fashion magazines to add to her collection. It wasn't unusual for him to make thoughtful gestures towards his friends either, so it wasn't that Jude didn't understand, it was just that carriage rides felt like forced romance to him, in the same way a game of charades would have felt like forced fun, often resulting in the opposite of the intended effect. Although clearly Emily was choosing to believe he had no idea what he was talking about.

'Call it a hunch.' She grinned again and the strength of the urge to kiss her took him by surprise. It was a stupid idea, and one he'd never act upon, but there was no denying it was there. He didn't doubt physical attraction; it was just what so many people mistook for the feeling of falling in love. Thank God he wasn't that naïve. It was far easier to rationalise and dismiss it when you knew what those feelings really meant.

Rufus loved the park every bit as much as Jude had expected him to, although there was no way he was trusting the dog off the lead with so many deer around. He and Emily had talked about the book, and he'd told her he was beginning to make some revisions that he thought might sow the seeds of a believable relationship for McGuigan, with a woman he'd first met years before, during his initial police training. An item left at the scene of a murder McGuigan was investigating would reveal that the killer had attended the same training course, forcing McGuigan to suspect everyone, even his ex-girlfriend. It would tie together the light and shade in his protagonist's life, just as Emily had suggested.

'Shall we stop here for a bit? According to the timeline India gave me, the carriage should be along soon.' Emily gestured towards a bench at the side of the path.

'Sounds good.' Jude took off the leather messenger bag he had across his chest, removing a collapsable dog bowl and bottle of water. 'I think Rufus needs a drink too.'

'He brings out a different side to you.' Emily gave Jude an appraising stare. 'Maybe that's another way you could soften McGuigan up, having him bonding with his love interest over a dog. Perhaps they could reminisce about a dog they worked with during their training that they both have fond memories of. If Rufus can break through your defences, I'm sure it could work for McGuigan too.'

'Have you ever thought about writing? I think you could give Sophia a run for her money.' Jude chose to ignore her comment about breaking through his defences and resisted the urge to tell her that the storyline she'd suggested was far too schmaltzy for one of his novels. But he wasn't being flippant; he genuinely thought she had the potential to write something that could easily rival Sophia's stuff.

'I love what I do now, but never say never. I just love stories, all kinds of stories. That's why I think people-watching is such a great way to generate ideas. I sometimes do it to create a more rounded picture in my head of a character whose story I'm narrating, but as a writer I'm guessing you could give anyone you saw a whole backstory.'

'It's not usually how I work.'

'Isn't this whole thing about trying something different? Maybe you should give it a go. What about her?' Emily pointed to the woman who'd just passed them and was now about thirty feet away. She'd looked to be in her mid-fifties. She had dark circles under her eyes, suggesting a problem with sleeping, and she hadn't minded one bit when Rufus had rubbed himself against her leg as they'd passed one another.

'Her name's Samantha, she's fifty-four, and she's just coming out of the other side of a tough divorce that she thought might kill her, but she's just starting to realise she's got her freedom back.'

'That's a lot of detail.' Emily raised her eyebrows and gestured towards a young couple standing next to one of the trees, clearly trying to get a closer look at the deer. 'What about those two?'

'Okay, their names are Lily and Sam, both mid-twenties. Lily is a vegan who is passionate about the environment, and Sam is just pretending to be so that she'll sleep with him.'

'Wow. Cynical.'

'All right then, so what backstory would you give them?'

'Let's stick with Lily and Sam.' Emily leant forward in her seat. 'They're great names, and I think you're right about the ages too. I'd say they first went out together at school, lost touch when they went to different universities, and bumped into each other by chance just today, in one of the park cafés. She's an aspiring wildlife photographer, and he's struggling to get his career as a journalist off the ground.'

'And you said I gave Samantha a lot of detail.' Jude laughed.

'I'm not finished yet.' Emily screwed up her face for a moment. 'Spending time together today makes them realise they still have feelings for each other, and that they share a passion for wildlife that they could use as a basis to support one another's careers. Their walk in the park will lead to dinner, and a discussion about setting up social media accounts that showcase Lily's photographic skills and Sam's journalism side by side. They'll become an online sensation and—'

He couldn't stop himself from cutting her off. 'Wait, don't tell me. They'll get married, have three beautiful children and live happily ever after. The end.'

'And what exactly is wrong with that?'

'Nothing.' He shrugged, telling himself he should just leave it there, but somehow he couldn't. 'Except the truth is that even if Lily and Sam do get married, they're more likely to end up getting divorced than staying together. And even if they do stay together, statistics suggest the chances of them being genuinely happy are even lower.'

'Do you really believe a good relationship doesn't make people happier?' Emily was looking at him with something akin to sympathy, but there was no reason for anyone to feel sorry for him. He was realistic, and as far as he was concerned that gave him the advantage.

'I'm sure a good relationship would, I just don't think many of them exist.'

Emily took the flask out of her bag and set it down on the bench between them. 'Can I ask you a question?'

'Okay.'

'Who broke your heart so badly that it left you doubting whether a good relationship is even possible?'

'I've never had my heart broken, because I've never been stupid enough to put it on the line.' Jude bent down for a moment and fiddled with the clasp on Rufus's lead so that he wouldn't have to look Emily in the face. If he did, she'd realise he was lying. His heart had been broken by two women, it was just that neither of them had been the woman who'd walked out of their shared flat to go off with another man, and he didn't think Emily would understand that. The first woman to break his heart had been his mother when she'd died, and the second time it had been broken by the cruelty of his father's new wife. His experiences had showcased in technicolour what happened when you 'fell in love'. His father had been almost destroyed by Ros's death, and Sandra had done her very best to finish the job during their marriage. He didn't want to risk losing someone he loved, any more than he wanted to risk falling in love with someone who turned out to be another person entirely. That was a mug's game.

'I think that's really sad.' Emily poured hot chocolate into the tin mugs she'd brought with her.

'I take it you've had your heart broken and it still hasn't put you off trying to find love?' Jude did his best not to sound dismissive, but he wasn't sure he'd pulled it off.

'I'm not sure I've had my heart broken either, but I don't think it would put me off if I had. I want something like my parents have got. If you saw them, I'd defy even you to be cynical.'

'Ah, but that's from the outside looking in. No one can really know how it feels unless they're on the inside.'

'But how will you ever understand how it feels to be on the inside if you don't even try?' Emily gave him a look of exasperation, just as the distinctive sound of hooves clip-clopping along the path towards them filled the air and Jude had to grab hold of Rufus's collar to stop the dog trying to lurch forward, despite the fact his lead was tied to the bench.

He'd been about to respond and tell her that he'd got close enough to the inside of his father's relationship with Sandra to experience its ugliness first hand, but he was glad the carriage had come along to stop him. He hadn't spoken to anyone about how those years with Sandra had shaped him, and he had no idea why he'd come so close to opening up to a woman he barely knew. There was just something about Emily that made him feel he had to justify his beliefs, but he had no idea why that was either.

7

Emily was starting to feel guilty about taking Jude's money. She'd done her best to show him what falling in love felt like, but the comment he'd made yesterday in Richmond Park kept coming back to her. He was never really going to understand what that looked like from the outside; he had to *feel* it. Watching other people in real life was no different to watching a movie. It was too disconnected from whatever it was that had closed Jude off to the idea so completely. She'd tried asking him about his past, but it was like the shutters had come down. He'd insisted he'd never put his heart on the line, but she'd have bet three months' rent that someone or something had hurt him really badly. If he wasn't willing to share that with her, she had no idea what to show him that might help. All she knew was that her latest idea wasn't working. She'd arranged to meet him at the London Eye, after a tipoff from a callout she'd put on social media. A man had responded to say that he was planning to propose to his boyfriend after they got off the three o'clock flight, on the fourth anniversary of their first date. Emily and Jude had arrived in time to witness the proposal, but it was clear it had left him cold.

Now they were wandering along the South Bank Winter Market and Jude kept sighing audibly.

'What's wrong?'

'Do people really like this stuff?' He paused by one of the market stalls, the scent of mulled wine filling the air and a long queue forming to buy Belgian-style waffles.

'Of course they do, it helps make them feel Christmassy.'

'What, buying overpriced crap from garden sheds?' Jude shook his head, and Emily bit her lip. This wasn't working and she didn't want to admit how disappointed she was that stopping for a warming mug of glühwein and watching the sunset over the Thames was clearly the last thing Jude would want to do. She'd stupidly thought if she could capture a romantic moment they were part of, however tenuously, that he might actually feel something. But it wasn't going to happen and the fact she felt so disappointed was a clear indication that she'd taken the fantasy too far already. She had a habit of doing that, and maybe he was right; maybe that was a legacy of loving romance novels as much as she did. Except the idea of getting lost in a perfect moment made her every bit as happy as reading about them. So what if that kind of thing didn't often live up to expectations in real life? She still wanted to believe that it could. But it didn't matter what she did to try and convince Jude; he was never going to believe in those moments, and he was wasting his money paying her to try and teach him something he wasn't willing to learn.

'I think we should call it a day.' Emily didn't look at him as she spoke, because then he'd realise she was upset and she felt like a fool for letting this get to her as much as it had.

'I thought we were going to Grosvenor Square next.'

'I don't think there's any point.' Emily dodged to one side as a group of young women, wearing reindeer antlers and laughing loudly, passed by, taking up most of the path. One of them, clearly on her hen do, had a veil attached to her antlers.

'What do you mean there's no point?'

'I think this might have been a stupid idea. Me trying to show you how people look when they're in love. I thought Christmas was the ideal time but I think it's proving to be a distraction if anything. I suppose I didn't really believe you hated Christmas every bit as much as you hate the concept of romantic love.' Emily quickened her pace. For some reason her eyes were stinging, but she wasn't going to cry over Jude Cavendish, that was for sure. She just hated failing, that was all. 'Anyway, you were right. I started reading the first DCI McGuigan book and he'd never do anything I'd perceive as romantic. It was a stupid idea and I'm sorry. I can refund you the money. I should never have thought I was qualified to do this.'

'It wasn't stupid.' Jude sighed heavily. 'I'm just... not like other people, I suppose. But I don't want my money back. Talking to you has given me some solid ideas about how to introduce a relationship for McGuigan, even if that doesn't look like the type that Sophia would put in her books, and I'm pretty sure I wouldn't have got that far without you. I'd still like to go to Grosvenor Square, if you can bear my company one last time.'

'I just don't understand why you'd want to go, after everything you've said.'

'I think we've established that I'm sceptical about romantic love.' He laughed at the look that must have crossed her face. Sceptical didn't do it justice. 'Okay, okay, maybe it goes beyond that, but you said something about Grosvenor Square being a good way to observe other kinds of love. Maybe if I can find a way to reveal that side of McGuigan, I can write him a believable relationship too. It's got to be worth a shot, and we more or less pass Grosvenor Square on the way home.'

'I thought you said all love was just a form of transaction.' It had been a conversation they'd had after they'd seen a family of four together at the ice rink, and she'd made a throwaway comment about how it was impossible not to believe in love when you saw them together. Jude had suggested they were only together because they got something from one another – care and security for the children, and some form of fulfilment that the parents had been seeking. He'd made the argument that in years to come the family wouldn't be so close. The children would no longer need their parents in the same way, and their parents would have to find something else to fill the gap that was left behind. As for whether the mum and dad would still be together, he'd had doubts about that too. It was all so clinical, dissecting the parts of something beautiful and making it seem ugly instead, summing up love as just a transaction. She should have known even then that this was going to be a waste of time.

'And as I recall, you told me I was wrong and that Grosvenor Square would prove it.'

'Okay.' Emily didn't even try to inject any enthusiasm into her voice. This would be her last attempt to get Jude to understand what she was trying to show him, and if he didn't get it at Grosvenor Square, he never would. 'But I'm only doing it because it's in the same direction as Shepherd's Bush, otherwise I wouldn't bother.'

'Message received and understood.' Jude nodded, and she hated the part of herself that was relieved they had a bit more time together. She should just walk away now, but she'd promised to take him to Grosvenor Square, and if there was one thing Emily hated doing, it was breaking a promise.

* * *

The Ever After Garden consisted of twenty thousand illuminated white silk roses, spread out across Grosvenor Square. Emily had seen it in the daytime before, but never at night, and the sight made her catch her breath. She wasn't the only one.

'It's beautiful.' Jude stopped on the path, a sea of roses in front of them, and they watched as two young women handed something to a member of staff. There was a brief exchange as the women selected a rose and the young man carefully placed a small wooden plaque next to it. Jude turned towards Emily. 'Do you know what they're doing?'

'Dedicating a rose to someone they've lost. It's a way of remembering a loved one and bringing them into your Christmas, now they're no longer here. All the funds raised go to the Royal Marsden.'

'Do you have to have lost someone to cancer?' Jude was still watching the two young women, who hadn't moved away from the rose they'd chosen. They had their arms around one another and it must have been obvious, even to someone as dispassionate as Jude, that this was an emotional moment for them.

'I thought you'd have heard about this, living close by.' Perhaps Emily shouldn't have been surprised; to say that Jude didn't seem the sentimental type was an understatement.

'I try to avoid anywhere that might get touristy at this time of year.' Jude let go of a long breath. 'But it's surprisingly quiet here, and there's something about the atmosphere. It's almost as if the park understands what it's playing host to.' It was the closest Jude had come to saying anything emotional.

'I know what you mean, but to answer your question, no, it doesn't have to be to remember someone who had cancer. You can dedicate a rose to anyone. I've been thinking about doing one for my grandparents, but I wasn't sure if I'd get over here before I went home for Christmas.' Emily moved ahead of Jude on the pavement. 'Now I'm here, I'm going to do it. Why don't you read some of the dedications? I've got a feeling they'll all be written with love.'

'I want to dedicate a rose too.' If Jude had suddenly started clucking like a chicken, Emily wasn't sure she'd have been any more surprised.

'Oh, okay.' She desperately wanted to ask who he was dedicating it to, but she didn't want him to shut down before he'd even had the chance to allow himself to feel something. As it was, he disclosed the information without her having to say anything.

'It's for my mother. She died when I was ten, in a skiing accident, four days after Christmas.' And there it was, in one simple sentence – the reason why Jude hated this time of year so much. Suddenly, Emily had the urge to hug him, but she linked her hands together instead, waiting for the feeling to pass.

'I'm really sorry, that must have been so hard. I almost lost my mum in a car accident when I was a teenager, and it changed everything for me. So I can't even imagine how difficult it was for you.'

'It was a long time ago.' Jude tried to brush it off, but his eyes gave him away. Even after all this time, it still hurt. So he was human after all, and there was no doubt he'd been capable of love in the past. But she wasn't going to push him to talk about it if he didn't want to.

'Let's go and get our roses.' Emily led the way to the pop-up booth where three members of staff were taking payments for the dedications. She didn't want to encroach on Jude's moment and, as curious as she was, she was determined not to read the dedication he wrote for his mother. If he was ever going to get in touch with his feelings enough to translate them to his characters, he needed the space to do it. 'I'll go to the far side of the counter, if you want to go to the left. We can meet up once we've both finished and chosen our roses.'

'Okay, thank you.' When Jude turned to look at her, their eyes locked for a moment and the urge to hug him returned, very nearly overwhelming her this time. Instead, she turned towards the counter, taking out her phone to make the payment for the dedication. She forced herself not to look in Jude's direction, and by the time she'd selected her rose, and the member of staff had attached the dedication to it, he was already waiting for her.

'This was helpful, thank you.' Jude nodded, as if to emphasise his words.

'Are you telling me this was all you needed to believe in love?' She couldn't help smiling.

'Maybe not the romantic kind, but its's impossible to be here and see that... How does that awful song go? Love is all around. I suppose I can acknowledge that it exists for some people, even if I'll never believe in the truly unconditional kind, especially when it comes to romantic love. I still think that's an illusion.'

'If you read the dedications, I bet you'll find plenty of them dedicated to the partners of people who still love them, even though they're no longer here.' Emily held his gaze. 'Surely that's proof of romantic love?'

'If it does exist, it's a lot less common than people think and I'm struggling even more with the concept that it will for McGuigan. But I think he could feel this.' Jude gestured around him. 'Love for someone he lost and never recovered from. I always thought he was just a pessimist, too hardened by what he'd seen on the job to let anyone into his life. But I feel like I've got to know him better over the last week. I understand him and his motivations more now that you've helped me realise that his backstory needed to be deepened. I'm still not quite sure how his relationship will play out, but I'm much clearer now about why he struggles with it so much. If I can reveal that to readers, maybe they'll understand him more as well.'

'I think they will.' Emily wanted to tell Jude that she felt as if she understood him a little bit better now too, and to ask if he could see the parallels between himself and his lead character as clearly as she could, but she knew what his response would be. He'd laugh it off, maybe even ridicule the idea, and for some reason it mattered to her that they didn't part on a bad note. 'I'm really glad it helped, and at least I don't feel as if you've wasted all your money now, but let's drop it back to the hourly rate we originally agreed. I think that's fairer.'

'No, I want to pay you the higher rate. Otherwise you're less likely to agree to carrying on until I'm sure I've got a handle on how to give McGuigan a relationship my editor will go for.'

'I can't carry on. Like I said, I'm going home for Christmas.'

'It's the twentieth of November.' Jude gave her an incredulous look.

'I know, I bought myself a Maltesers advent calendar yesterday and I had to hide it under the bed to stop myself from opening it, but I'm still not sure I'll hold out for another ten days.' Emily laughed, even though it was no joke. 'But I'm going home tomorrow. I've got some prep work to do for books I'll be working on in the New Year, and I've booked a few slots at a studio in Truro to do some recordings, but I'll be home with my family for six weeks.'

'Six weeks with your family?' Jude pulled a face, as if he couldn't imagine anything worse, before seeming to regain his composure. 'We could meet up in Cornwall.'

His suggestion made Emily catch her breath for a moment and she just stared at him in shock without saying anything at first. It seemed like a crazy idea for him to come all the way to Cornwall just to see her. The village where she'd grown up felt like a completely different world to Emily, away from the one where she'd somehow ended up as a romance consultant on a crime writer's novel. The thought of Jude being a part of that other world was strangely unnerving, and it somehow felt far more personal than seeing him in London. Yet she couldn't deny the frisson of something that felt a lot like excitement at the prospect of continuing to see him, but it really was madness.

'Why on earth would you want to trek all the way down there to meet me, even if there was anything more I could think of that would help?'

'Because I've got to resubmit the book to my editor in the New Year, and because I'm spending Christmas in Cornwall too.' Jude pulled another face.

'Are you? Why?'

'I was brought up there and my father and his family still live there.' Jude seemed to stumble over the mention of his father's family, but it said a lot that Jude didn't see them as his family too. Emily was struggling to work out what possible reason he could have had for not mentioning he'd grown up in Cornwall before. She'd told him that was where she came from the day they'd gone to the ice rink. Either way, it was hardly like they'd be around the corner from one another, and it wouldn't be as easy to meet up as it had been in London. Her family had a saying about Cornish miles taking far longer than the same distance anywhere else; it was the narrow country roads, and there was no racing from A to B. It was a good enough reason for her to turn down his suggestion, even if the real reason was more about self-preservation.

'I don't have to tell you that Cornwall's a big place, then. We can't just jump on the Tube to meet up.'

'I know, but you said your family lived in Port Agnes, didn't you?' He paused as she nodded. 'Well, my dad's place is just outside Port Tremellien. So we'll virtually be neighbours.'

This time she couldn't stop herself from asking why he hadn't told her any of that before. 'Why didn't you mention it when I told you where I came from?'

'It didn't seem relevant at the time.' Jude shrugged, and Emily furrowed her brow. She wasn't sure she'd ever understand him, but she suspected he hadn't felt the need to tell her about the link they shared back then because he hadn't envisaged them staying in touch. He probably hadn't been sure if her input would be of any use, and it was only now that he'd apparently decided it was that he seemed willing to make some kind of personal connection. She wasn't sure why the idea annoyed her so much – after all, he was paying her very well for her advice – but for some reason it did.

'Okay, but I still don't know why you'd want to meet up. I've shown you everything I wanted to show you here. You just need to use that to flesh out McGuigan's character a bit and take it from there.'

'You said if I met your parents, I'd know what real love looked like.' Jude's blue eyes were still striking, even in the semi darkness of Grosvenor Square.

'You want to meet my parents?'

'Yes, if you think it would help.'

'Absolutely not. I wasn't being literal.' There was no way on earth she was putting her parents through that. They weren't animals in a zoo for Jude Cavendish to stare at.

'Fair enough.' He shrugged again, not looking remotely put out by the strength of her objection. 'But I'd like you to show me some of what a Christmas back home means to you, and why you still call it home, despite having lived in London for eight years.'

She was thrown off guard for a moment by the fact that he'd

remembered that, but she still didn't understand what he wanted from her. 'You must know what a Cornish Christmas looks like. You grew up there too.'

'I suspect my upbringing was very different from yours.' There it was again, that little chink in the armour that allowed her to glimpse another side of Jude. A side that made her far more inclined to continue helping him than she would have been otherwise. He clearly wasn't going to stop trying to convince her that he needed her help either. 'You could read some of the revised draft for me too, give me your opinion on whether readers will buy into the relationship and care how it turns out.'

'You could email it to me.' For a moment he seemed to consider her suggestion, and she was already regretting making it, because despite how infuriating he could be, for some reason a big part of her didn't want this to be goodbye. But then he shook his head.

'I'll be there anyway and I'll need an excuse to get away from my father's family for a while. So you'd be doing me a huge favour.' There it was, that choice of words again – *my father's family*. She had no idea what the story behind it was, but it persuaded her to agree.

'Okay then, but I'll have to let you know how much time I can spare you when I get down there and work everything out.'

'I'll be spending most of my time writing, so that works for me. Just let me know when you can meet.'

'I will.' Emily held out her hand and Jude shook it. If it had been anyone else, she might have given him a kiss on the cheek to say goodbye, but for some reason it felt like that would have been a mistake with Jude. 'I'll see you in Cornwall then.'

'Can I walk you back to the Tube station? It's getting late.'

'I'll be fine. There are plenty of people around, but thank you.' She turned and began walking away from him before he could protest, but she was strangely touched by the fact he'd offered. That was the thing about Jude; he only revealed crumbs of insight into who he might really be, but those crumbs were oddly compelling. She knew she'd make time to meet up with him when she got back to Cornwall, because she couldn't deny she wanted to find out more about him, even though there was a good chance she might not like what she discovered.

8

Even as Jude authorised the payment for the holiday let he'd just booked for the next week, he wondered what the hell he was doing. The decision to rent somewhere wasn't the issue; there was no way he could face spending that amount of time with his father, even if he and Viv had been willing to put up with Jude for that long. It was the fact he was going to Cornwall at all, and that he'd rented an apartment overlooking the harbour in Port Agnes, in the same village where Emily would be. He told himself it was because, when the property had come up, he hadn't been able to believe his luck. Puffin's Rest was beautiful, and the views from the windows were breathtaking. It was the perfect place to hole up and get some writing done.

When he'd contacted the owner, the man had explained that the apartment was only available because the renovations on it hadn't been due to complete until the end of January, so they hadn't taken any bookings until February. When the work got finished early, he'd decided to list it; less than half an hour before Jude had found it and made the enquiry. Maybe it was fate, but the fact that he'd included Port Agnes in his search at all meant he couldn't really call it that. The truth was he'd never have included the village where Emily lived if he hadn't known that was where she'd be.

Puffin's Rest had an enclosed courtyard, but it was at the bottom of a steep flight of stairs. Still, there were wonderful walks along the coastal paths for Rufus right on the doorstep. And getting away to a new location had to help fire his imagination and get him inspired to complete the revisions on his book. It also meant he'd be spared December in London when the throngs of crowds could surely make even a diehard Christmas fan long for January, let alone someone who found the holiday season as difficult as he did.

Even the sight of a holly wreath on someone's door could get to Jude. There'd been one hanging on the door of the church when he and his father had gone to see the vicar about his mother's funeral, the day after her body had been flown home, when they should all still have been having fun on the ski slopes together. Christmas couldn't be over fast enough for him. When the owner of Puffin's Rest had asked if he'd like a Christmas tree to be delivered, Jude had declined. He'd much rather look out at the sea and enjoy its dramatic moods. It felt far more suited to this time of year than fairy lights and tinsel. Maybe renting an apartment in Port Agnes for the best part of two months wasn't such a crazy idea after all, although it meant he had absolutely no way of avoiding spending Christmas with his family.

'Well, this is unexpected.' Jude's father, Charles, had a way of making every phone call feel as if it was unwelcome, and today was no exception.

'I just wanted to call to talk about Christmas.' Jude was heading off to Cornwall first thing in the morning, but he had no intention of dropping by his father's place the moment he arrived, or pretty much any time before Christmas Day.

'Viv messaged you about that and she's still waiting for an answer.'

'I know, I'm sorry, but like I said, that's why I'm calling.'

'Don't you think, out of courtesy, that you should be speaking to Viv about this instead? After all, she's the one who contacted you about making arrangements.' Charles's tone was even, but it was still on the tip of Jude's tongue to ask his father whether he thought he should have been the one to invite his son for Christmas Day, but there was no point. Charles had always been the kind of man who was able to compartmentalise the different facets of his life. When it came to Jude, it had been out of sight, out of mind. While he was at boarding school, as far as Charles was concerned, he was under the care of the staff, and it didn't seem to occur to him that Jude might still need his father. Now that he was married to Viv, he seemed equally happy to leave it to her to be the channel for communication between him and his son. Jude didn't know whether it would have made any difference if his father had been the one to reach out and ask him to spend Christmas with them, but he couldn't deny he would have liked him to try.

'I'll message Viv straight after this, but I wanted to talk to you first.'

'Okay, but like I said, she's the one who knows all the plans. Who's coming when, what days we're at the various get-togethers she's accepted invitations to and whatnot. I'll probably only mess up if I suggest when you should come down and how long you should stay for.'

'I won't be staying with you.' Jude couldn't keep the hint of bitterness out of his voice. He couldn't envisage ever having children, but if he did one day become a father, he couldn't imagine not wanting them to come back home as adults whenever they felt like it. It shouldn't matter to his dad whether Jude might be there at the same time as other guests, or when Viv and his father had plans elsewhere. Their home should feel like his home, not like he was a guest in a hotel who couldn't be left there without someone 'on duty'.

'Don't tell me you're staying in that flat on your own for another Christmas?' For a moment he thought his father might be disappointed, or concerned. But then Charles added the line Jude should have known was coming. 'It'll really upset Viv if you turn down another invitation to Christmas.'

Charles could have said, *I really want to spend time with you*, or even, *It would be brilliant to have you here*, like Viv had said, but he didn't. His father wasn't worried about seeing his son at Christmas, he just didn't want his wife to be upset. Viv was his only priority, just as Sandra had been his only priority when they'd been together. The only difference was that Viv was a lovely woman, who Jude could bear to be in the same room as. In truth it was more than that; he enjoyed Viv's company, he just wished it didn't come hand-in-hand with having his father's company too. There was far more baggage there.

'I will be spending Christmas Day with you. I just won't be staying over.'

'So you're staying in a hotel? Surely that's an unnecessary expense?'

'No, I'm not staying in a hotel, I'm—' Jude's father didn't even let him finish.

'Please don't tell me you're thinking of driving all the way down here for one day. That's even more ridiculous.'

'I've rented an apartment, a couple of villages away.' For some reason, Jude didn't want to tell his father exactly where he would be.

'Why on earth would you do that, when you know there's room for you here?'

'Is there?' This time Jude didn't give his father a chance to answer. 'Look, I'm treating it as a bit of a writing retreat. I've got some major edits to do and I thought the change of scene and getting away from London for a bit would help.'

'Hmm.' His father sounded doubtful, even before he went on. 'I'm not sure how swapping sitting in one apartment on your own for doing exactly the same thing in another will make a lot of difference, but I'm sure you know best.' It was crystal clear from Charles's tone that he didn't think so at all.

'It'll make it easier for me to see you all without having to impose.' Jude paused for a moment, but his father didn't even try to counter the idea that his presence might be a nuisance. In the end, it was Jude who broke the silence. 'I'll text Viv to sort out the details, but I just wanted to let you know I'll be seeing you on Christmas Day.'

'Just make sure you don't forget to tell Viv.' That was it. Not even the slightest hint of enthusiasm about the news that Jude was 'coming home' for Christmas, but then he shouldn't have expected any other response.

'I will, don't worry. I'll see you on the twenty-fifth then.' He had even less intention now of seeing his father before Christmas Day, despite the fact he'd only be a few miles away for the next five weeks.

'All right then. Oh, and Jude…' This was his father's chance to say something that would prove his son wrong and show him just how much his coming home meant.

'Yes?'

'Make sure you text Viv today. I think she's ordering the turkey soon, so she needs to know how many of us there'll be.'

'No problem. Bye, Dad.' As Jude disconnected the call, his shoulders slumped. Suddenly the thought of going back to Cornwall for Christmas seemed even more stupid. But he reminded himself why he was going. He needed to get this book into shape, and he couldn't deny the difference the help Emily had given him was making. He was going to Port Agnes to finish the job he'd started, to get his career back on track and stop Marty pulling the plug on the DCI McGuigan series. Opening his contacts, his fingers hovered over Emily's name for a second or two as he wondered whether he should text to offer her a lift down to Cornwall. She'd said she was leaving tomorrow too, and it seemed a waste for him to drive down there with an empty car. Then he remembered how long the journey took and just how interminable it could feel if you got stuck in a traffic jam. He wasn't sure Emily would still be speaking to him if they were confined together like that for hours on end, let alone willing to continue acting as a consultant on his book. So he thought better of it. Instead, he fired off a quick text to his stepmother.

> Hi Viv. Thanks so much for the offer of coming to you for Christmas. So sorry for the delay in responding, but I've been up against some deadlines for my next book. It would be great to spend Christmas Day with you, Fiona and the family. I won't be staying over, I've rented somewhere nearby as a writing retreat and at least it saves you the hassle of having to make up the room before and after. See you then and thanks again.

His stepmother must have had the phone in her hands ready to type her response, because her reply came through almost straight away.

> Hey Jude! Sorry, I know, but I don't think I'm ever going to stop doing that! Can't wait to see you and, if you change your mind about staying over, it's always a pleasure to have you here, never a hassle. You're welcome any time, I hope you know that. Off to order the turkey now, good luck with the deadlines! Lots of love, Viv xx

He stared at the message, unable to stop himself wishing that his father was just a tiny bit like Viv. He wondered how different things might have been between them if Charles had been warmer, or if he'd met Viv sooner, instead of putting them both through his ill-fated marriage to Sandra. But it was pointless wondering about that, just like it was pointless wondering how things might have been different if his mother hadn't died. His relationship with his father was what it was, and he doubted very much there was anything either of them could do about it, even if they'd been willing to try.

* * *

As usual, Emily had broken her journey to Cornwall in Exeter, staying the night with her sister Charlotte and her young family. She loved spending time with her six-year-old niece, Bronte, and the tornado of energy and excitement created by her four-year-old twin nephews, Ellis and Arthur. How Charlotte had the time to brush her teeth with them around amazed Emily, let alone how she continued to run a small accountancy business from home. Her husband, Jake, was very hands-on too, but his work as a health and safety consultant took him away from home fairly frequently, and Emily had a feeling that was her brother-in-law's version of down time.

'I wish I could stay longer, and I wish I could help out more on a regular basis.' The guilt in Emily's chest as she said goodbye to her sister weighed almost as heavily as her nephews clinging to her legs on either side. They'd woken her up just after 6 a.m. by bouncing on her bed and whacking each other with a pillow. Every moment she spent in Charlotte's house gave her a new level of respect for her sister.

'I wish you could stay longer too, but I know you've got recordings to prepare for and that you want to go with Mum and Dad to the hospital appointment on Tuesday.' Charlotte had hugged her tightly and long enough for Emily to wonder if she was having trouble letting go. 'I'll see you soon anyway. We're going to come down as soon as the kids break up from school, but I need you to let me know if you think Mum and Dad can cope with having us staying there for over a week. If not, we'll see if we can find an Airbnb.'

'I'm sure it'll be fine. There's plenty of room.' Their parents' house had four bedrooms and a big downstairs study with a sofa bed, so there was lots of space for everyone, but Emily knew that wasn't what her sister had meant.

'I'm not talking about how much room there is; it's whether it'll all be too much. You've seen what the kids are like and with Mum—'

Emily interrupted Charlotte, knowing what her concerns were without her needing to voice them, and keen to put her mind at rest. 'The last thing Mum will want is to miss out on having an entire week with you. I'll be there the whole time. With you, me and Jake, we'll be able to do one-on-one marking with the kids. And if Dad wants to take you and the kids out somewhere and Mum doesn't feel up to it, I can keep an eye on her to give him a break. It'll be good for all of us.'

'Okay, but if you get there and you think differently, just promise you'll let me know.'

'I will.'

Charlotte had given her another hug, and Emily had eventually managed to peel her nephews away from her legs, with promises of taking them out to the soft play centre in Port Tremellien when they were all down in Cornwall. The journey from Exeter to Port Agnes had been uneventful. Emily's father, Richard, had told her to call when she was due to arrive so he could pick her up. It was only a ten-minute walk from the station to home, but with six weeks' worth of packing, not to mention the Christmas presents she'd already bought, she was wrestling with one large case and one medium-sized one. Charlotte had insisted on picking her up in Exeter, and Jake had dropped her back to the station, but even loading and unloading on the train had been tricky. So walking home wasn't really an option. There was no way she was calling her father out though, because he'd worry about her mum the whole time they were gone if she did.

Her mother's falls had become far more common in the past eighteen months, and Emily had been shocked by the toll that Parkinson's disease had taken on Patsy's body. It was obvious her condition was progressing, and Emily was almost certain that the consultant would say that Patsy was starting to need support to get dressed, and was reliant on a walker to get around the house. After she'd had a fall while Emily's father was out at work, he'd decided to take early retirement.

'She was lying on the floor for almost two hours before I could get home.' He'd had tears in his eyes when he'd recounted the story, but when Emily had offered to move back home to support them, he wouldn't hear of it.

'I signed up for better, for worse, in sickness and in health, and I meant every word of it. Looking after your mum is my responsibility.' He'd stopped then and shook his head. 'No, not my responsibility, it's my privilege.'

It didn't matter how often Emily repeated the offer, both her parents had declined every single time. In the end it had started to upset Patsy, and Emily had agreed to her father's pleas to stop mentioning it.

'She can't bear the thought of this curtailing your life in any way, so the best thing you can do is to keep going out there, doing what you love, and making us proud.'

Emily had got her love of books from her mother, who read voraciously. She'd even witnessed Patsy trying to do the hoovering and read a novel at the same time once, because the book was quite literally too good to put down. It was no wonder Emily had developed the same sort of habits. Patsy had fallen in love with the novels of the Brontë sisters as a child and it was why her daughters had been christened Charlotte Anne and Emily Elizabeth. Charlotte had ended up carrying on the tradition, settling on Bronte for her daughter, and naming her sons after two other members of the Brontë family. Her parents' house had bookshelves in every room and, just like after the car accident, Patsy had told Emily that escaping into novels had been her salvation when the Parkinson's began to take away more of her independence. Patsy had got hooked on audio books too, and Emily knew her mother would be anxious to hear everything about her upcoming projects, so she couldn't wait to get home to tell her.

There was no long line of taxis outside Port Agnes station in the winter, like there would have been outside any station in London, but if you were very lucky there was sometimes a taxi waiting outside. Thankfully, Emily's luck was in, and Clive, who drove the only year-round taxi that serviced Port Agnes station, was free to take her home.

'I thought you were going to call.' Emily's father got up from the table in the kitchen and threw his arms around her as she came in through the door at the side of the house. 'I didn't even hear your key in the lock, and Gary Barlow certainly didn't.'

Emily grinned at the mention of her parents' dog. He was a Border terrier, who'd been named in honour of her mother's favourite singer. Patsy had fallen in love with a song he'd written when she'd been recovering from the car accident. The song had already been a few years old by then, but she'd heard it on the radio and the lyrics had really resonated with her. After that, she'd started listening to every song he'd ever written, and she could probably answer questions about Gary Barlow as her specialist subject on *Mastermind* if the need ever arose. Whenever anyone in the family was talking about the dog, they always used his full name, to avoid confusing him with their next-door neighbour, Gary, and it had just kind of stuck. The only time the dog's name ever got shortened to Gary was when he was out on a walk and they needed to call him to come back. Emily's father had said there was no way he was putting up with the strange looks people gave him when he stood on Port Agnes beach, calling out at the top of his voice for the lead singer of Take That. Why her parents hadn't just called him Barlow was a mystery no one could answer, but after eight years it was far too late for a rethink now.

'Is he starting to go grey?' Emily knelt down to where Gary Barlow was sitting, in his basket by the wood burner, and planted a kiss on top of his head. It was covered with of wisps of wire-like hair. If he'd been a human being, there was no way she'd have kissed him, but somehow it was different with dogs.

'It seems like it.' Her father sighed. 'But he still gets really excited whenever we're about to go out for a walk, so there's life in the old dog yet.'

'You're going to live forever, aren't you, boy?' Emily stood up and took one of the dog treats out of the jar on the Welsh dresser. Gary Barlow might have been getting on a bit, but there was nothing wrong with his sense of smell, and she almost lost a finger with the speed he whipped the treat out of her hand. 'How's Mum?'

'She had a bit of a fall again yesterday.' Her father's tone was falsely bright, but she didn't miss the way his jaw clenched. Even when her mother had broken her wrist in February, her parents had insisted that she'd only had *a bit of a fall*. It wasn't until Emily had come for a long weekend over Easter that she'd discovered her mother had broken her wrist in two places.

'I know you two and your "bit of a fall" description. Am I going to go through to the front room and find her lying on the sofa with her leg in plaster?'

'No, I promise.' Her father gave her a watery smile, and her chest ached at how tired he was suddenly looking. He was only sixty-two, but his once bright ginger hair had long since washed out to a very faded mix of auburn and grey. There were grooves etched along the skin on his forehead which looked new, and a deep crease between his eyebrows. The last few years had been tough. Emily's mother had been diagnosed with Parkinson's disease two years after the car accident. At first the symptoms had been mild and the doctors had been confident that the medication would ensure the progress remained slow, and that Patsy would have the same life expectancy as everyone else. But then the medication had stopped working as well, and Patsy's symptoms had begun to get worse as she moved from stage one through to stage three, and now, it seemed, it was worse still. 'It's so lovely to have you home, darling, and your mum is going to be really thrilled to see you.'

'I know. I'm so happy to be home with you guys too.' Emily hugged her father again, meaning every word. She knew how lucky she was to have parents who adored her, and a sister who might have been her best friend if they weren't related. Not everyone had a family like that, and she couldn't help thinking of Jude in that moment. He'd looked horrified at the thought of going back to Cornwall to spend time with his family, and she had a feeling that explained a lot about him. She still hadn't got to see many of the chinks in his armour, but what she had seen suggested that his mother's death was at the heart of everything. Emily was determined to do what she could to help Jude get past that so that he could finish his book, and she wouldn't have to feel guilty about just how much money he'd paid her. But for now there was only one mother on her mind – her own – and she was about to give Patsy the kind of hug reserved especially for her. And just like when Charlotte had hugged her goodbye, Emily wasn't sure she'd ever be able to let go.

9

Emily had been home for two days without venturing outside again for anything more than a dog walk. She'd missed her parents so much and it had been really lovely just to hang out together and not have any plans. But today she was meeting up with an old friend from school.

'You look lovely, darling. Give my love to Rosie.' Emily's mother looked up at her from the armchair next to the wood-burning stove in the kitchen. Gary Barlow was lying by her feet, snoring softly.

'I will, Mum, and thank you.' Emily leant down and kissed her mother's cheek. She'd always appreciated how lucky she was to have the parents she did, but ever since she'd started working with Jude, that feeling had been heightened. He'd lost his mother at an early age and hinted at a difficult upbringing, which she was certain had affected his decision not to let anyone get close to him. The easiest way to do that was to write off love as a concept altogether.

'Thank you for what?' Patsy gave her a questioning look.

'For being such a lovely mum. Sometimes I forget how lucky I am.'

Her mother caught hold of her hand. 'I'm the lucky one. Having you, Charlotte, and your dad.'

At that precise moment the dog opened its eyes and lifted its head. 'Oh, and Gary Barlow of course! I can't forget you, can I, sweetheart? You'd never let me.'

'I can take him for a walk when I get back if you like, before we go to the hospital.' Her mother's appointment wasn't until four o'clock, and she'd arranged to meet her friend, Rosie, for breakfast, before she started her shift. Rosie had just begun working at the Port Agnes Midwifery Unit, after previously having worked in Truro. It meant she was back living with her parents until she found somewhere to rent, and she'd told Emily she needed to get out of the house before she and her mother had another row. Emily couldn't imagine what it would be like to have a relationship like that with her mum. Despite all the health challenges she'd faced, Patsy had always been easy to be around.

'It's okay, darling, Dad is going to take him when he gets the papers. Just have a nice time with Rosie.'

'Okay, see you later. Love you.' Emily blew her mother a second kiss and turned towards the door, still thinking about how different her life would have been if she'd had a different sort of relationship with her parents, and trying not to think about why Jude Cavendish's life was occupying so many of her thoughts.

* * *

Port Agnes was beautiful all year round, but she loved the way the village was decorated at this time of year. There was a huge Christmas tree in the main square, and rows and rows of festoon lights strung between the houses on the narrow streets. A second tree had been constructed by the harbour from lobster pots. It might not have had the glitz and glamour of some of the decorations in London, but as far as Emily was concerned, it still beat the big city hands down. Her old school friend was already waiting by the make-shift Christmas tree when she arrived.

'Am I late?' Emily hugged Rosie as she reached her.

'No, I was here a bit early, just hanging around hoping to spot a handsome fisherman looking to land the catch of the day.' Rosie grinned.

'I thought you were off men after Ollie?' Emily had heard many times how Rosie would never trust a man again after discovering her husband of two years, who was a paramedic, had been sleeping with his crewmate since before they were even engaged. Admittedly, the last time she'd seen Rosie face to face had been months ago, but she'd been just as adamant then as she'd been when they first broke up.

'I'm not off men. I'd be up for a casual fling. As Ollie so kindly demonstrated, human biology doesn't support monogamy. I was fighting a losing battle all along, so it's just long-term relationships I'm done with.'

'You sound just like...' Emily shook her head, trying to get Jude out of it at least for a little while. 'Like a lot of people who seem to be saying the same sort of thing lately.'

'But not you eh, Em?' Rosie grinned and linked her arm through Emily's in a companionable way. 'We can still rely on you to believe in love and romance, while the rest of us turn into bitter old cynics.'

'I hope so, although God knows why. It's not like the relationships I've had have encouraged that belief, but growing up with parents like mine makes it hard not to believe it's true.'

'Ah, yes, Patsy and Richard, the couple who give us all hope.' Rosie squeezed Emily's arm. 'How's your mum doing?'

'Her symptoms have definitely got more severe, but hopefully she just needs a change of medication to stabilise things again. We're going to see her consultant this afternoon.'

'Give her my love, won't you?'

'I will, and she said the same to you.' Emily could smell freshly baked bread drifting on the air from Mehenick's, a bakery with its own café. Sometimes, Emily would lie in bed on a weekend in London and dream about toast made with one of their farmhouse loaves, or their giant cinnamon swirls that were big enough for two but which no one wanted to share. She turned to look at Rosie, silently praying that the smell of the bread would be enough to lure her friend too. 'Have you got anywhere particular in mind for breakfast?'

'Mehenick's? I'm starting my shift at the unit at eleven and I need to do some serious carb loading first.'

'Sounds perfect.' Emily stopped to let Rosie go ahead of her as they reached the door. It was busy inside, and her friend weaved quickly through the tables to find a vacant spot. It was only after Rosie had grabbed the last table that Emily realised someone she knew was sitting on the table behind. And that someone was Jude.

'Should I be worried that you're stalking me?' He gave her a slow smile, and she didn't know whether to laugh or be annoyed. He had that effect on her, and bumping into him had been the last way she'd expected to start her day.

'Oh, I'm sure you're used to being followed by fans all the time.'

'I can't walk down the street without being mobbed.' He smiled again, and this time she couldn't help joining in. There was something very attractive about someone so successful who didn't take themselves too seriously, but she needed to go carefully with Jude. And the more she got to like him, the more careful she needed to be.

'That must be tough, but if anyone is doing the stalking I'd say it was you. My family lives in Port Agnes, but I thought you were staying in Port Tremellien.'

'Mehenick's is famous across the whole of Cornwall.' Jude's statement wasn't an exaggeration, so there was no reason to doubt his excuse for being there, but he wasn't finished. 'As it turned out, there were no suitable Airbnbs near my father's house and, when one came up here, I figured it was more than close enough to family.'

'Makes sense.' Emily didn't want to say anything else in front of Rosie. Jude had already hinted that he had a tricky relationship with his father, and she knew he wasn't the sort of person who would relish being questioned about that, especially in front of a stranger. Instead, she turned towards Rosie, suddenly aware of having left her friend out of the conversation.

'Sorry, this is Jude. An author I've been working with.' Turning back to look at him, she continued the introduction. 'And this is Rosie, one of my best friends from school.'

'Nice to meet you.' Jude smiled at her. 'I'll let you get on with catching up.'

'Why don't you join us?' The words were out of Rosie's mouth before Emily could do anything to intervene.

'I don't want to intrude.'

'Don't be silly.' Rosie patted the seat beside her. 'Emily might get to meet interesting people in her job, but most of the people I meet are either screaming in agony or throwing up on me.'

'She's exaggerating,' Emily said as Jude's eyes widened. 'Rosie actually has the best job in the world. She's a midwife.'

'That's amazing.'

'It is brilliant, but it's definitely not all about cuddling babies.

There are things I do far more often, but you probably wouldn't want to hear about any of them over breakfast.' Rosie pulled a face. 'Being an author must be incredible, though.'

'Put it this way, there's probably just as much screaming in my job, but I'm the one doing it.'

Rosie gave a hearty laugh in response and it was clear she wasn't going to take no for an answer when it came to Jude joining them. Having rearranged the table, and carried Jude's coffee over, it was a fait accompli before Emily knew it. They spent the next hour together, with Rosie asking him questions about his books and regaling him with the most entertaining experiences from her job, most of which she'd shared with Emily in the past. It wasn't how Emily had expected to spend their time together, and she'd felt a bit like a third wheel, but she couldn't say it wasn't interesting. Jude and Rosie had both insisted that there was no such thing as romantic love, but the way her old friend was hanging off his every word suggested she might be experiencing more than a spark of attraction towards him. Jude was giving far less away, as always, although he did look visibly moved by one of the stories Rosie told him about a woman who'd delayed cancer treatment in order to save the life of her unborn baby. It was an act of love not even he could attempt to deny.

'Oh God, is that the time?' Rosie started fumbling in her bag. 'I've got to get to work, but I'll leave you some money to pay for my breakfast.'

'I'll get it.' Jude took the words out of Emily's mouth, but she wasn't going to let him do that.

'No, it's my treat. I haven't seen Rosie since she got her new job, so I was planning to buy her breakfast to say congratulations.'

'Okay, but I need to thank Rosie too. My original storyline with the pathologist just doesn't work and I was thinking of having McGuigan get involved with an ex, but I'm now wondering if his partner should be a nurse or a midwife. Someone who helps him see that there are still good people in the world.' As Jude looked at Rosie, Emily's scalp prickled in response. She couldn't have begun to justify why, but she hated the thought of him using her old friend's job to make the revisions to his story instead of the things she'd suggested.

'You could always buy me dinner instead.' Rosie looked at Jude, and the prickling on Emily's scalp became more intense. Rosie didn't go as far as fluttering her eyelashes, but the flirtatious tone to her voice was unmistakeable. 'In the meantime I'll leave you both to argue over who buys me breakfast. I've got new lives to bring into the world. I'm a superhero!'

She laughed, but Emily suspected she was only half joking. Rosie clearly wanted to impress Jude, and he had every right to be impressed. Her friend did an amazing job; all Emily did was read stories other people had written. Deep down, she knew it made a difference to people; she'd had messages from people telling her that. Only right now she felt completely inadequate. There was a twinge of something else too that she'd rather not acknowledge, but it felt uncomfortably like jealousy. Rosie was single and gorgeous, and she'd already stated that she was up for a fling. It would be perfect timing with Jude being in Port Agnes over Christmas, and it had been obvious that Rosie was attracted to him. The only problem was that Emily absolutely hated the idea, and she didn't even want to think about why that was.

'Are you really considering making McGuigan's love interest a midwife?' She fiddled with the paper napkin in front of her once Rosie was gone.

'I don't know. It's just an idea. I can't work out how I can link it back to his past in the same way I could if it was someone he trained with. But I like the idea of the contrast to his job, one that's all about murder and the horrors of this world, and another that involves bringing new life into the world, like Rosie said.' He paused for a moment, but when she didn't look up or respond, he continued. 'It all goes back to what you were talking about, providing light and shade.'

'So you're saying that whatever option you choose it was my idea?' This time she was the one who delivered the slow smile, and he laughed.

'I guess so.'

'It's interesting that it got you thinking the way it did. Surely you must admit, after hearing Rosie's stories, that some types of love can't be denied; like the love between a mother and her child.' As soon as the words were out of Emily's mouth, she wanted to stuff them back in again. Jude's face had fallen and she'd realised, far too late, that she'd put her foot in it. Here she was, talking to a man who'd lost his own mother when he was still just a boy. 'I'm so sorry, I shouldn't have said that. I can only imagine how hard it was for you to lose your mum when you were so young. It was a stupid thing to say. I just meant that some kinds of love have a power that defies logic.'

'Maybe, but that's not always the case, even between a mother and her child. And certainly not always between a father and his child, at least not in my experience.' He held her gaze for what felt like an eternity, as if he was weighing up whether to continue, but then he did. 'I told you about losing my mum, but what I didn't tell you was that she was my adoptive mother.'

'Oh.' Jude had a habit of making revelations that left her with no idea what to say in response. She wanted to reach out and comfort him in some way, but she didn't know if he'd welcome it, or whether it was even the right thing to do. She didn't want him thinking she viewed adoption as something to be pitied. That wasn't why she felt so sad. It was because he'd lost his adoptive mother, and it didn't sound like his father had done anything to try and minimise the impact of that loss. She still didn't know what the right thing to say was, but for some reason she ended up blurting out a question she strongly suspected she shouldn't ask. 'Are you in contact with your biological parents?'

If Jude was fazed by the question, he didn't show it. 'After the skiing accident, my father didn't even want to talk about my mother any more, and just a couple of years later he'd remarried. It felt like I was the only person who remembered Mum, and we'd never had the chance to talk about how she might feel if I wanted to find my biological mother. She was the most loving person I've ever known, and she always put me first, so I didn't want to do something she might have hated, just to track down a woman who chose to give me away.'

'I doubt it was easy.' She couldn't seem to stop herself from crossing the line. Something inside her wanted to defend this faceless and nameless woman and to make Jude believe in the power of love. 'I can't pretend to know the facts about your adoption, but I do know that the vast majority of women whose babies are adopted do it out of love, because they want the best possible life for their child. And it sounds like your mother gave you that kind of life before she died.'

'She did.' Jude's eyes locked with hers again. 'If I was going to buy into your view that love isn't always some kind of transaction, she's the one who could make me believe it. But the rest of my childhood made it difficult to remember what that felt like. My father didn't show me love, and my stepmother definitely didn't. Sandra hated me even more than I hated her. She couldn't wait to get me packed off to boarding school and my father didn't put up any objection.'

'I'm so sorry.' Emily's fingers twitched with the desire to reach out and take his hand, but she balled them in her lap beneath the table instead. 'I can understand now why you didn't relish the idea of coming home for Christmas.'

'Thankfully Sandra moved on quite quickly, but that didn't change the way my father acted towards me. He was still just as distant as ever. His third wife, Viv, is lovely, but my relationship with my father is never going to change now.'

'I don't blame you for feeling that way, but I'd have thought you might believe in second chances more than most.'

'Because I'm such a ray of positivity?' It was good to see the smile back on his face, but she wasn't going to let his self-deprecation get him off the hook.

'No, because you're writing about DCI McGuigan, a flawed character who changes into a better version of himself when he experiences love. The relationship is his chance of redemption. So you must be able to envisage a scenario in which your father is capable of the same thing.'

'How do you know so much about McGuigan?' He was watching her now, his eyes never leaving her face, and she had to look down again.

'I've read both books in the series so far, and the notes you sent me from your editor.'

'Really?' Jude tilted his head to one side as she nodded. 'It's slightly concerning that you might know McGuigan better than I do. Although I guess that's exactly what I needed, a fresh perspective from someone who understands storytelling.'

'Where are you going?' She called out to Jude as he stood up and turned away from their table, only looking back to respond to her question.

'I'm going to pay the bill and then I'm going home to have another look at the revisions Marty wants. I need to think about them again from the perspective you've just given me.' He reached out and touched her hand for such a brief moment she almost wondered if she'd imagined it, before he stepped away again. 'Thank you, and we're not arguing over it any more – breakfast is on me, and I want you to bill me for your time today. It's given me a lot to think about.'

'This wasn't a consultation. It was just friends having a chat.'

'Friends?' He raised his eyebrows, and colour flooded Emily's face. He clearly didn't feel that way, and she suddenly felt like the biggest idiot in the world for thinking that the arrangement between them was anything but professional.

'Not us.' The heat from the blush intensified; she was making it worse. 'I just meant that Rosie and I are friends. We were chatting, and that just happened to help you when you joined us. I'm not charging you a consultation fee for that.'

'Oh, okay.' If she hadn't known better she would have sworn he looked disappointed, but then his expression cleared. 'The offer is open if you change your mind, but next time we're settling the money in advance. Like I said before, I can't ask you to keep helping me if you don't let me pay you.'

'If it makes you more comfortable, next time I'll charge you my usual hourly rate.' A middle-aged woman who'd just come over to join a table to the side of them shot Emily a disgusted look, which broke the tension, making them both laugh. It was only when Jude had paid the bill and said goodbye that she realised he'd never answered her question about whether he thought his father was capable of change. Sadly, she was almost certain she knew the answer.

* * *

Jude's attempts to get stuck into the revisions of his book after he got back to Puffin's Rest came to nothing. He couldn't stop thinking about how much of his past he'd revealed to Emily and wishing he hadn't. Jude had friends he'd known for decades who he hadn't been that honest with, and he couldn't work out what it was about Emily that brought out that side of him. He kept trying to tell himself it was because he needed to be honest with her if he was going to get the most out of their working relationship. Inevitably, authors put aspects of themselves and their life experiences into the stories they wrote, and he was no different. That didn't mean that DCI McGuigan's story wasn't fictional, it was just that Jude's approach to storytelling was shaped by those experiences, and Emily needed that insight to understand how that might impact on the development of McGuigan's character. Except if that was the reason, he should have told Marty about his childhood years ago, but he never had. He needed to clear his head.

'Come on, boy, let's go for a walk.' Jude clipped a lead on to Rufus's collar, the two of them taking the stairs down from the apartment to the courtyard at a steady pace. He had to keep a firm grip of the dog's lead to stop him hurtling from top to bottom far too quickly. He allowed Rufus to pick up the pace as they headed towards the coastal path. Jude didn't want to stop and chat to anyone, not even to exchange pleasantries about the crisp late-November weather, or for a stranger to remark on what a handsome dog Rufus was. He already felt weirdly over-exposed after the conversation with Emily, and he just wanted to hide in plain sight as they made their way out of the village.

Jude slowed the pace again once they reached the path and some of the tension left his body as they started the climb. There was something about getting higher and higher above the houses, and the people below, that was helping him put things into perspective. It didn't matter what he'd told Emily; it had just been a story. He hadn't talked about how all of that had made him feel, how lost and alone he'd been as a ten-year-old boy suddenly left without his mum, wondering what he'd done to deserve losing not one, but two mothers. His father's lack of emotion had made him question whether he was unlovable, and then Sandra had come into his life and answered the question unequivocally. It was what had taught him that love was transactional. People didn't offer it if they didn't get something they wanted or needed in return. He clearly hadn't had anything his father needed, and Sandra demonstrated just how little she wanted him around. What had happened with Mia had just compounded those feelings. She might not have broken his heart, but she'd proved what he'd suspected all along. He hadn't felt truly loved since his mother's death, and it was easier to believe that love didn't really exist for anyone than to face up to the fact that maybe it just didn't exist for him, and that it never would because he couldn't be what anyone wanted or needed long term.

If Jude had told Emily all of that, she'd have understood him on a level he was only just coming to terms with himself. The truth was he tried not to scratch the surface of that too often because there was probably a whole lot more underneath that he hadn't even thought about. Jude had gone into survival mode when his mother had died, and that had only intensified when Sandra had come into his life. It was liked he'd covered his heart in layers of bubble wrap to try and prevent it from further damage, which was probably why Mia leaving hadn't affected him nearly as much as it probably should have done. Then suddenly Emily had come along and popped the first layer by making him reveal things he'd never spoken about. All he had to do was remember why those layers of protection were so important and not allow her to remove any more of them. He could do that; he was used to doing it. He'd probably only had those kinds of conversations with Emily because he was being forced to look at McGuigan's problems with relationships, and that had brought up some difficult issues. He was reading far too much into it by thinking this was all about her.

'Right then, boy, how far do you want to go today?' Jude patted the dog's head once Rufus had bounded back towards him. 'Because I really have got to get on with a bit of work.'

The dog's only response was to race off ahead again, making it clear he had enough energy to keep going for as long as his master could. And then Jude's phone pinged with a text from Emily.

> Hope you're okay. Sorry if I asked too many questions today, but I hope it ended up helping with the revisions. Thanks again for breakfast.
> Em x

Jude stared at his phone for a moment. She hadn't mentioned anything personal, and yet there was still something intimate about the message. Emily was getting under his skin in a way he couldn't remember anyone ever doing. He was going to have to tell her that he didn't need her help with the revisions any more. Except when he attempted to respond, he couldn't seem to string the words together. Shoving his phone into his pocket, he quickened his pace again to try and catch up with Rufus. He'd deal with the Emily situation later. He just had to work out how.

10

By the time Patsy's appointment with the consultant was over, it was getting dark and the cold was turning their breath into clouds of smoke in the air.

'I don't know about you, but I need a drink after that.' Emily's mother reached up and put a hand over where her husband was grasping the handle of the wheelchair. She'd started using it when she was out and about a few months earlier. She could still walk short distances using a frame, but she needed help getting in and out of a chair, and it had just become more traumatic than it was worth to resist using a wheelchair if she needed to walk further.

'I didn't think you could drink alcohol with your medication?' Emily's tone was gentle. She could understand why her mother might want a glass of wine after getting confirmation that the disease was progressing, but she was usually very sensible when it came to ensuring that she maximised the chances of her medication working.

'I can't – well, put it this way, I'm not *supposed* to. But I didn't mean alcohol, I meant a nice big hot chocolate and preferably an even bigger slab of millionaire's shortbread to go with it.'

'Oh, I think that can be arranged. There are plenty of cafés nearby and some of them should still be open,' Emily's father said as he pushed the wheelchair across the car park.

'Or we could get into the car and go down to Lemon Quay. The Christmas market has started.'

'Now that sounds like a good idea. We don't want to come all this way and not have a bit of fun. Onwards to Lemon Quay, and don't spare the horses.' Patsy pretended to swing a whip in the air. It was nice for Emily to see her mother so animated, and she seemed to be reacting calmly to what the consultant had told her. The main change, if her mother agreed to go ahead, was to have a minor operation so that her medication could be administered via a tube directly into the small intestine. It would maintain a more consistent level of treatment, which should help with some of the symptoms Patsy had been experiencing with her movement and motor skills, as well as the anxiety which seemed to have become worse in recent months. It all made sense, although Emily found it difficult to believe there was anyone with a diagnosis like her mother's who wouldn't feel anxious about it, especially when it seemed to be getting worse.

In around twenty minutes they'd transferred Patsy back into the car, driven down towards the market and found a parking space. Then they'd walked the short distance to the Boscawen Street market, with a plan to head on to the bigger market afterwards. It was just after five o'clock on a Wednesday evening, so although the markets were bustling, they weren't so horribly busy that it was impossible to move. After checking out the stalls at the first market, and sampling the best clotted-cream fudge Emily had ever tasted, they moved on to Lemon Quay. Patsy was already one festive hot chocolate down, having sampled a peppermint flavoured one, complete with candy canes, but she wasn't done yet.

'I want to find a gingerbread hot chocolate this time, or one of those Ferrero Rocher ones if they do them, and I haven't forgotten about the millionaire's shortbread either. Someone here must sell it, but if not I will settle for a brownie at a push.'

'Last year there was a stall further up on the left that did amazing brownies. Let's head up that way and see what we can find.' Emily squeezed her mother's shoulder gently and exchanged a look with her dad. Her mother was still so upbeat, but she knew Patsy sometimes wore a bright expression to mask her fear. She'd done it ever since her diagnosis, to try and stop her family worrying even more than they already were. She'd made a comment once about having put the family through enough when she had her car accident, but none of her health issues were her fault and Emily wanted her mother to be able to talk about her fears. They'd all seen the mask slip from time to time, but never for long. It meant that Patsy was carrying a heavy load she ought to be able to share with the people who loved her.

'Did you say you're driving home, Em?' Her father paused, waiting for her to respond.

'Absolutely. I thought you could have a drink. I bet they've got Baileys hot chocolate, and glühwein.' Emily's father wasn't a big drinker, but he'd always enjoyed a couple of drinks with his friends at the end of the working week, and when he'd first retired he still went occasionally. Recently he'd stopped going altogether and these days he wouldn't even have a drink at home at the weekend, in case anything happened and he needed to get his wife to the hospital.

'I might go wild and have a mulled cider. I'm sure I can smell it.' Emily's father closed his eyes and took a deep breath. There was a definite hint of apple and cinnamon in the air, as well as what smelt like hot fresh doughnuts.

'Why don't you guys go and grab a spot under the covered seating area and I'll track down some gingerbread hot chocolate, the mulled cider and some amazing cakes.'

'Okay, sweetheart.' Richard gave her a brief hug before pushing her mother through the crowd. Emily was as good as her word, quickly finding the drinks her parents had requested. She hadn't been able to track down any millionaire's shortbread, so she'd settled on some very indulgent-looking brownies and a bag of hot doughnuts.

'Have I missed anything?' Emily asked as she took the food and drinks over, and Patsy pulled a face.

'Your father was just telling me that it's okay to admit that I'm worried about having to have an operation. But Dr Alexopoulos was very reassuring and she told us it was only minor, so God knows why he thinks I'm going to make a fuss about it.'

'She's great at making things sound straightforward.' Emily smiled, but she couldn't help wondering if her expression looked as false as it felt. Her mother's consultant had been wonderful. She and Pasty had developed such a good relationship that Emily's mother hadn't wanted to move to another consultant, even after the opening of St Piran's Hospital just down the road from them. It was why they still came to Truro. But despite how much they all trusted Dr Alexopoulos, the operation was a big deal. It was another step along the road of a progressive illness, and that would be scary for anyone. 'We all know what you're like for trying to pretend everything's okay, Mum. Charlotte and I were only talking about that the other day. But you don't need to cover up how you're feeling for our benefit.'

'That's what all mums do, sweetheart.' Patsy smiled. 'I hope you discover that one day, I really do.'

'Not all mums are as selfless as you are. I hit the jackpot.' Emily laid her hand over her mother's. She couldn't help thinking about Jude and the things he'd told her. Her heart had ached for what he'd been through, losing his mother so young and then being faced with a stepmother who seemed determined to make his life hell. She couldn't imagine how painful that had been, and she'd wanted to do something to try and take some of that hurt away, but there was nothing she could have done or said. It had clearly affected Jude deeply; she'd been able to see it in his eyes as he recounted the story, and it had played on her mind ever since. It had been a stark reminder of just how blessed her own childhood was.

'Hmm, I'm not sure about that.' Her mother pulled a face. 'I can't help you or Charlotte out nearly as much as I'd like to.'

'You're always there to listen and support us, and that's far more important than anything you might not be able to do.' Emily hoped her mother believed her, because it was true. 'I met someone recently who made me realise how fortunate I am to have the family I've got.'

'You've met someone? Did you hear that, Richard? She's met someone.' This was typical of her mother. All she seemed to want was to see both her daughters settle down, and Emily almost didn't want to admit that her relationship with Jude was strictly business.

'I did hear that, Patz. And are we allowed to ask any more details about this someone, sweetheart?' Her father reached for the mulled cider as he spoke, and Emily attempted a casual shrug.

'His name is Jude and before you get all excited...' She knew it was already too late for that particular caveat, but there was no point in giving them any false hope about Jude. He couldn't have been less likely to fulfil her mother's dream of seeing her youngest daughter settling down with someone. 'He's an author from the same publisher as Sophia, and I've been working with him on his book.'

'Doing the audio recording?' Her mother's assumption was a natural one and it would have been far easier to just go along with it, but Emily knew her mum. Patsy would want to know when she'd be able to listen to the book, just as she had with all the other novels Emily had narrated. If she tried to fob her off, her mother would start digging. So she might as well be honest.

'No, not exactly. Jude's editor told him he needs to give the main character in his series a meaningful relationship, something that makes readers invest in staying with the series long term and root for the character. So he asked for my help.'

'But you're not a writer.' Her father narrowed his eyes. 'And I love you to bits, Em, but you could hardly put "expert in relationships" down on your CV, could you?'

'Not unless they want a specialist in picking wrong 'uns.' Her mother started laughing, her father quickly following suit. Emily might have been offended if it wasn't so great to see them laughing together. In any case, it was true; she'd developed a talent for dating the wrong sort of men over the years. The trouble was a lot of them were so good at pretending to be something they weren't at the start. At least with Jude she knew who he was from the beginning. The novels she loved might have given her high standards, but she wanted someone who believed that with the right person, love could last forever. If she couldn't have that, she'd rather be on her own, no matter what her mother or Jasmine might think about it. Jude would have laughed at the concept of forever. So it didn't matter how attractive he was, they couldn't have been more wrong for each other if they'd tried.

'If you've both finished laughing your heads off at my expense, I'll explain.' Emily couldn't help smiling at the sight of her parents with their heads pressed together, still grinning in her direction. 'I might not be a writer, but I doubt there are many people who've read as many romance novels as I have. And Jude thinks I can help him create a relationship that his readers will become invested in, but which doesn't make him want to repeatedly slam his head in the laptop.'

Jude had said those exact words in an email when he outlined more about what he was trying to achieve after their initial meet up in Covent Garden. He didn't want to alienate the readers who had no interest in DCI McGuigan's relationship status, especially as he counted himself among them.

'I'm sure you've given him some great pointers, and I don't care what you say, I still think you could write a book yourself if you put your mind to it.' Her mother had been saying the same thing Jude had for years. 'But why can't he draw on his own experience of relationships? Isn't that what authors are supposed to do? And his track record can't be any worse than yours.'

'He doesn't believe in love.' Emily wasn't surprised to see the disbelieving looks on her parents' faces, and she was about to make it worse. 'Not just the romantic kind either. He doesn't really believe in any kind of love, unless there's a transactional value to it. According to Jude, people only give what society calls love if they receive something tangible in return.'

'That's a pretty sad concept.' Emily's father shook his head. 'He sounds a bit bitter.'

'Jude's a lot nicer than I'm making him out to be, and I think he'd call himself a realist. He's been through a lot. He was adopted and—'

'*Adopted?*' Patsy cut her off, and Emily nodded. Her mother had been a counsellor before retiring, and it was no surprise to hear she had a theory about why Jude was the way he was. 'His adoption could be at the heart of his inability to believe in love. If he has any unresolved feelings of rejection, he might not have the kind of solid foundation people need to form successful relationships. Depending on how well he got on with his adoptive parents, it's possible he might even have a form of attachment disorder.'

Emily had got used to her mother psychoanalysing every friend she brought home over the years, so she should have guessed her mother would do the same thing to Jude. That didn't stop Emily feeling strangely disloyal for even mentioning his adoption to her mum. She had a feeling he didn't talk about it a lot and it felt like she'd betrayed a confidence, even though he hadn't asked her to keep it to herself.

'I don't think I'll mention that next time I see him. It might be overstepping the mark.' Emily pulled a face. Despite feeling uncomfortable talking about Jude, she realised she wasn't finished. What her mother had said made perfect sense, and it felt as if she knew him on a slightly deeper level. 'Do you think it could affect him so much that he'd struggle to even create fictional relationships in his books?'

'If he had a tough time with the adoption, his norm when it comes to relationships probably doesn't feel the same as yours or mine would. If that's true, he needs to work on resolving it. Otherwise it probably won't matter how much advice he gets. He won't really be able to believe in what he's writing.'

'Can I ask you both something else?' Emily looked at her parents, the two of them answering in unison, like they were perfectly attuned with one another.

'Of course.'

'If you'd adopted me, how would you have felt if I'd wanted to find my biological parents?'

'I'd have been worried about the possibility of you getting hurt if you were rejected, but I'd want to support you and I'd understand why.' Her mother's response was no surprise, given her previous occupation, but when Emily turned to her father, he was frowning.

'What about you, Dad?'

'I'd want what was best for you, and if not knowing who your biological parents were was negatively affecting you, I'd want you to find them. But I'd be scared of losing you to them, I'm not going to lie.' He looked so sad for a moment that Emily had to step forward to hug him. Part of her wanted to tell her parents that Jude's mother had died when he was ten, and that his father probably couldn't care less whether Jude went in search of his biological parents, but that would have betrayed his trust in an even bigger way than she had already. It was time for a change of subject.

'Thank you, both, that might help with one of the plot lines Jude is working on. But I've got a much more important question for you now. Brownies or doughnuts?' Emily stepped back from her father and opened the bag of brownies, releasing the rich, chocolatey aroma.

'Well, it is Christmas, so how about both?' Her father smiled, and Emily wanted to hug him again. She really was lucky to have the parents she had, and she wasn't going to take that for granted. With the progression of her mother's illness, she was feeling the pull home to Port Agnes more and more. What she hadn't expected was the pull she was feeling to contact Jude again, to ask him when he next wanted to meet. Her mother was probably right that there was very little she could do to make him understand the concept of love in a way that he could translate to his writing, but for some reason she still wanted to try.

* * *

Jude had been trying for two days to think of a reason to contact Emily. He'd told himself he didn't want her help any more and that the uncanny ability she had to make him open up about himself wasn't something he wanted in his life. So he had no explanation for his reaction when he got her text.

> How's Rufus coping with country life? I wondered if you fancied meeting up for a dog walk, although I should warn you about my parents' dog's name. It's a bit embarrassing.

He found himself smiling at the thought of seeing Emily, and he responded straight away.

> I think Rufus is missing lampposts and there are just too many trees to choose from. Do I have to guess your dog's name?

Her response came through just as quickly.

> You can try, but you'll never guess it.

> Rumpelstiltskin?

> No.

> Dog?

> Wrong again. I'll give you a clue. It's two words.

> The Dog?

> This could go on a while... Maybe you should ask Rufus to guess. It might be quicker.

Jude laughed and looked at his fox red Labrador, who was far too busy dragging his bed around to send his master a telepathic message. He was going to have to buy more time.

> Rufus said he needs another clue.

He's the lead singer of Take That.

> Bloody hell, is he? Rufus kept that really quiet.

You're an idiot! Not Rufus, my parents' dog.

Jude laughed again as he read the text. He'd never met Emily's parents, but he liked them already.

> Your parents' dog is called Gary Barlow?

Uh huh. It's a long story. I'll explain when we go for our walk. If you're up for it?

He hesitated for less than ten seconds before responding. It might not have been sensible, but he wanted to see Emily again, and what could possibly happen on a dog walk?

> Rufus has always wanted to meet Gary Barlow, but he might get a bit star struck. Where and when do you want to meet?

By the harbour, in about half an hour?

> Perfect. See you there.

As Jude put down his phone, he looked at Rufus.

'Right then, boy, we're off out for another a walk, and you better be on your best behaviour.' If anyone had asked, Jude couldn't have explained why he was putting on aftershave, or why he'd agreed to meet up with Emily in the first place. All he knew was that he wanted to.

11

Rufus and Gary Barlow had bonded instantly. When they were off their leads in an open space, they played a game where they'd both zoom around for a bit, then Rufus would suddenly stop and stand completely still as Gary Barlow darted underneath him and then shot out the other side before Rufus gave chase. It was like watching joy and energy collide, and it made Emily and Jude laugh every time it happened. She told herself that was why they'd been on so many walks together over the last few days, sometimes twice a day. Gary Barlow had never had so much exercise in his life, and he'd been waiting for her by the door when she got back from the studio in Truro late in the afternoon. It was 1 December and already dark, but she hadn't been able to meet Jude for a walk before she left, so they'd agreed to meet by the harbour and stick to the roads around there, rather than venturing up to the coastal path. It meant there'd be no zooming games tonight, but there'd be plenty of opportunities for the dogs to have a sniff around.

'I've already walked him today, sweetheart, so don't feel like you've got to go out again. It's bitter out there.' Emily's father had shivered at the thought of venturing outside, but it hadn't put her off.

'I won't be long, but I want to go and see the boats while it's dark. I love it when they're all lit up.' It wasn't a lie. She'd always loved seeing the fishing boats bobbing in the harbour, illuminated by fairy lights in all different colours. Over the years, the boat owners had got more and more competitive, trying to outdo one another, and in the end it had been turned into a proper competition, with the winner announced on Christmas Eve. Anyone could pay a pound to vote for their favourite and all the money raised went to help fund the local lifeboat station. But that wasn't the only reason she wanted to go out. All day she'd had that nagging feeling, as if she'd forgotten to do something really important and, try as she might to deny it, she knew it was because she hadn't seen Jude. This wasn't paid work any more; they were hanging out together because they both seemed to want to. She liked talking to him and they'd spoken about all kinds of things, including the aftermath of their mothers' accidents. Emily had felt his pain as he'd described Ros's last days, when the doctors had said she was never coming out of the coma. He'd lost his mother at such a young age, and that could so easily have been what happened to Patsy. It had deepened something between them to share those experiences, and it turned out they had a lot more in common too. Some of it quite surprising.

'Have you got plans to get together with any more of your friends while you're down here?' Jude had asked the question as they were walking along the clifftop to Dagger's Head, in the neighbouring village of Port Kara.

'Yes, a few. I'm having a night out with the girls I went to school with at the weekend. A bit of a Christmas get-together.'

'Let me guess, you're going over to the hotel on the Sisters of Agnes island for cocktails and dinner?'

Emily had laughed. The Sisters of Agnes island was cut off from Port Agnes at high tide. The island's only building was a former convent, but it had been turned into a hotel after the last nuns had left. It was far too high-end for the kind of night Emily and her friends had planned. She was flattered that Jude thought she was the sort of woman who dined in five-star hotels, but on this occasion he couldn't have been more wrong. 'Sadly, we're not that classy.'

'So what are you up to?' He'd turned and looked at her, and when she didn't answer he'd grinned. 'It's all right, I'm not going to ask to tag along.'

'I very much doubt you'd want to tag along with what we're doing.'

'Now you've really got me intrigued. I'm picturing a *Magic Mike* night in the village hall.'

Emily had laughed again. 'Okay, if you must know, we're going to an Abba tribute night and, yes, we will be dressing up. I know it's kitsch and that I'm far too young to love Abba as much as I do, but I don't care. I think they're brilliant and it was my turn to organise the Christmas get-together, so that's what we're doing.'

'I love Abba too.' She'd been certain at first that he was joking, but then he'd explained. 'My mum used to play their songs all the time when I was growing up. She'd been huge fan of theirs when they were at the height of their fame, and she'd never stopped loving their music. I was probably the only eight-year-old at my school who knew all the lyrics to "Dancing Queen" and "Waterloo". I listened to their music all the time after Mum died, and of course Sandra even tried to ruin that for me, telling my dad I must be gay, as if there would have been something wrong with it if I was. That summed Sandra up. She was bitter and hate-filled, so it shouldn't have been any surprise that she was homophobic too. Her insistence that I needed to be more masculine was one of the reasons she used to persuade my dad to send me to a boarding school, where I could play rugby and learn to be a man, as she put it. She just wanted shot of me, but it was her way of justifying it. But even she couldn't kill my love of the music that meant so much to Mum, and I'm not ashamed to admit that I've got the Abba Gold album downloaded to my phone. It's still my go-to when I need cheering up. It just makes me think of her, and a time when we were both really happy.'

'Maybe you should come with us then.' Emily hadn't been able to stop herself from inviting him along. There had been so much she wanted to say to Jude in response to what he'd just told her, but every time they talked about anything personal she let him lead the conversation. It was far easier to avoid overstepping the mark that way and having to watch him shut down on her again as a result. She'd been itching to ask him if he thought being adopted might be at the root of the way he felt about relationships, especially given everything that had happened after Ros died. Instead she'd found herself making an offer she suspected would be all too easy for him to refuse.

'Oh, I'm sure your friends would love that!' Jude had laughed this time.

'Actually I think they probably would.' What Emily hadn't admitted was that she knew for a fact her friends would have been delighted to have Jude's company. None more so than Rosie, who'd asked Emily to pass her number on to Jude the day after they'd bumped into him in Mehenick's. Rosie had no idea Emily hadn't done it yet, and she couldn't have justified the delay to her friend if she'd asked why. She couldn't even justify it to herself.

'Maybe next time. I might need a while to source the right outfit.' Jude had laughed again, before changing the subject and that had been that. It was another moment when he'd shown

Emily a side of himself that he almost instantly seemed to regret revealing, but bit by bit she was piecing the real Jude together and she liked him more and more.

'You look like you're about to head across the Antarctic,' Jude called out to her now as he walked towards where she was waiting, just in front of the lobster pot Christmas tree. 'I wasn't even sure it was you at first, until I saw Gary Barlow.'

Emily loved the fact that Jude was happy to call the dog by the silly name he'd been given. When they'd first met, she'd thought he was arrogant, maybe even a bit stuck up, but that slightly cold persona he sometimes adopted definitely wasn't the real Jude.

'My dad insisted on the furry deer stalker, and these wellies were a Christmas gift from my Great-aunt June last year, who I suspect still thinks I'm about seven. But you're going to have to shout because I can't hear anything with these ear flaps.'

'One of the things I really like about you is that you're so authentically yourself.' She was almost sure that was what Jude had said, but she lifted the flap of the fake fur hat so she could check. 'Sorry, what did you say?'

Jude laughed then and shook his head. 'I said I really like the fact you're your own person. I don't think I know anyone else who'd wear a furry deer stalker and bumble bee wellies, happily introduce her dog as Gary Barlow to anyone who asked, or who would be quite so open and honest about their hopes for a happily ever after in a world where we're all supposed to be far more cynical.'

'Hmm, I'm not entirely sure whether I should take that as a compliment.' Emily smiled all the same, hanging on to the fact that he'd said he really liked her for exactly who she was. Surely that had to be a good thing.

'It's definitely a compliment, and this was a great idea. I'd forgotten how much effort they make with the boats.'

'You must be able to see them from your place.' When Emily had discovered that Jude was staying at Puffin's Rest, she'd felt a pang of envy. She'd seen the apartment online when it had gone up for rent, but she could never have afforded it, even if she hadn't been living in London. She hadn't realised it had gone back to being an Airbnb, but she couldn't really have justified booking it for a weekend when it was less than ten minutes' walk from her parents' house.

'The windows look out to sea in the other direction, and I've been mostly working when I haven't been out with Rufus. So I haven't been out in the evenings. The last time I came down just to look at the lights was with Mum, a few days before we left on the skiing trip.' A mask of sadness almost swallowed Jude's features for a moment, and Emily's throat burned as she looked at him with the desire to cry tears she had no right to. This wasn't her pain, but it was so palpable and she wanted to put her arms around Jude and try to absorb some of the hurt for him, just for a little while, but she had no idea how he'd react.

'I'm sorry. It must be so hard when memories like that hit you.' She spoke softly, resisting the urge to reach out for him, as much as she wanted to.

'It's nice to remember the good times. She always loved Christmas and the lights down here, but for a long time all of that was associated with the time of year we lost her.' Jude seemed to shake himself, turning to her with a smile, clearly ready for a change of subject. 'So where are we headed off to? Are you going to take me on a tour of all the dark alleys that no one born outside Port Agnes know exists?'

'What, and have my wicked way with you?' Emily clamped a hand over her mouth, suddenly wishing the ground would swallow her up. It was the kind of throwaway line she'd have made as a joke with almost anyone, but with Jude it felt far more inappropriate, and not just because the basis of their relationship was a working one.

'I should be so lucky. I mean, with that deer stalker and those wellies...' He let out a long whistle, breaking the tension, and she laughed.

'Well, I'm afraid my ears are the only bit of myself I'm going to be revealing to you tonight. No, I was thinking we could head down King's Street first, the gallery there always has a good display at Christmas, then up Mariner's Stairs to Seaview Road. There's a house there my dad insists has Christmas lights that are visible from space. Well, maybe not space exactly, but his best friend Barry swore he spotted them flying back into Exeter airport.'

'Your dad sounds great.' Jude didn't look at her as he spoke. They were already walking in the direction of King's Street, but there was a wistfulness to his tone that he couldn't disguise.

'He is. Although it's probably Dad that I get most of my quirkiness from. He's always had his own way of doing things. Ever since he retired he's been doing stuff to try and keep his brain active. His latest thing is learning Spanish, and he practises by speaking it to the dog when he doesn't think any of us are listening. Gary Barlow is probably ready to sit his GCSE by now.'

'Brilliant.' The smile was back on Jude's face, and Emily's shoulders relaxed in response. It gave her a warm feeling when she made him smile. The natural thing would have been to ask about his own father, but she already knew how he would respond to that, so she decided to focus on work.

'How are you getting on with the edits?'

'They were going well.' Jude's hand accidentally brushed against hers, and her skin tingled. There was no point trying to deny the attraction, because her body had started overruling her brain a long time ago. She didn't want to enjoy his company as much as she did or think about him all the time when they weren't together, because before too long their business arrangement would be over and she already knew she was going to miss him. She just had to keep pushing those emotions down, focus on what he was saying, and wait for the feeling to pass. 'I thought I'd cracked it. I decided to stick with Plan A and McGuigan's relationship with an old flame, whose brother, a former friend of McGuigan's, has been identified as a suspect for a series of murders, which she may or may not be covering up. It gave the relationship a tension based on McGuigan's difficulty in opening up to someone, and the fact that the woman he's falling for second time around might be protecting a serial killer.'

'That sounds great, and it won't have any of the... What was it you said? Gushy hearts and flowers you were so worried about.'

'You'd think not, wouldn't you? But when I read through what I'd written, it still sounded shoe-horned in, and so unlike McGuigan. I just don't think readers are going to buy into it.'

'Maybe it's just because you don't.' There was a heaviness in Emily's chest. Even after all the time they'd spent together, Jude still couldn't accept the idea that a relationship might add something to his character's life. 'Have you shown any of the changes to your editor?'

'Marty keeps nagging me to see them. But he's Sophia's editor too and, I'm not being rude—'

'Why do people always say that when they're about to be rude?' She cut him off, her defensiveness of Sophia and her brilliant books already kicking in.

'I'm really not, I promise. All I was going to say was that if sections of my book read like Sophia has written them, it's going to jolt my readers out of the story.'

'You're too close to it to be objective. You said before that you might want me to look at some pages, and I'm happy to do that.'

'Thanks, but it's not about a lack of objectivity. I can tell it's crap.' Jude sighed. 'But that's got nothing to do with you. You did a great job of opening my eyes to why so many people want to believe in love, and the kinds of things people who think they're in love do and say. I just can't make those things sound anything other than stupid when they're coming out of McGuigan's mouth.'

They'd reached the window of the gallery by now and usually the sight of it would have left Emily feeling all warm and fuzzy. Someone very talented had recreated a miniature version of part of Port Agnes in the window, complete with a winding street of cottages, covered with a dusting of snow, waves sparkling with what looked like ice crystals, and a tiny recreation of the lobster pot Christmas tree, flanked by a family building a snowman on one side and Father Christmas on the other. It was beautiful, but all Emily could feel was a sense of irritation, and try as she might, she couldn't let it go.

'Why do you have to say people who *think* they're in love? Why can't you admit that for some people it is real, even if it's never happened for you?'

'Because it's a chemical reaction at the start and then, like everything else, it becomes transactional, and it only—'

'Not this again.' She cut him off for a second time. 'My dad has been looking after my mum ever since her Parkinson's progressed to a level where there are a lot of things she can no longer do independently. He doesn't do that because he gets something back from it, he does it because he loves her.'

'But he does get something back from it, can't you see that? Look at how you're talking about him, admiring what he does because it's out of the ordinary. You wouldn't need to do that if this was really about love, because everyone would just accept that's what someone who loves another person does for them. What your dad gets out of this at the very least is a sense of purpose, of doing something worthwhile. And if we're honest, the chance to be seen as a hero is no bad thing either.'

'Don't you dare suggest that my father doesn't love my mother.' Emily's scalp tightened and her voice rose an octave, making both dogs tilt their heads to one side. She knew all the things she was about to say would cross a line that couldn't be uncrossed, but she couldn't seem to stop herself, and the truth was she wasn't sure she wanted to. She'd almost certainly lose the friendship that had been building between her and Jude, but she was certain now that if she really wanted to help him, this was the only way. 'You've got no idea about my parents' relationship, you've got no idea about anybody's, because you're so messed up by your own childhood. You might not admit it, even to yourself, but the reason you don't believe in love is because you doubt that anyone really loved you. Ros showed you love, but when she died you didn't get it from your dad or Sandra, and in the end that even made you doubt what you had with your mum. I think the reason you won't work through your feelings about the adoption is because you're terrified you'll discover that your biological mother didn't love you. That's why you can't write about McGuigan being in love. You're never going to buy into the idea until you believe it could happen to you, and you can't do that if you have doubts about whether you've ever been loved.'

The words had come out in such a rush of emotion that Emily could barely catch her breath.

'Are you finished?' The look Jude gave her was so cold, and all she could do was nod in response. 'Good, because I think we are too.'

He didn't give her a chance to respond, pulling Rufus's lead as he turned his back on Emily and disappearing into the night.

* * *

Gary Barlow had whined desperately when Emily had refused to let him follow Jude and Rufus, and he was still making pitiful sounds every few steps as they headed home. It made her want to cry, and so did the biting wind that seemed to have come out of nowhere, which was now whipping at her face. That had to be why her eyes were streaming with tears; it couldn't be because of the argument she'd just had with Jude. Although in truth it would have been hard to call it an argument, because all the outpouring of emotion had been on one side. She shouldn't have let her feelings get the better of her like that, but Jude had touched a nerve with his comment about her parents, and it was too late to take back anything she'd said.

'I should have kept my mouth shut.' Emily said the words out loud, the wind carrying them away. Wishing she'd done things differently was futile; all she could do was hope that somewhere, deep down, they'd resonated with Jude in some way. She might wish she'd approached it differently, but she still thought he needed to hear what she'd had to say.

Just as she reached her parents' house, Emily's phone began to ring, her heart plunging much harder than she'd ever imagined it would when she realised it wasn't Jude.

'Hi, Jas.' Her voice sounded falsely bright even to her own ears. 'How's everything going?'

'Good. I was just ringing to check on life in cream-tea land. Where the hell are you? You sound like you're in a wind tunnel.'

'I just got back from walking the dog, give me a sec.' Not wanting to disturb her parents, or have them overhear her conversation with Jasmine, Emily opened the side gate and went into the summerhouse, quickly flicking on the light and praying that a mouse or something even worse didn't run across her foot. Gary Barlow gave her a curious look, clearly wondering why he wasn't already inside warming up by the wood-burning stove, and she made a silent promise to make it up to him with a treat later on.

'Sorry, it's turned really wild out there.'

'What are you doing out walking Gary Barlow in the dark anyway?' Jasmine sounded concerned. 'I know Port Agnes is nothing like the mean streets of the big city, but even so, it can't be a good idea walking around this late by yourself.'

'I wasn't by myself. I met up with Jude so we could walk the dogs together.'

'Again?' There was a teasing tone to Jasmine's voice, but Emily didn't feel like laughing.

'I was in the studio all day and I just wanted to go out and get some air, that's all.'

'I bet it looks very romantic down there. The pictures you put on Instagram of the Christmas tree down by the harbour are lovely.'

'Yeah, it's really pretty.' Her voice was almost robotic by now. She couldn't think of the harbour without picturing Jude, up in Puffin's Rest, hating her guts for saying all the things she'd said and, even worse, feeling all the emotions he'd worked so hard to bury. She'd forced him to confront them without any idea if he knew how to deal with them.

'What's up, Em? You don't sound like yourself.' The concern was back and, when she didn't answer, Jasmine upped the stakes. 'If you don't tell me, I can call your mum and dad.'

'That's not fair. You know I don't want to worry them.'

'Good, so tell me what's going on, because you're worrying me and that's not fair either.'

'Jude and I have been spending a lot of time together in the week or so since I got down here, and before you start getting any ideas, let me finish.' Emily was employing what she termed her headteacher's voice, and it had the desired effect.

'Okay.'

'Things seemed to be going well with the book, so we started hanging out more as... I don't know, I suppose you could call it friends. It was mostly walking the dogs, but we were finding we had things in common and the more I got to know him, the more I liked him.'

'Right, so then what happened? You jumped his bones and realised he wasn't your type after all?' Her friend gave a throaty laugh and Emily sighed.

'You said you were going to let me finish. Anyway, how long have you known me? You know that's not how it works for me. I do relationships first.'

'And then the meaningless sex!' Jasmine started laughing again, but when Emily didn't join in, she finally seemed to get the message. 'I'm sorry, I know I'm being an idiot, but I'm just trying to cheer you up.'

'I know, it's just been a rubbish night. Jude opened up to me about some stuff and I had this theory that some unresolved issues from his past were stopping him from being able to finish the book the way his editor wants him to.'

'And you told him that?' The incredulity in Jasmine's voice was obvious.

'I never meant to, but he started talking about how love doesn't really exist, and when I told him about Mum and Dad, he said something about Dad doing it to be seen as a hero.'

'You should have punched him! Your dad's amazing.'

'I know, but I just wish I'd handled it differently. Jude's been through a lot and I'm supposed to be helping him with the book, but I doubt he'll ever want to speak to me again.'

'So what? It's not your real job anyway.' Jasmine suddenly sucked in a breath. 'Unless you're worried it will affect other authors wanting you to narrate their books.'

'It's not that, it's...' Emily couldn't seem to finish the sentence, but it turned out Jasmine could.

'It's just that this has gone way beyond a business arrangement and whatever this friendship-slash-consultant-slash-dog-walking thing is between you, you don't want it to end. Am I right?'

'Uh huh.' Emily's response was barely audible, but it felt like a huge admission all the same. She'd only known Jude for about three weeks, but they'd seen each other almost every day and their conversations had been so personal that it felt more like years. She wasn't ready for it to be over.

'Well, apologise then and take it from there. You both said things you shouldn't have, but you can be the bigger person. If he won't accept your apology when he owes you one too, that tells you all you need to know about who he really is.'

'And if he does accept it?'

'Then you, my friend, might well find yourself in unchartered territory.' Emily wasn't completely sure how she felt about that idea; it was a mixture of terror and excitement, but she had no idea which one was winning. All she knew was Jasmine was right and that she didn't want whatever she had with Jude to end. She was just going to have to discover where the unchartered territory took her and hope it didn't turn out to be somewhere she'd end up getting hurt.

12

Rufus had been pacing around the apartment like a caged animal all day. Jude took him for a long walk at lunch time, thinking that the dog would spend the afternoon stretched out and snoring, as he usually did after a walk, but Rufus went straight back to pacing as soon as he came back. The only time he stopped was to go and sit by the door for a little while and make whining sounds, as if he'd been left on his own for hours instead of having Jude's company all day. Rufus wasn't the only one feeling hemmed in either. Jude had lived in the city all his adult life, and much of that time he'd spent living in flats or mews houses. He was used to enclosed spaces, and Puffin's Rest didn't even feel small because of the full-length windows with seemingly endless views out to sea. So he couldn't rationalise why all of a sudden he felt so hemmed in, and why it had been impossible for him to settle down and get any work done at all. Or why the hour-long walk he and Rufus had taken along the coastal path hadn't done anything to stop either of them feeling restless. Even before he got the text from Emily, he knew the unsettled feeling had something to do with her.

> I'm really sorry about last night. Gary Barlow wouldn't look at me this morning when he realised we weren't meeting you and Rufus for a walk. I should never have said the things I did, it's none of my business and I overstepped the mark. If you can forgive me, we'd both love to meet up with you for a walk tomorrow and if my apology isn't enough, maybe this picture is.
> Sorry again xx

Emily's text was accompanied by a photograph of Gary Barlow looking very miserable with his head resting on his paws. A smile crept across Jude's face before he even realised it and some of the tension in his shoulders relaxed. A huge part of him wanted to text her back straight away and tell her he was sorry too, that he'd had no right to talk about her father the way he had, but the strength of his desire to see her again made him hesitate. He wasn't used to feeling this much pull towards someone and he didn't like how exposed it made him feel. Jude had prided himself on being self-reliant ever since he'd left school. He didn't want to need anyone the way he seemed to need Emily.

He was still holding his phone when it started to ring. It was his editor, and for a moment he considered not answering, but he'd have to take the call eventually, so he might as well get it over with.

'Hi, Marty, how are you doing?'

'I'm just wondering how my number one author is getting on with the revisions to the next DCI McGuigan story.'

'So you've passed my book on to Sophia Wainwright to work on, have you? You better give her a call if you want to know how she's getting on.'

Marty laughed. 'Don't be like that, Jude, you know you're still my favourite. I just want you back at number one in the charts too, where you belong.'

'The revisions *were* going well. I gave McGuigan a relationship and then I put it in jeopardy by tying it to a murder case. Potentially there's enough there to get the investment you wanted from readers in the relationship, but I'm still not sure it feels believable.'

'Sounds like Emily's help has moved things on a lot, that's great.' The relief in Marty's voice was tangible. 'As for whether or not it's believable enough, why don't you let me be the judge of that?'

'Because with all due respect, Marty, whether you believe in it or not isn't the issue. This is my book and I need to believe in what I've written.' Jude looked out of the window as he spoke, a lone boat bouncing across the waves. He'd always thought that being alone was preferable to allowing his happiness to be impacted by someone else, and yet somehow Emily had got under his skin and made him question whether solitude really was the best option. He still didn't know the answer, but he didn't feel nearly as certain about anything any more, and that included the approach he'd taken to editing his novel.

'I've known you for a long time, Jude, and I'm not sure you're capable of making any kind of judgement about the validity of a relationship.' There was no edge to Marty's voice; he was just stating the facts as he saw them. 'The trouble is we haven't got forever. Have you considered showing Emily what you've written? Or I'm sure I could ask Sophia if there's any advice she can offer.'

'No.' Jude couldn't believe what he was about to say to Marty, but they'd worked together for years and something that might be described as friendship had grown between them. So he might as well be honest. 'I wouldn't want McGuigan's storyline to look like anything Sophia might write, and having her look at it wouldn't solve the problem of me believing in what I've written. Emily seems to think I need to face up to some things that have happened in my life in order for me to be able to view McGuigan's relationship with an open mind, and I'm coming to the conclusion that she might be right.'

'I don't know what you're paying that girl, but you should double it!' Marty laughed again, but as he continued, his tone became more serious. 'I don't need to know the details, but I've suspected as much for years. You're a great writer, Jude, but I think you could be exceptional if you found a way of unblocking some of that emotion you find it so hard to translate to the page.'

'Oh God, Marty, please don't ruin a great working relationship by going all deep and meaningful on me.'

'I won't as long as you promise me you'll take Emily's advice and do whatever you need to in order to get things sorted. Just don't take too long about it. You've got a January deadline to hit that we're not going to be able to extend any further.'

'You can rely on me.'

'I hope so, Jude, because it's not going to be great for either of our careers if we don't pull this off. Just call me when you've got good news.'

'I will. Bye, Marty.' Jude breathed out as he ended the call. His editor spelling out the bottom line seemed to relieve the pressure rather than add to it. A firm deadline was about as tangible and emotionless as it got, and something about that gave Jude comfort. If he could use that to take the emotion out of facing up to his past, it suddenly felt far easier to do, and he was going to make a start on looking at the edits again before he changed his mind. There was just one other thing he needed to do first.

Opening the last message from Emily, he typed a reply.

> I'm sorry too, we both said things we probably shouldn't have, but you were right, I do need to work through some of the stuff around my adoption. As for meeting up, Rufus has already made it clear he'll be leaving home if I don't let him meet up with Gary Barlow again in the next twenty-four hours and he's not afraid to pee in my shoes in the meantime if I don't comply. So how about tomorrow morning at ten down by the harbour?

After he'd pressed send, he stood for a moment staring at the phone, willing a reply to come through, but it was going to drive him mad watching and waiting. Setting down the phone instead, he walked over to his laptop and flipped open the lid. It was time to face his past, whatever it might reveal.

* * *

Emily had the kind of butterflies in her stomach that she usually only got when she was reading reviews on Audible about a novel she'd narrated, waiting to hear whether listeners thought she'd done the book justice or completely ruined it. Thankfully the vast majority of her reviews were good ones, but she wasn't nearly so confident that the outcome today would be as positive. Even though Jude had agreed to meet her, she had no idea if they could get back to the burgeoning friendship they seemed to have developed since they'd both arrived in Cornwall. It shouldn't have mattered to her as much as it did. Emily had done what she could for him in terms of advising him on his book, and it wasn't like she was hoping he might choose her to narrate one of his novels. She didn't have the right voice for crime, at least not the kind of stuff that Jude wrote. She'd narrated cosy crime before, but she'd found her niche in romance and women's fiction, largely thanks to the big break Sophia had given her.

Despite all of that, she still cared about what happened after this meetup with Jude. She didn't know whether it was because she hoped they'd be friends, or as Jasmine had guessed, that a part of her wanted something more, despite his view of relationships. One thing she knew for certain was that Jude needed a friend. She suspected he'd opened up to her more than he'd intended to, and she'd been told in the past that it was a knack she had with people. She wanted to help Jude, if he'd let her, but she'd learned her lesson about pushing him too far.

Gary Barlow saw Rufus and Jude before she did, turning around in circles and barking in delight at spotting his canine friend and his master.

'Hello.' Emily's voice was low, and an eternity seemed to pass before Jude smiled.

'Hello. I didn't realise all this was going to have appeared when I suggested meeting here.' Jude gestured towards the small stage that had been erected on the far side of the lobster pot Christmas tree. There were posters dotted around Port Agnes about upcoming Christmas events. The first of them was a concert by a local rock choir, who'd apparently be singing 'all the Christmas classics' and raising funds for the Friends of St Piran's Hospital, situated in neighbouring Port Kara.

'It seems to be getting busier every day, and tomorrow is the farmers' market, so they'll be putting up some stalls for that later. We might be better off heading out of town a bit. We could take the coastal path in the opposite direction to usual, towards the kissing gate.'

'The kissing gate?' Jude's eyebrows shot up and he grinned as heat flooded her face. She hated how easily he had that effect on her.

'I didn't mean...' She shook her head. 'I just thought it would make a change from always taking the route that leads towards Dagger's Head.'

'I'm up for a change. I think it's about time.' Jude looked as if he was about to say something else but, when he didn't, Emily decided to stick to a relatively safe topic as they began to head out of the village. 'What's the best Christmas gift you ever got?'

'Buzz Lightyear.' There was no hesitation on Jude's part. 'I must have been about five or six and it was the year the first Toy Story film came out. I was certain I was going to grow up to be an astronaut. My whole room was space themed, but in the meantime I wanted a Buzz Lightyear toy more than anything. Everyone did and it must have been hard for my mum to track one down, but she'd have done whatever it took to make me happy. She always did.'

'She sounds amazing.'

'She was.' The wistfulness in Jude's voice made something twist in her chest, but then he turned to look at her. 'What about you?'

'My parents bought me a car the Christmas after my seventeenth birthday, but I don't think even that beat the guinea pig Santa Claus bought me when I was nine. His name was Geraldine.' She laughed at the expression on his face. 'We thought he was a girl for a long time; that's what the sales assistant at the pet shop told my dad. The vet put us right in the end, but it was far too late to change his name by then. Why are you laughing? It's really hard to work out a guinea pig's sex.'

'I'm sure it is.' He didn't seem to be able to stop laughing, and she couldn't help joining in. It was great to see him looking so much happier. 'I'm just amazed at your family's ability to give your pets such unique names. Don't tell me, I bet you've got a goldfish called William Shakespeare.'

'Not quite, but my mum has got a penchant for paying tribute to the people she admires. She named me and my sister after the Brontë sisters.' Emily shrugged. 'I must admit I thought you might give me a bit more of a ribbing about still believing in Santa when I was nine. When did you realise he wasn't real?'

'Santa Claus isn't real?' Jude pulled such a convincing face of horror that just for a split second she wanted to apologise, and then he started laughing again and she gave him a gentle nudge in the ribs. It set the tone for the rest of the walk up to the kissing gate. Just as she'd hoped, they'd found their way back to easy conversation, joking back and forth. It was like they'd been before she'd given him her unsolicited opinion on what he should do to sort out his life. Offering further proof that if they avoided certain subjects, they had a lot of common ground.

The air was getting colder as they approached the kissing gate, and there were crystals of frost clinging to the blades of grass and shards of ice in the puddles they passed.

'It's lovely here, isn't it? The view captures a snapshot of the whole Three Ports section of the coast.' Emily stopped about twenty feet before the gate, at a spot where the curve of the bays at Port Agnes and Port Kara continued along the headline to Port Tremellien.

'I'd forgotten just how beautiful Cornwall is. It's been a few years since I've been back.' Jude's face was impassive, and just like before, she didn't push him to elaborate.

'I know what you mean. I come back whenever I can, but it still takes my breath away every time. I think when you're born somewhere like this, it's in your blood somehow and, wherever you go, it will always draw you back again.' Emily was expecting him to dismiss what she'd said as stupidly sentimental, but he nodded.

'I was born over there.' Jude pointed to the stretch of coast between Port Kara and Port Tremellien. 'There used to be a cottage hospital there. I couldn't believe it when I found out how close I was born to where my parents raised me. For a while I wondered if they knew my biological mother personally, but it was just one of those weird coincidences.'

'I didn't realise you knew those sorts of details.' Emily spoke carefully, desperately trying not to overstep the mark again.

'When I was eighteen my father gave me all the details he had, including my birth mother's name and where I was born. My parents had also been told that I was born on her twentieth birthday. Apparently, she asked for me to be placed with a family in Cornwall. Social Services couldn't guarantee it, but my parents had been waiting for a baby for three years and they were deemed a good match in other ways.' Jude sighed. 'I've often wondered whether my biological mother wanted me to know which county I was in because she was planning to come looking for me. But she never did.'

'Even if she knew the county, it wouldn't be easy.' Like so many times before, Emily felt an almost overwhelming urge to reach out to him, but she gripped the dog lead tighter instead. 'Isn't the onus on the child to reach out first?'

'Yes, but like I said before, I never wanted to.' He turned to look at her. 'Until now.'

'You're going to find her?' Emily couldn't keep the surprise out of her voice. She was shocked by how much of a turnaround this seemed from the impression he'd given her before. She didn't know if the things she'd said had influenced him, but she hated the idea that she might have pushed him into a situation where he could face more rejection. The thought of him getting hurt again made her shiver, but she could see he needed to do this, and she'd do anything she could to help.

'I'm going to try.' Jude let go of a long breath. 'I still feel as if

I'm being disloyal to Mum, but she must have known there was a possibility of me meeting my birth mother one day, with us living so close to where I was born. So the idea can't have bothered her too much.'

'From what you've told me about your mum, I get the feeling she'd just want you to do whatever you thought was best.'

'I think you're right. I'm just not sure whether this will turn out to be for the best. It could open a whole can of worms that I'll wish I'd left alone, but I think I'll spend my whole life wondering "what if" if I don't do it. I just have to go into it prepared to hear that my biological mother gave me up because she didn't want me.'

'Giving something up implies sacrifice to me, and sacrifices are far more likely to be made out of love than for any other reason. I can only imagine what it feels like to take a risk on something like this, but if you do decide to do it, I might know someone who can help.' She watched for his expression to shut down, and when it didn't she continued. 'My dad's best friend, Barry, is married to Gwen. She was a midwife in the area for well over forty years. If there was a cottage hospital where babies were born close by, you can bet she worked there. She seems to know everyone around here too. So even on the off-chance she never worked there, I bet she knows someone who did. Gwen would be a great place to start. If you want me to put you in touch with her?'

'Thank you, but I don't want to contact my birth mother unless she's willing to hear from me. I added myself to the adoption contact register last night, but it can take weeks to hear back and there's always a chance she hasn't put her name on the register.' Jude's tone was neutral, but there was muscle going in his cheek. Emily longed to tell him she was sure that wouldn't be the case, and that of course his biological mother would want to hear from him, but she couldn't know that for certain. In the end she didn't say anything, allowing Jude to continue instead. 'I know my biological mother's name was Phillipa Judith Johnston. I don't know how my parents knew her full name, but my father seemed certain about it.'

'Is that why you're called Jude?'

'Yes, he said Mum wanted to give me a name that linked me to my birth mother, and I'm glad I got Jude instead of Phillip.' When he looked at her again, the tension in his jaw seemed to ease. 'I'm just glad she didn't take a leaf out of your mum's book, otherwise I might have been called Benny or Björn.'

'Or maybe even Agnetha, and do you know what? I think you could have carried it off.' She grinned as he laughed again, the sound fast becoming one of her favourite things. As the realisation of that hit her, Emily caught her breath. Jasmine was right; she was in unchartered territory, and it was too late to stop herself getting involved. She was already in far too deep.

13

When Jude had first suggested meeting Emily's parents, she'd completely dismissed the idea. Despite knowing that they were capable of convincing anyone about the concept of true love, she hadn't wanted them to be used as some kind of social experiment, or just to entertain Jude. When her mother had first been diagnosed, one of the things she'd struggled with the most was the assumptions people made about her symptoms. She'd been accused of being drunk on multiple occasions, mostly when the tremors that had been the first symptom of the disease had been uncontrolled and obvious. It had made Emily's mother reluctant to be around people she didn't know. Thankfully, for a long time the medication Patsy had been given was successful in reducing most of her symptoms, but it was no longer working as well as it had been, and the reluctance to be around new people was back too. She could cope with big events like the Christmas market, when she had her family around her and she could get lost amongst the crowd, but not anywhere she felt she might be under scrutiny. It was why Emily hadn't been prepared to allow Jude to meet her parents, not even to prove to him that he was wrong about love, but then her mother had taken her by surprise and asked her to invite him over.

'I read one of Jude's books.' Patsy's tone had been light and there was no way of knowing from the expression on her face what she'd thought of the novel she'd read.

'Did you like it?' When Patsy had wrinkled her nose in response, Emily had found herself getting defensive. She'd read Jude's books; he was extremely talented and for some reason she hated the thought that her mother might think otherwise.

'I can see why he needed your help. The murder storylines are great; he makes them feel so believable, and the lives of the victims are complex and multi-layered. So it's odd that his lead character appears so one-dimensional. It's like you can't scratch the surface of who DCI McGuigan really is.' Patsy had paused for a moment, her eyes locking with Emily's. 'Is that what it's like with Jude?'

'It was at first.' She hadn't intended to be so honest, but her mother had always been able to make Emily open up to her. Maybe it was because she'd been a counsellor for so long. 'I felt like he was shut down and standoffish, but the more time I've spent with him, the more I suspect that's how he protects himself. I think you're right about the adoption having affected him even more than he realised, but he's decided to try and find his birth mother.'

'Wow, that'll be quite something after all these years. I wonder if she's been hoping and praying all this time.' There'd been a spark in Patsy's eyes that Emily remembered from before her mother had been forced to retire. She'd loved working with complex cases, and this kind of situation would have been right up her street.

'I just hope he can find his biological mother and get some answers. He's added his name to the adoption contact register, but he was born at the old cottage hospital near Port Tremellien and I wondered if Gwen might have been there at the time. It's a long shot and I don't know if she'd be able to tell him anything even if she was there, but I'm sure an adoption would have stuck in her mind if she knew about it.'

'Maybe, but sometimes the proper channels are the best way of doing things. That way Jude can access some support if he needs it.'

'You're right, and he said he doesn't want to approach his biological mother unless he's sure she wants to hear from him, so he didn't seem all that keen to speak to Gwen when I mentioned it.'

'I can sound her out, so he's got options if he does decide to go down that route, but why don't you invite Jude here for dinner in the meantime?'

'What for?' Emily had known the reason, but she'd wanted to see if her mum would be honest about it.

'He hasn't got a lot of support by the sounds of it, and I'd like him to feel like he can turn to us if he needs to.' Bingo. Her mother's response hadn't surprised her at all.

'You don't even know him, and I'm just someone he hired to help him revise one of his books.'

'You keep telling yourself that, Em, but it's pretty obvious it's gone a long way beyond that, and I think I could help him too if he was willing to let me.'

'He won't want a counsellor, Mum, and you don't even practise any more.' Even as she'd protested, she'd known it was futile. Her mother would have kept suggesting inviting Jude over until Emily eventually backed down. It was stupid not to make the offer, especially when he'd already said he wanted to see for himself what made her parents' relationship so special.

That was why she was standing in their lounge now, trying

not to make it obvious that she was staring out of the window so she could see when Jude arrived. She wanted to be able to answer the door before her father got to it, but she didn't want Jude to think she was standing there waiting with bated breath for him to arrive. She had no idea why she was overthinking this as much as she was.

'Ooh, there he is.' The words came out despite Emily's intention to play it cool, and her mother shot her a knowing look. Thankfully her father was in the kitchen, so there was no chance of him getting to Jude first and saying something embarrassing that might give away just how often his name had come up in conversation lately. *Emily's always talking about you.* No, she didn't want Jude hearing that.

'Hi, come on in.' Emily suddenly felt strangely shy now that Jude was standing on the doorstep of her family home. His dark hair was artfully messy, as if someone had styled him to look as though he'd been running his hands through his hair while working through the draft of his book. The intensity in his blue eyes made it feel as if he could read her mind, and that was definitely something she didn't want.

'Mum's in the lounge, and Dad's insisting on making pizza. It's against his religion not to have pizza on the first night of Christmas movie month, and tonight's the night.' She stepped to the side and ushered him in to the hallway.

'That sounds like the kind of religion I could get on board with.' Jude's generous mouth curved into a smile. 'Although I'm intrigued to know what else Christmas movie month involves.'

'We've done it ever since Charlotte and I outgrew all the traditions little kids enjoy. We always start in the first week of December to fit everything in, but it would probably sound awful to anyone else, watching the same films every year.' Emily shrugged, not really caring what other people – even Jude –

thought of Christmas movie month, because she loved it. 'We have a list of all the Christmas films we love the most and absolutely have to watch in the run-up to the big day. We schedule them in and share it on our family WhatsApp group. If we aren't all together, we still make sure we watch the same films on the same day. So Charlotte and her family will be watching *Home Alone* at their place, and after you've gone we'll watch it too. No doubt Dad will recreate a scene from the movie – probably the aftershave scene – and post a picture of it in the group. It's a way of getting into the spirit of things together even when we're apart. It's silly, but I love it. We all do.'

'It doesn't sound silly.' Every time that wistful tone came into Jude's voice, she wanted to reach out to him physically and emotionally, but she was pretty sure that was the fastest way to make him shut down. Instead, she just smiled as he handed her a large hessian bag. 'I've brought some chocolate and some flowers. I was going to bring wine, but I wasn't sure if your parents drink.'

'You didn't need to bring anything, but that was really thoughtful. Thank you. They don't really drink any more; it affects Mum's medication, and Dad doesn't like drinking in front of her, or when he's taking care of her.'

'The more I hear about your dad, the more I wish he was mine.'

'Even if that made us siblings?' It was a throwaway comment, but she still wished she hadn't said it. She'd thought stopping her father answering the door would save her from embarrassment, but now she wasn't so sure. Maybe there'd be safety in numbers. 'Shall we go through so you can meet them both?'

'I'd like that.'

By the time they got through to the lounge, her parents were sitting side by side on the sofa.

'Mum, Dad, this is Jude.' Something about being around him

always made her feel clumsy, and Emily knew she was stating the obvious, but there was no other way to do the introductions. 'And these are my parents, Patsy and Richard.'

'It's good to meet you both, thanks so much for inviting me over.' Jude extended a hand to Emily's father, who shook it, but when he attempted the same with Patsy, her tremor was painfully apparent and she was struggling to keep her hand steady enough to take his. Now that the medication was no longer working, the tremors seemed to have come back with a vengeance. If it fazed Jude in the slightest, he didn't give it away, gently reaching forward to take her hand.

'We had to invite you over, we've heard so much about you.' Emily should have known that it would be her mother who was at most risk of embarrassing her, although she seemed to be determined to do a good job of it herself.

'Of course I'm going to talk about Jude. This is the most interesting job I've ever been offered.' Emily knew she was protesting too much, but she didn't seem able to stop and she needed to take the focus off herself. 'I told him that if he ever met the two of you, he wouldn't be able to deny that true love existed.'

'It must do, otherwise I'd have stabbed him through the eyeball with a fork years ago for snoring so loud it sounds like someone felling a tree with a chainsaw and, until very recently, never changing the toilet roll.' Patsy smiled. 'Whereas I'm an absolute breeze to live with.'

'You are, Patz, you are.' Emily's dad winked. 'What would I do without your freezing-cold feet on me in bed and the way you've always been able to somehow burn and undercook pasta all at the same time.'

'I'm just glad you realise how lucky you are.' Patsy leant into her husband, and he dropped a kiss on her head, making it obvious that teasing one another was just another sign of the affection between them. Emily wanted what they had one day, but they were a hard act to follow and she wasn't prepared to settle for anything less.

'Sit down, Jude, there's no need to stand on ceremony for us.' Richard gestured towards an armchair opposite her parents. 'I hope you're okay with pizza.'

'Love it, but you really didn't need to cook for me.' Jude took a seat as he spoke.

'I'd hardly call pizzas cooking, but Patz would never forgive me if a guest went away hungry.'

'Jude bought chocolates and flowers.' Emily held up the bag. 'The roses are beautiful, so I'm going to put them in some water.'

She was gone less than five minutes, checking on both the pizzas and her makeup before she went back in. She told herself it was because the blast of hot air from the oven had made it feel as if the mascara had clumped her lashes together, but that didn't explain the slick of lipstick, or the spritz of perfume she'd applied. Emily could hear the laughter coming down the hallway as she headed back from the kitchen.

'I can't believe you did that!' Her mum's eyes were shining in response to whatever it was they'd been laughing about, and Emily felt like someone watching an inside joke she didn't understand. It made her feel left out and it was something else that mattered more than it should have done when it came to Jude.

'What's so funny?'

'I just admitted to your mum and dad that I bought my first stepmother a sweatshirt that said *Merry Christmas You Filthy Animal*.' Jude grinned. 'My dad said I had to get her something, and I knew she'd have no idea what *Home Alone* was. She thought I'd had it specially made and was completely outraged. Her reaction was the best gift I got that year.'

'Jude's going to stay and watch the movie with us.' Her

father's statement was a fait accompli, and Jude looked as if he'd been one of the family for years. The worst thing was that a big part of her wished it was true, and that unchartered territory Jasmine had warned her about suddenly felt scarier than ever.

* * *

Jude hadn't wanted to leave the cosy warmth of 10 Lowenna Close, and not because the temperature outside had plummeted well below freezing. The air caught in his throat, cold and sharp, making it hard to take a deep breath. Frost clung to the grass and settled in the cracks of the pavement, making it look, in the glow of the street lamps, as if someone had taken a giant pot of silver glitter and spread a blanket of it all over Port Agnes. Jude slipped on a patch of black ice as he crossed the road, heading back towards Puffin's Rest. Thankfully the couple on the pavement opposite were too busy kissing to notice that he'd almost fallen over. Even as Jude tried to remind himself that he didn't think that way, he could suddenly understand how a winter's kiss in the glow of the moonlight might be considered romantic. It was time to get home before any other ridiculous notions entered his head.

Rufus might sulk for a little while when he arrived, making his displeasure about Jude's prolonged absence clear. He'd promised the dog he wouldn't be long, offering up the reassurance as if Rufus understood every word. Apparently dogs had no concept of time, but his faithful Labrador was more than capable of giving him the dirtiest of looks when he'd been out for too long. Although on a night like this, Rufus was far more likely to be sprawled out snoring, taking advantage of having the place to himself and no one to tell him to get off a sofa that didn't belong to them. The trouble would come when Rufus picked up the scent of another dog on Jude. Gary Barlow had sat on his lap for almost the entire evening, claiming the spot before the opening credits of *Home Alone* and not moving again until Jude got up to leave.

Rufus would be very put out that he hadn't been invited to spend the evening with his best friend. Although Jude suspected his dog would have been welcomed with open arms by Patsy and Richard had he turned up with Rufus in tow. They wouldn't even have minded if he'd left big, muddy footprints down their hallway, or snagged a bit of pepperoni pizza when no one was looking. They were just those sorts of people, relaxed, and friendly and warm. Not to mention every bit as devoted to one another as Emily had said. That was the real reason he didn't want to leave 10 Lowenna Close. Being inside their home was what it felt like to be in the heart of a real family, with private jokes and a kind of shorthand that meant speaking to one another often didn't require full sentences, or sometimes even words. He might have assumed that Emily had no idea how lucky she was, except that they'd had the kind of in-depth conversations that proved she did. No one was left out; the WhatsApp messages flying between Charlotte in Exeter and her family in Port Kara meant she might as well have been in the room. He understood for the first time how easy it must be for someone like Emily to believe in love, and maybe she was right. Maybe there were families like this all over the place, who chose to spend time together just because they wanted to, not because there was some kind of obligation or transaction taking place between them. Maybe Jude even had a family like this somewhere, one with a space on the sofa, waiting for him to fill it.

Now you really are being an idiot. Jude shook his head. Romanticising a reunion with his biological family was a dangerous game. In the very best scenario it would live up to expectations, but it was far more likely to fall significantly short of the ideal he was picturing. Life had taught him that it was better to have no expectations and to assume the worst, because it was far harder to end up disappointed that way. Perhaps if his mother hadn't died, they'd have had their own version of what Emily and her family had. He couldn't imagine his father ever being the warm-hearted patriarch that Richard was, but he could picture his mother laughing at *Home Alone* and telling him she loved him, the way Emily's mother had done so casually when her daughter had brought in her favourite lemon cheesecake. Jude wasn't sure if his father had ever told him he loved him. If he had, Jude certainly couldn't recall it. Maybe that explained a lot about his views on love. If he'd asked his father whether he loved him, he'd almost certainly have got a response along lines of 'of course I do'. But that would have been transactional; Charles would have said it because Jude was his son and that meant he had a duty to love him, not because he couldn't stop the words from bursting out of him.

There was a sense of duty nagging at Jude too. He needed to tell his father that he'd put his name on the adoption contact register. He should visit and have that conversation face to face, he knew that, but he also knew he didn't want to. For a moment he considered just texting it, but then another memory of his mother suddenly popped into his head.

'Never take the coward's way out, Jude, even when that feels easier. It's the difficult conversations that teach you the most.' He'd been ten when she'd told him that, the summer before she'd died. He'd kicked a football far too enthusiastically and it had sailed over their fence and smashed through a pane of glass on their neighbour's greenhouse. Jude had begged his mother to be the one to go and tell Mr and Mrs Pike what had happened, or failing that to be allowed to leave a note, but she'd urged him to do the right thing and speak to them himself. He'd been terrified, but their neighbours had praised his honesty and had told him they were planning to replace the greenhouse soon anyway, and that Mr Pike could patch it for now. There'd been no negative repercussions, but having to face that situation had still made Jude far more careful about where he kicked his football in future. As always, his mother had been right. She'd almost certainly have wanted him to go and see his father face to face, but he was just as sure she'd have preferred him to phone Charles rather than text him with the news.

Jude looked at his watch. It was almost ten o'clock. He should wait until the morning really, but suddenly he didn't want to. As tempting as it was just to call, he didn't want to wake his father or Viv, or make them worry that something serious might be wrong. Standing under the light of a streetlamp, he texted his father a short message.

> Are you still awake? Just need to call you about something, but it's nothing to worry about.

As Jude pressed send it crossed his mind that he wasn't sure what would worry his father when it came to him. Would he be horribly upset if something happened to his only son, or would he shrug in that resigned way of his and carry on with a life that didn't involve his son in any significant way?

> Still awake, I'm staying up for Newsnight.

That summed it up. Richard and Patsy were *Home Alone* people, and his father's idea of festive viewing was *Newsnight*. It was probably more worthy, but it sure wasn't a lot of fun, and it was the way Charles had always been. Jude texted his father again.

> I'll call you now then, it won't take long, you won't miss Newsnight.

He sent the message via WhatsApp and waited until the two blue ticks appeared before calling his father.

'Hi, Dad.'

'Hello, Jude.'

'How are you?'

'Fine. How are you? How's the holiday apartment?'

'Good. Rufus loves it, although the seagulls seem to live to torment him.' Jude smiled at the thought of the dog barking madly at the birds who pecked on the glass, seemingly with the sole purpose of winding him up. 'How's Viv?'

'She's fine. Asking when you'll be coming to see us.'

'Is she?' Jude wondered if his father would ever have even mentioned it if he hadn't called.

'Yes. Let her know, will you?'

'I will.' He hadn't intended going before Christmas, but that sense of duty was prodding at him again. There was something else he needed to say first though. 'I wanted to call you to let you know that I've put my name on the adoption contact register.'

'Right.' His father's response didn't give any indication of how he felt about it and Jude wasn't sure whether he'd even understood.

'It means my biological mother will be able to contact me, if she's on the register.'

'Right.' It seemed to be his father's new favourite word, and Jude still had no idea how he felt about it, so he was going to have to ask.

'Do you mind?'

'Why would I?' It was a reasonable enough question, but it was one Jude couldn't answer. There might have been adoptive parents who'd feel threatened, or jealous, sad even, but they probably had very different relationships with their children than Charles had with Jude.

'Do you think it would have upset Mum?' He held his breath, willing his father to say something that would make him feel closer to Ros again, even just for a moment. He still missed her so much, even after all this time, but he'd pushed that down for years, hiding it, even from himself. It had been Emily who'd made him face it.

'No.' It hadn't been the reply Jude had wanted. It was too simple, too easy, and anger surged inside him, making him snap back in response.

'How can you possibly know that?'

'Because we talked about it.' His father sighed lightly. 'When we discovered where you'd been born, we knew your biological mother must be local and I wanted us to move away. I thought it would cause problems when there was such a big chance of crossing paths with her, but your mum wouldn't hear of it. She wanted it to be easier for you to find the woman who'd given birth to you if you wanted to one day. Even if that never happened, she thought it was important you maintained a link to your other family. Even if that was just by staying close to where your roots were. It would have been hard for her, I'm sure, for you to suddenly have these other people in your life, but you always came first to your mother and she'd have wanted whatever you did.'

There was a note of something in his father's voice that Jude couldn't define. For a moment, he wondered if Charles might find it hard to see his son with another family, but his father could hardly complain about that. After all, he already had another family of his own. Asking Charles the question would probably just cause more hurt. The least said between them always seemed to be for the better.

'It helps to know she would have been okay with me doing it. Thank you.' Jude wasn't sure what he'd expected his father to say in response, but he should have known what was coming.

'Don't forget to let Viv know if you're coming to see us before Christmas.'

'I will. Bye, Dad.' There'd been no wishes of good luck, and no requests to let him know if Jude's search came to anything. It clearly didn't interest Charles, because it didn't involve him, and the fact that the outcome might matter so much to his son didn't even seem to come into the equation. It had been so easy to believe that love might be everywhere when he'd been at 10 Lowenna Close, but all of a sudden Jude was back to being far less certain that it was.

14

The conversation with his father had strengthened Jude's desire to search for his biological mother. He needed to know the circumstances of his adoption, but more than ever he wanted to know how it had felt for her to give him up. Had she spent her whole life waiting for him to get in contact, or had she not even put her name on the register? He'd spent hours googling when he'd got home, and all he'd got for his efforts was a growing sense of frustration and impatience.

The waiting time to hear back from the adoption contact register suddenly seemed interminable. He knew his mother's name, but he couldn't find anyone who seemed to be a match on social media, unless of course she had a different surname by now. It was like trying to find a needle in a haystack. By 2 a.m., Jude was considering checking the marriage register, but he had no idea what he was doing and there was a voice in his head warning him that he was poking a hornet's nest.

Leaving the process to the official channels was safer and, as much as he wanted to know what had led up to his adoption, he didn't want to contact someone who was desperate not to be found. But then he thought about how long it might take and the looming deadline for the revisions to his book, which he seemed completely incapable of concentrating on, and he knew he had to do something. That was when the googling started again and he eventually hit on the idea of using an intermediary service. It was getting light by the time Jude sent the email to the one which seemed the best fit, explaining what he wanted and giving them his name and number. He'd had no idea that the call back would come so quickly, and he was still asleep when it did.

'Oh, hi, is that Jude Cavendish?'

'It is.' Jude's head felt fuzzy, as if he'd been up drinking all night rather than spending it down a virtual rabbit hole on the internet, trying to work out the best way of finding his biological mother.

'Great, I'm Courtney Davies, from Reunion Connections, and I understand you'd like to use our service to find your biological mother?'

'That's right. I've already added myself to the adoption contact register, but it feels like a long wait to hear back from them, and of course there's a chance she might not even have added her name. So I wanted to try and speed up the process of finding her.'

'Our service might not make the process any quicker, however we do have a dedicated team who will follow up queries with local authorities and government agencies when responses are slow. If that feels like something you might not have time to do yourself.' Courtney sounded like she was reading from a script, but Jude didn't need much convincing. He didn't want to get involved in the bureaucratic process, because he could already see how easily it could become all-consuming, and he had a book to rewrite.

'I can see the benefits of leaving all that to you.' Jude had seen on their website that the agency had a fixed fee, so he knew what he'd be getting into if he asked them to act on his behalf, and it felt more than worth it.

'Okay good.' Courtney sounded a bit more enthusiastic. 'And I understand you believe you have your biological mother's name?'

'Yes, that's right, that and her date of birth, as well as where I was born. My father gave me the information when I was eighteen, but it's only in the last couple of weeks that I've wanted to find her.'

'It's possible that the name your father was given wasn't correct.' Courtney's statement was matter-of-fact, but her words made Jude catch his breath. She was right; he had no way of verifying that what his parents had been told was true. He'd just taken his father's word for it and held that name in his head for years, never wanting to act on it, but knowing he could if he changed his mind.

'Is there a way of finding out?'

'Yes, there is.' Courtney clearly wasn't going to give him any pointers, in case he decided to do it on his own, but he wanted to make it clear to her that wasn't an option.

'I started looking for her online, and I thought about checking the registers of births, marriages and deaths, but there's so much information to go through and I don't want to find someone who doesn't want to be found.'

'I think that's a great way to approach this. As I said, whilst we can't guarantee making the process any quicker, we can help protect the people involved. Not everyone chooses to add their name to the contact register, but that doesn't always mean they aren't open to being found. If your biological mother does want contact, we can pass on the details.' Courtney paused for a moment, before continuing. 'As I'm sure you know, some individuals choose to veto contact. This can be absolute, which vetoes any kind of contact, or it might be a qualified veto, where contact can be made in certain circumstances. Even in the case of an absolute veto, it's sometimes still possible to pass on key information, such as hereditary medical conditions. It's very unusual for us not to be able to pass on some kind of information as a result of the search, and we truly believe it's a far better option than going it alone, or signing up to a DNA website, as some adopted children choose to do.'

'I don't want to pursue that option. I have no interest in finding a second cousin in Milton Keynes. I'd just like the chance to have a conversation with my biological mother, even if it's only once.'

'I understand that. I'll email you some information about how to get the process started and what we'll need from you. Then we'll run some initial checks using the name you were given. Our first goal is always to establish that the person we're searching for is still living, and there are a couple of ways to do that quite easily. After that we can get going with the next phase of the search, but please remember these things are rarely as quick as we'd like them to be.'

'Okay, I understand that. Thanks for all your help and I look forward to hearing from you.' As Jude ended the call, he suddenly shivered, a sense of foreboding settling on him for just a moment, before he shook it off. It was understandable that this felt like a big step, and of course he was going to question whether he might be making a mistake, but he'd already examined the worst-case scenario. If all his biological mother wanted to do was forget he'd ever existed, then at least he'd know. Ignorance had stopped being bliss a long time ago.

* * *

Emily had a biscuit tin under one arm and Gary Barlow under the other as she climbed the steep stairs up to Puffin's Rest. Her parents' dog never went upstairs and it turned out he didn't even seem to know how. He'd put his front two paws on the second step up and then refused to go any further, even when she'd given a gentle tug on the lead.

'We could just have met down by the harbour again.' Emily's pronouncement as Jude opened the door to her was only partly because of the effort of carrying the dog up the stairs. The idea of being alone with Jude in his flat suddenly seemed like a risk she didn't need to take. He was making them lunch, and he'd finally asked if she minded reading some pages from his reworked novel to get her perspective, which she'd offered to do before they'd even come down to Cornwall.

They'd met the day before, for their usual walk with the dogs, and Jude had told her about his decision to contact an intermediary agency to move forward the search for his biological mother. It was clear this was a big step, but it was just as clear it was one he needed to take so that he could free up some head space to finish his book. His editor had called him when they'd been out with the dogs, checking on his progress. She just hoped she'd be able to tell him the pages he'd reworked were brilliant, because she was all out of ideas about how to help him write a believable relationship for DCI McGuigan. He'd met her parents, and she got the impression he'd liked them every bit as much as they'd liked him. They hadn't stopped asking when he was coming round again and, on her way out of the house, her mother had instructed her to check whether he was coming to watch *Elf* with them over the weekend. She'd also given Emily a tin of Christmas cookies to pass on.

'Meeting down by the harbour for lunch would probably have been a good idea. It would have got me out of the flat and away from the computer for a bit longer.' Jude stepped back to allow both her and Gary Barlow inside. 'That way I might actually stop checking my emails every five minutes.'

'Are you waiting for some news about your books?' Emily remembered Sophia jumping at the phone every time it pinged when they'd been out together the previous year. One of her books had been optioned by a TV company, and there was a meeting that day to discuss whether it had been selected for production. Sophia hadn't been able to relax while she was waiting for the news. After about the third time she'd leapt on her phone to check a message, even Emily was feeling jumpy.

'No. I know it's stupid, because it's almost certainly going to be weeks before I hear anything, but I can't stop myself from checking whether there are any messages about the adoption search.'

'That's understandable.' Emily followed Jude through to the open-plan living area, and he invited her to take a seat. No one would ever have guessed it was less than two weeks to Christmas judging from the décor. There wasn't a single strand of fairy lights on display, never mind the kind of six-foot Christmas tree that would have looked stunning in front of the full-length windows looking out towards the sea. 'If you want something to distract you from checking your emails, Mum and Dad have been nagging me to invite you over to watch *Elf* tomorrow night. Apparently, you told Mum it was your favourite and after the children break up from school, you won't get the chance to see any more films in peace because my sister and her kids will be there in person for every movie night after that.'

'Watching *Home Alone* with all of you was the first time in a long time that I've got the kind of Christmassy feeling I remember from when I was young. I'm not sure if the kids will appreciate me being there once they arrive, so I better take your parents up on the offer while it's quiet. That's if you don't have any objections?' Jude gave her a questioning look.

'Of course I don't.' Emily tried her best to sound casual; she didn't want him to know how much she wanted him to accept the invitation. 'I think you'll be fine with my sister's kids, though. They're pretty full on, but it's hard not to get swept up in their excitement about Christmas. You must remember what that was like, and that being around other kids made you even more excited?'

Jude shook his head. 'I never really got to hang out with other kids that much over Christmas, or at any other time. When Mum was alive, she made things special, but that didn't really involve other kids. It was just us and, looking back, I suspect that was because my father didn't want a house full of kids. After she died and Sandra came along, I don't think they even wanted me in the house, let alone other children. I know she didn't. There were the other kids at boarding school of course, but we were too old for all the Santa stuff by then.'

'What about now? With your stepsister's children?' Jude had told her about Viv's daughter, Fiona, and it had sounded as if he was fond of her and her family, but he shook his head again.

'I don't spend time with them either, at least not as much as I probably should. Sandra's dislike for me was so obvious, and I struggle to believe that Viv doesn't feel the same way, even though she never gives any indication of it.' Jude shrugged. 'It's just easier for us all if I don't get too involved.'

'I guess.' Emily nodded. She didn't really agree with him at all, but the last thing she wanted to do was dismiss the way he felt. It must have been incredibly sad to believe that his own family, the people who were supposed to love him most, didn't really want him around. She didn't think for a moment it was true, because once you got below the surface and Jude revealed his true self, there was so much about him to love. He was clever, kind, generous and funny. It was just that he preferred to hide it all away and keep his emotions firmly in check. Emily was certain if he gave his family even a hint of wanting to be a part of their world, that they'd welcome him in with open arms, and it made her sad to think he might never do that. She'd never have believed a few weeks ago that Jude would open up to her as much as he had, and as he busied himself setting food out on the table, having refused her offer of help, she decided it was her turn to open up to him.

'Working on this project with you has made me think about a lot of things, especially as Mum's Parkinson's disease is progressing again. The consultant is hopeful she can get it under control and that Mum can enjoy a normal life span, but there's a chance she won't and that it'll escalate to stage five instead. Even if they can stabilise things for now, the new symptoms might still limit what we can do in the future. I just don't want to waste any opportunities to make the most of the time we've got.' Emily tried to keep her tone level, but she didn't quite pull it off, her voice cracking on the final line. Right from the time of her mother's diagnosis, the whole family seemed to have made an unspoken pact to look on the bright side, but things had got worse recently and the thought of what might happen if the new medications didn't work made it impossible not to get emotional.

'I'm so sorry about your mum, she's such a lovely lady, but I think what you said is really important.' Jude looked across at her and she had to fight not to drop her gaze. 'There's nothing specific I wish I'd done with my mum while I had the chance, I just wish I'd treasured the time we had far more than I did and realised how precious it was. Although I guess you don't understand the true value of important moments until you know for certain that it's impossible to recreate them. I just wish I'd told her how I felt about her.'

'And how was that?'

'I loved her.' Jude smiled at the look that must have crossed her face. 'All right, all right, you've got me. I did love her, but it doesn't detract from my theory that love can often be broken down into a series of transactions. I got a lot from my mother and I loved her in return. She desperately wanted a child, and I needed a mother. There's your transaction right there.'

'I don't think you really believe it's as simple as that.' She was pushing Jude now, knowing she risked him shutting down on her, but she couldn't seem to help it. For some reason, it was really important that he acknowledged the existence of love, in a way that went beyond what he needed to finish his book. 'There are plenty of parents who don't do a great job, but their children still love them. Or children who commit terrible crimes, and yet their parents stand by them. Neither of them are getting what they want or need from each other, yet the love is still there.'

'Is it really though? Maybe it's a sense of duty on the parents' part, or what society expects them to do. That's a different kind of transaction.' Jude shrugged.

'And what about the children who still love their parents, even in the face of fundamental selfishness, or something much worse like neglect?'

'That's harder to explain.' Jude's face clouded for a moment. He was such a clever person, always ready with an answer, but he was clearly struggling. Then he seemed to recover. 'I don't know, maybe it's because those children are desperate to believe that they are loved, despite the way the parents have acted. So they excuse the behaviour and want their parents to be a part of their lives more than ever, in the hope that they'll suddenly change and become the kind of parents the children need.'

'That's a complicated transaction that I'm not sure even you really believe.' Emily raised her eyebrows, and she had a feeling from the look on Jude's face that she might be right. He'd been so certain of his theory about love when they'd first met, but she'd seen the edges of that start to soften a bit, even if he was nowhere near ready to admit it.

Emily could have taken her argument further and asked Jude about his dad. Did he love Charles despite his failings and, if so, was it only because he was hoping his father might change? But they'd come so far since they'd got to Cornwall and she didn't want to push things any more than she already had. Not today at least. She just hoped she'd done enough to give him a new perspective, one that could help him finally finish his edits. Either way, she'd find out when she read his pages.

Not mentioning his father ensured that the conversation flowed easily. Jude had made a pasta dish that smelt delicious and tasted even better. Gary Barlow sat by her feet on one side, with Rufus on the other, both of them staring up at her and waiting for something, anything, to be dropped.

'Can I interest you in dessert?' Jude asked as he cleared away the dishes from lunch. She'd been about to answer when his phone started to ring.

'Sorry, do you mind if I get this? It's the intermediary agency. They probably just need some more information.'

'Of course not. I'll finish clearing the dishes.' Jude didn't have time to object if he wanted to take the call before it went to voicemail. Emily felt suddenly awkward in the open-plan space, and she didn't want him to think she was eavesdropping, even though it was impossible not to. Clearing the plates away was the next best thing to being in another room. It was still impossible not to hear Jude's side of the conversation, and even if she hadn't been able to, she'd have known something was wrong by the look on his face.

'Right... so you were able to verify that for sure?'

'That's good, at least I haven't had the wrong name all this time.'

'That makes sense... Okay, so you found her name there?'

'Really? When? Thirty-four years ago... I'd thought about the possibility, but I didn't really think it would be the case. I've got to admit I'm a bit shocked.'

'Okay, I understand. I don't know, I'm just... I need to think about it... Yes, I'll let you know... That's okay, thank you.'

As Jude ended the call, Emily balled her hands into fists, digging her fingernails into her palms. She wanted to ask him if everything was okay, but she already knew it wasn't. And the truth was she had no right to ask him anything. It was up to him whether he wanted to tell her.

'My biological mother died just after my first birthday. From meningitis.' Jude didn't look at her as he spoke, but she could see the tension in his jaw as he struggled to process what he'd just been told.

'I'm so sorry.' Emily had no idea what to say to help, so she just went with her gut.

'Me too. I never really thought about it ending this way. Courtney said they were able to verify that her name was Patricia Judith Johnson from the record of my birth they were able to access online. She told me when I first got in contact that they always run some initial checks to see whether the person they're trying to find is still alive. Apparently the first stage is an NHS check, alongside a review of the register of deaths, because the last thing they want is to give a client false hope. I didn't expect to hear anything for weeks, but the fact that she's dead made the search easy. I can't believe she's been gone for almost my entire life.' Jude's voice cracked on the final few words, and he took an audible breath before continuing. 'They told me they could try to trace other members of her family, but I don't know if I want that. I don't think there's any way it can give me the answers I need.'

The look he gave her was one of such utter desolation that she couldn't do anything except cross the room to hug him. Part of her expected him to pull away, regain his composure and try to convince her that it didn't really matter, but to Emily's surprise he held her close.

'I'm so sorry.' She was repeating herself, but she didn't know what else to say.

'Me too.' He moved back just enough to look at her, and time seemed to stop altogether for a moment before he closed the space between them, his mouth finding hers, their bodies pressing together again as she responded to his kiss. Her brain was still trying to override the desire pulsing through her body, but it had no chance. This was what she'd wanted, deep down, almost from the first moment she'd seen Jude. Except it was more complicated now. The physical attraction had given way to something far deeper, and the kiss took that to another level. It was exhilarating but terrifying too, because she knew, after this, that if he walked out of her life, it would hurt her even more than before. Despite all the emotions racing through her head, the kiss was incredible and she wasn't sure how she'd ever have stepped back from him if Jude hadn't pulled away first.

'I'm sorry, I shouldn't have done that.' His hands dropped to his side, his face suddenly blank, as though the moment they'd just shared hadn't happened, and then he changed the subject in such a drastic way that it took Emily's breath away. 'Did you say whether you wanted some dessert?'

'No, thank you, I'm fine.' It was the biggest lie Emily had told in a long time; she was anything but fine. She was going to have to find an excuse to leave, and take Jude's pages with her. There was no way she could sit in the same room as him and read the words, or take the dogs out along the coastal path together afterwards like they'd planned. She had to get out of there and away from Jude as soon as possible, before she made an even bigger a fool of herself than she already had. She was so confused, certain that she hadn't read the situation wrong, but Jude was acting like it was the kind of mistake he couldn't wait to move on from. Embarrassment mingled with a disappointment she didn't want to feel. He'd told her from the start where he stood, so allowing her feelings to deepen as much as they had was incredibly stupid. Emily only had herself to blame for the crushing sense of regret that came from wanting something that had never been an option in the first place.

15

Jude didn't know what to do with himself. He'd been so certain that finding his biological mother would finally allow him to fill the void in his life, one he hadn't fully realised was there until he'd met Emily. But the void felt even bigger because it could never be filled now. He'd reached the point where ignorance about his birth story was no longer bliss. He couldn't remember feeling true contentment since his adoptive mother's death. But even not knowing had been better than this; the absolute knowledge that he would never know how the woman who'd given birth to him felt about handing him over to someone else.

Jude had tried to convince himself that Emily's theory had been rubbish. He didn't want to believe that his inability to write about love was down to his desire to protect himself from the consequences of the truth. But she'd chipped away at the barrier he'd built around himself, and he'd finally decided he needed to test her theory. After discovering that Patricia was dead, he realised how right she'd been. She was the one person he wanted to talk to about what had happened, but he couldn't. Emily had got under his skin and made him feel things he hadn't ever felt before. If he saw her now, he wouldn't be able to stop himself from opening up to her again, and it was safer to keep some feelings boxed up. He'd already paid the price for forgetting that. Jude had pulled out of going to her parents' house to watch *Elf*, and he'd fobbed Emily off when she'd texted him about meeting up with the dogs. He just couldn't face seeing her.

He couldn't deny that he'd wanted to kiss Emily from the first day he'd met her, and that desire had deepened as he got to know this bright, insightful and beautiful woman who made him look at the world differently, even when he didn't want to. It was hard to believe he'd only known her for four weeks. But as much as Jude had wanted to kiss Emily, and as amazing as it had been, he shouldn't have done it. He'd crossed a boundary he'd been determined to maintain, but far worse, he'd allowed her to see him at his most vulnerable, in the wake of the news that his biological mother was dead. The news had hit him like a sledgehammer, and he'd been shocked at just how devastated he had felt.

He should never have listened to Emily in the first place and allowed her to convince him that finding his mother was the key to connecting with his characters on a deeper level. Jude should have kept in mind what life had taught him – that people always let you down in the end, one way or another. Whether that was through deliberate action, like his father, or by dying, like both his mothers. If Emily managed her usual trick of getting him to talk, it would just rake over pain he couldn't do anything about, and all he wanted was to bury it along with every other bad thing that had happened to him. He doubted very much there was anything she could say that would help him sort out the mess his head was in, let alone his book.

The novel was far worse now than before he'd started the revisions; he knew that without having to show Marty the changes. Jude had felt he was getting somewhere, but now, as he reread it, the story seemed completely unbelievable. Why would McGuigan risk his career, his life even, for someone who'd just let him down in the end, whether she meant to or not? And how could McGuigan's girlfriend love such a flawed and complex man? Love couldn't be worth that kind of sacrifice; it took far more than it gave and set you up for so much hurt. It was illogical, a game you couldn't win. Everyone lost in the end, one way or the other. Except when he thought about Emily, a tiny part of him could acknowledge something stronger than logic. A pull between them that couldn't be explained. If their professional relationship was over, why did it feel like something was missing when he wasn't with her?

Jude couldn't give Emily what she deserved, even if she wanted to be with him. She deserved what her parents had, and Jude was far too broken to be able to offer her anything close to that. Since his adoptive mother had died, every lesson he'd learned had reinforced the belief that he was unlovable. His father's disinterest, Sandra's blatant hatred, and a string of relationships that had never felt right, as if somehow they weren't enough. Mia had been the only one he'd got as far as living with, and it was probably the only relationship that could be called serious, but looking back, even then, he'd been holding a part of himself back. He'd blamed the ending on Mia and the fact she'd left for someone else, her disloyalty making the relationship fail, but it hadn't been that. It had been set up to fail from day one, because of Jude's inability to allow himself to fully invest in the relationship and put his heart on the line. It was almost certainly why Mia had been so open to Bexter's advances. He might never have realised it if Emily hadn't made him see that he was the one who wasn't enough. It wasn't some failing on the part of the women he'd become involved with. He'd been so busy trying to protect himself from getting hurt again that he'd closed a big part of himself off. Emily had made him open up and admit that he did want to know his biological mother's story.

What he hadn't acknowledged was the hope he'd felt; hope that finding her would stop him feeling like that little unwanted boy, whose father, stepmother and birth mother hadn't loved him. Any concept of love had died along with his adoptive mother, but Jude had felt the embers of it reigniting since meeting Emily, and now they'd been snuffed out again. He missed her, just as much as he missed the hope he'd secretly been nurturing since adding his name to the adoption contact register, and he hated how out of control those emotions made him feel.

Jude snatched up his phone when it began to ring, the hope that it would be Emily rising and falling as he looked at the display. It shouldn't have been any surprise that she wasn't calling. After all, when she'd texted about meeting up to walk the dogs, he told her he was busy with edits and couldn't make it. She'd followed it up by wishing him luck with it, and telling him to message her if he wanted to meet up once he had time. All he'd texted back in response was 'will do'. He was an idiot, but he couldn't risk giving the feelings he had for her any more power; they were already taking over his subconscious.

When he was writing the new scenes, the only way he could buy into the story was to imagine Emily as the person McGuigan was falling in love with. He'd even changed the description of McGuigan's girlfriend so that she had the same dimples as Emily. He could imagine loving her, and that scared the crap out of him, because the one thing he absolutely couldn't imagine, the same thing that was blocking him from being able to write McGuigan's relationship in a believable way, was the idea of Emily falling in love with him.

When Jude realised it was Marty calling, he almost let it go to voicemail, as he had when his editor had called the day before, and the evening before that, just a couple of hours after Jude had discovered that his biological mother had died. He'd ignored several messages and emails from him too. He couldn't bear to give Marty another update, letting him know that the novel was still a steaming pile of horse manure, but he couldn't keep dodging his friend and editor forever either. He might as well face the music.

'Hi, Marty.'

'Bloody hell, Jude, I was beginning to think you might have died!' Marty sounded genuinely relieved. 'I've been ringing you and messaging you. I was about to ask Sophia for Emily's number. I thought maybe the two of you were together.'

There was a note of hope in Marty's voice in the final sentence, but Jude was going to have to disappoint him again. 'I haven't seen her since the day before yesterday.'

'In that case, I hope you're going to tell me that the revisions to the manuscript are almost complete?'

'I've made a lot of changes.' That part wasn't a lie. Jude had made changes, altered them again, and in some instances changed them back to how they'd been in the first round of edits. Before he'd kissed Emily, he'd wanted her to look at some of the key pages and give him feedback about whether or not they were as big a mess as he feared. Only now it felt like he'd already revealed far too much of who he was. He didn't want Emily to see anything else that exposed the flaws in his character, flaws that were mirrored in the description of the characters in his book.

'That's great. So when do I get to see these changes?' Marty's tone was almost always upbeat, even when he was delivering not so great news, probably because he tried to see the upside in every situation and find solutions that worked for the publishing house and for Jude, if things weren't panning out the way they'd hoped. He'd always felt like an ally, someone who wanted Jude's career to flourish every bit as much as he did. Jude knew how lucky he was in that respect. He wasn't just a pound sign to Marty. Only now there was a far more serious, insistent tone to his voice. 'I need you to deliver on this, Jude, for both our sakes.'

He'd suspected that Marty might have put his neck on the line with the team at Foster and Friedmann, by championing the DCI McGuigan series and insisting that the diminishing sales could be turned around. Now he knew it was true, and Jude's stomach roiled at the thought of letting Marty down. It was time to be honest. 'I can send them to you, but I'm still not sure I've captured what the readers want. To be truthful, Marty, I'm not even sure I've got what it takes.'

'Yes, you have, you just don't believe in yourself. You've always been the same, Jude. Christ, when I got your manuscript from Daniel Beckham, I wasn't even going to read it.' Marty sighed. Jude had been thrilled to find an agent, but he'd had no idea Daniel Beckham had set up his literary agency, with no experience and hardly any contacts. 'We'd all had manuscripts from him that weren't worth the paper they were written on. He was signing anyone, in a kind of scattergun approach, with the hope that something would land and make him some money.'

'That's why he took me then, because he was taking anyone?' Jude could joke about it now, but when he'd first heard this story from Marty it had knocked him for six. It had just been more proof that Jude was nothing special, and it had only been Marty's faith in him that had stopped him giving up on writing altogether.

'Yeah, but you were the one he got lucky with. I know you've heard all of this before, but I think it's a good time to remind you. I wasn't even going to look at your novel, but it had become a standing joke sharing stories about how bad the latest Daniel

Beckham submission was. So I thought I'd read a couple of pages to give me a funny anecdote to tell, and that was all it took. I realised I'd found a diamond in the rough. I knew it wasn't the story that was going to be your breakthrough, but I also knew I wanted to work with you on one that would be. The biggest barrier to your career has always been your belief in how good you are. I want this next novel to prove that to you, so we've got to get it right.'

'I'm lucky to have you, Marty.' It was as mushy as Jude was ever going to get. 'And maybe you can make a silk purse out of this sow's ear. Although I'm chopping it up and churning it over so much it's probably more like salami by now.'

'I think we need to take a different approach. That's what I've been trying to get in touch with you about.' Marty let out a long breath. 'I know you're probably not going to like this, but I've set up a meet and greet for you at Cecil's Adventures. It's a fabulous bookshop in Holly Bay, about half an hour from where you're staying. They've had all the big names in there and they contacted us a while back to see if you and Sophia would be willing to go in and give a talk to some of their readers. I knew what you'd say, so I didn't even bother to ask, but Sophia accepted. Only now she's got the flu and it's completely wiped her out. The owner of the bookshop was putting on a brave face when she spoke to Sophia, but she'd already had another author cancel this month. That's when Sophia asked me if there was anyone else who might stand in for her and I thought maybe you would. It could be a great way of connecting with readers and hearing from them first-hand what it is that makes them invest in a character's story.'

'Sorry, Marty, but no. It's a ridiculous idea. Why on earth would fans of Sophia want to see me instead?' It didn't matter how big a debt he felt he owed his editor, or how worried he was about the state of his novel, there was no way he was agreeing to this.

'The team at the bookshop have been doing an all-out blitz, locally and online, to let people know there's a change of author, and they've had lots of responses from readers who want to meet you, not Sophia.'

'They're already advertising the fact I'm going to be there?' Jude raised his voice. This felt like a stitch up.

'Look, when I couldn't get hold of you, I had to make a decision and I really think this could help you see how to make any final changes the novel might need.'

'No, I'm sorry, Marty, but no.'

'That's a real shame, because it means Emily is going to have to carry the whole event by herself.'

'What do you mean?' Jude frowned, trying to work out what possible role Emily could have in all of this.

'Sophia asked if she'd go along and do a reading of her new book for anyone who shows up, not realising there's been a change of author.' Marty gave a theatrical sigh. 'I mean, I suppose we could ask her to do a reading from your book too, but it's a lot to put on her, especially when people are expecting to meet you.'

'Bloody hell, Marty.' Jude wanted to be angry, but the thought of seeing Emily again was making it impossible to summon up the same kind of response he'd have given otherwise. 'When is this thing?'

'Tonight, at 6 p.m.'

'*Tonight!*' Suddenly, Jude found himself laughing. It was so ridiculous, so far out of the realms of anything he thought he'd ever agree to, and yet he knew he was going to say yes, because of Emily. 'Okay, but you owe me one, big time.'

'I'll just offset it against the ten thousand or so things you owe me.' The upbeat tone was back in Marty's voice. 'I'll get someone from marketing and promotions to send you all the details. Have fun, and more importantly, listen to what the readers have to say so you can get that bloody book of yours finished.'

'I'll do my best.' As Jude ended the call, he felt his shoulders slump. The thought of seeing Emily again had lifted a weight off him, but now it was back. He had no idea if agreeing to this ridiculous meet and greet would do anything to improve the novel, and even less idea of how Emily would feel about seeing him again. He wasn't even sure which of those things bothered him the most.

* * *

Butterflies were soaring and dipping in Emily's stomach. There were far more people in the bookshop than she'd expected. She'd done lots of readings in the past, but never without Sophia there. Added pressure came from the fact that her parents were sitting in the audience, alongside her father's best friend, Barry, and his wife Gwen. The bookshop was like something out of a Hallmark movie. A huge Christmas tree was decorated with baubles depicting characters from unforgettable stories, everything from Paddington Bear to *A Christmas Carol*. There were rows of gold fairy lights hung in swathes along the top of the bookshelves, and the children's corner had a candy cane lane leading to a sleigh filled with beautifully wrapped parcels; classic children's books slotted artfully between them hinting at just how perfect a Christmas present they would make.

The shop was Emily's idea of heaven and usually not even her nerves would spoil that for her, but she was also going to have to face Jude. She'd let her attraction to him show, and when he'd kissed her it had been impossible to believe the feeling wasn't mutual. Except he'd decided almost instantly that it was a mistake, and his actions since had hammered the point home. It was embarrassing enough to realise that the kiss had been a full stop for him, in terms of moving beyond the friendship she'd been so certain they were building. But now it seemed he didn't even want that. She'd suggested meeting for a walk, in the hope they could get back to where they'd been before the kiss, because she'd only have been lying to herself if she didn't admit how much she liked spending time with Jude. He was complex and guarded at times, but not far below the surface he was warm and funny, and kind. When Jude had come over to meet her parents, Patsy had ended up telling him about her favourite ever Christmas gift – two Ladybird classic fairytales, *Cinderella* and *Rapunzel*. Her mother's face had lit up when she'd described looking at the pictures, huddling under the bed covers with the light of a torch she'd been given that same Christmas. Emily had made a mental note to do some research to try and track down copies to give her mother as a Christmas gift, but before she could even start looking, a parcel had arrived at her parents' house on the same day Jude and Emily had shared that fateful kiss. The package contained copies of the original Ladybird books from 1964 and 1968, along with a printed note from Jude.

> Dear Patsy, thanks so much for inviting me over. Anyone who doesn't believe in time travel doesn't understand the power of stories. When you talked about reading the Ladybird books, it took me back almost thirty years to when my mum read The Elves and the Shoemaker to me. It brought back so many good memories and I hope rereading these books does the same thing for you. Jude X

It had made Patsy cry for all the right reasons, and it had deepened the feelings Emily had been trying to fight. She'd been planning to tell him how much the books had meant to her mother, but things had escalated so quickly after the call from the intermediary agency and everything that had followed. Now he was barely responding to her messages. Hearing that his biological mother had died must have hit Jude hard, and she could understand why his emotions were all over the place, but she wished he hadn't just shut down on her again. Maybe he blamed her for opening himself up to the hurt, and maybe he was right. All she knew was that she missed him, which was crazy when they barely knew one another really, except that wasn't really true either. They might not have known each other long, but the focus of their relationship had been to prove in the existence of love. It meant their conversations had gone far deeper than they might have done in months or even years, otherwise. They'd told each other the things that defined them, and yet suddenly he was a stranger again, fobbing her off when she suggested meeting. All of which meant that the thought of having to face him was uncomfortable to say the least.

Emily had seen him arrive about five minutes before she was due to do her reading and had drained the glass of ice-cold Pinot Grigio that one of the bookshop staff had liberally topped up when they'd passed by. Maddie, the owner of Cecil's Adventures, had gone all out to make it feel like a proper Christmas party, and Emily felt sure the attendees wouldn't feel short-changed for the cost of their tickets, even if her reading turned out to be a total disaster. Either way, she was about to find out.

After Maddie had introduced her, Emily gave a short introduction to the story she'd be reading an extract of. She talked about how meeting and working with Sophia had changed her life, and that even if she hadn't believed in the magic of chance meetings before then, she certainly would have done afterwards. It was the perfect setup for Sophia's latest romance novel, where a Christmas gift delivered to the wrong house resulted in the kind of happily ever after Jude definitely wouldn't have believed in. She was aware of him as she was speaking, on the right-hand side of the room, already gathering a crowd. She didn't want to look at him, but somehow her eyes were drawn towards him against her will. She'd been expecting to see Jude speaking in hushed tones to the people around him, or signing books, anything so he didn't have to listen to the utter twaddle he no doubt believed Sophia's story to be. Except he wasn't. He was looking straight at Emily, seemingly oblivious of the people around him. And in that moment, her nerves almost took over completely. Emily wanted to get off the raised platform at the front of the bookshop, or hide behind the huge cardboard cutout of the Gruffalo that was positioned to the side of her. Instead, she dropped her head and continued to read, letting herself get lost in the words Sophia had written and shutting out the rest of the world, even Jude. He'd been right about one thing – books could transport you to another time and another place; you just had to let them.

'That was amazing, thank you so much, Emily.' Maddie hugged her tightly after she'd finished the reading, and the audience's response was every bit as enthusiastic. It was a relief, because they'd ended up being an odd mixture of diehard Sophia Wainwright fans and those who loved Jude Cavendish's far grittier novels, and who'd made the effort to be there despite the very last-minute change of speaker. A smile tugged at the corner of Emily's mouth as she thought about how Jude's upcoming talk might be perceived by Sophia's fans. God help him if he dared to say that love was an illusion. He'd probably get lynched.

Within minutes Emily had her answer. Maddie had introduced Jude and opened up the floor to the promised Q&A session. He'd had the audience in the palm of his hand, and he had a great line in self-depreciating humour. When an aspiring writer in the audience had asked him how to cope with being rejected, he'd told a story about using rejection emails from agents and publishers as target practice for Rufus's toilet training when he was a puppy.

'They thought my novel was only good for toilet paper; well, two can play at that game.' He laughed then, the intensity in those blue eyes softening for a moment, and Emily could see the man he really was. It was easy to underestimate childhood trauma if you hadn't been through it, but she could see what losing his mother and being rejected by his father and his stepmother had done to Jude. Despite the fact, he didn't seem to want her support any more, she couldn't help wishing there was something she could do.

'Right, I think we've got time for one last question.' As Maddie made the announcement, a collective moan went up from the audience. She gave an apologetic shrug and turned towards Jude. 'Would you like to select someone to ask the last question?'

'Actually, I'd like to ask the audience a question instead, if that's okay?' Jude widened his eyes, and Maddie nodded. 'I know there are a mix of people here tonight, those who read my books and those who love Sophia's novels, so I wanted to pose a question that might best be answered by having those two groups of people put their heads together. I'm working on some changes to the next DCI McGuigan novel, at the suggestion of my editor, and he wants to see McGuigan change as a result of falling in love. It'll mean making sacrifices he'd never have thought possible. So I'd love to hear from the audience about the biggest sacrifice you've ever made for love, and whether you came to regret your decision.'

Emily wasn't sure whether anyone would want to share that

kind of information in a room full of strangers, but within moments the audience was sharing stories. There was a woman who'd donated her kidney to a sister she no longer spoke to, but who had no regrets because it meant her niece and nephew had experienced a far better childhood. A man who'd moved to a new country to be with a woman he loved, leaving behind everyone else he cared about, only for that relationship to fall apart. Yet there was no regret from him either, because he'd later got together with the woman who'd become his wife, and they'd never have met if he'd still been on the other side of the world. There were a few people who had minor regrets, but most of the stories the audience shared had resulted in a positive impact in some way, despite the results not always being what they'd hoped for. It supported what Emily believed and nothing Jude could say would change that. Love wasn't a transaction, because giving it didn't mean you always got back what you wanted in return, but at the very least it could teach you something about yourself, and that thought was like a lightbulb moment.

Jude was fixated on love changing McGuigan, because suddenly everything was right in his personal life, but that story-line had resulted in a relationship he couldn't believe in. What Jude hadn't grasped was that McGuigan's relationship didn't have to be perfect; it didn't even have to work, it just needed to show he was still capable of changing and evolving, and holding on to some kind of hope for a future that might be better. That was all Jude's readers needed to keep investing in the story, and Emily was sure it would sit better with him than trying to shoehorn in the kind of happy ever after he might never be ready to believe in. She was certain now that she could help him finally finish his book; she just needed to persuade him to talk to her first.

* * *

'Oh darling, you were brilliant!' Emily's mother smiled brightly as she walked over to where her parents were standing with their friends.

'You really were.' Her father pulled her into a hug. 'And so was Jude. Oh, speak of the devil, here's the man himself.'

Emily's father pulled back to shake Jude's hand.

'I hope that's not what I am, Richard, the devil.' Jude smiled. 'Although I know I pulled out of watching *Elf* with you, so I probably do deserve that.'

'As long as you join us for *The Muppet Christmas Carol* on the twenty-fourth we'll forgive you.'

'I'm sure he has far better things to do than that, Dad.' Emily couldn't look at Jude, mortified at what he must think of her father's suggestion. He happened to be at their house for one Christmas movie; that didn't mean he wanted to sign up to the entirety of their annual tradition.

'Something far better than *The Muppet Christmas Carol*? I highly doubt that.' Her father shook his head, as if nothing could convince him that such a thing existed. 'We were just saying how great you and Em were. We were bursting with pride watching the pair of you, weren't we, Patz?'

Her dad was doing it again – making out Jude was suddenly a part of the family when they'd spent one night with him. Admittedly, it had been a night filled with laughter and the kind of conversation that had gone way beyond the superficial small talk they might have expected. Emily was beginning to suspect it was a superpower Jude had no idea he possessed, the ability to reveal just enough of himself to make people want to tell him all about their own lives and to hear more about his. Either way, it was clear her parents had taken Jude to their hearts and that they wanted to spend more time with him.

'Emily was brilliant, wasn't she?' There was no suggestion in

Jude's voice that he was just being polite; he really sounded as if he meant it.

'We're biased of course, but we think so.' Patsy beamed again. 'Oh sorry, Jude, these are our friends Barry and Gwen.'

'I love your books and you probably get sick of hearing this, but I'm a huge fan.' Barry shook his hand with as much enthusiasm as his words conveyed.

'There are some things a writer gets sick of hearing, but that's definitely not one of them. Thanks so much.' Jude smiled. 'Great to meet you both.'

'You might have met Gwen before actually, Jude.' Patsy looked from him to Gwen and back again. It had taken less than two seconds, but the action seemed to plunge the whole world into slow motion as Emily suddenly realised what her mother was about to say. She wanted to tell her to stop talking, but her tongue seemed to have become glued to the roof of her mouth.

'Oh really, where?' Jude waited for the response, and it was Emily's last chance to intervene and stop him from finding out just how much of his personal story she had shared with her mother. They'd talked about Emily contacting Gwen on his behalf, but he'd said he didn't want that, so she hadn't pursued it. Her mother had also felt it was best to leave things to the professionals, but she had a horrible feeling Patsy might have changed her mind after meeting Jude. He'd mentioned his adoption to Emily's parents, and her mother hadn't given away the fact she already knew. But he hadn't told them where he was born, so he'd know that information could only have come from Emily. She'd decided not to tell her mother what the intermediary service had discovered, because it had felt like Jude's story to share with whomever he chose. So her mum had no idea that the search for his biological mother had already hit a dead end, or how cut up Jude had been. Patsy would have been certain she was helping by mentioning it to Gwen, even though Jude hadn't asked for her help. Like mother like daughter. Emily had to stop this conversation, but before she even opened her mouth to speak, Gwen had answered Jude's question.

'I worked at the cottage hospital near Port Tremellien where you were born, and I remember your mother.' Her smile was warm, but for a moment Jude just stared at Gwen, as if she was speaking a language he didn't understand. When he finally responded, his tone was tight.

'You remember Ros?'

'No – Patricia.' As Gwen said the name, a series of emotions seemed to flit across Jude's face. He didn't say anything, but his expression somehow told the whole story – confusion, anger and sadness all competing to win the war. In the end it was Gwen who spoke first. 'I'm sorry, I probably shouldn't have just come out with it like that. There's a reason I've got a reputation as a big mouth. It's just that I used to work there and when Patsy told me that's where you were born and that you'd been adopted, I knew it had to be you. By 1990, adoptions were few and far between, and there were only a handful of births happening in the cottage hospital each year by then. So it was a case that I've never forgotten.'

Jude still didn't respond and Emily desperately wanted to tell him she was sorry and to try to explain why she'd spoken to her mother about him. But as she turned to look at him, a muscle was going in his cheek, and she wasn't sure she could deal with what he might say to her in response.

'Jude, sorry to drag you away, but there's someone I want you to meet.' Maddie suddenly appeared at his shoulder, her singsong voice cutting through the tension that had felt as though it might suffocate Emily. 'George is one of my best customers and he preorders all your books from the shop, so I promised him I'd introduce you.'

'Great.' Somehow, Jude managed to smile in response to Maddie, and turning back to the group, he offered an apology for his departure that anyone who hadn't witnessed the last few moments would have been certain was genuine. 'Sorry, you'll have to excuse me.'

Jude's smile was mask-like, but it was the look in his eyes that gave away what he was really feeling. It was almost as though there were subtitles telling Emily that not only was this conversation over, but so was every other conversation they might have had. And it was all her fault.

16

Something inside Jude had begun shifting when he was watching Emily at Cecil's Adventures the night before. Her utter conviction about the love story she was reading made him start to believe it too. It was listening to Emily that had made him ask the audience about what sacrifices they'd made in the name of love. He'd wanted to hear that she was right, and that love didn't always have to be some kind of transaction. She'd already told him she thought his biological mother had made sacrifices when he was adopted – sacrifices that were out of love for him, rather than because she didn't want to sacrifice her freedom in order to be a parent. He had no way of knowing that for certain now that Patricia was dead, but Emily had helped him believe in the possibility, and so had every answer the audience at Cecil's Adventures had given him.

He'd wanted to tell Emily after the reading that he was sorry for the way he'd reacted on the day they'd kissed, and that it was because of how he felt about her that he'd shut down, the way he always did in order to protect himself. He might not have been quite that honest, but he'd have started with an apology at least and the admission that he wanted to keep seeing her in a way that had nothing to do with revisions to his book. He'd really wanted to talk to her about the option the intermediary agency had given him of trying to trace other members of his biological mother's family, and to ask what she would do in the same circumstances. It wasn't that he thought Emily had all the answers, but he trusted her to be honest with him and to tell him what was in her heart rather than what she thought he wanted to hear. That was the kind of perspective he needed when he'd got so used acting with his head rather than his heart.

Jude had walked towards Emily and her family, ready to tell her all those things as soon as they had the chance to talk on their own, but then he'd been blindsided by the conversation with Gwen. It had been dropped in his lap like a hand grenade, and suddenly all the trust he'd had in Emily had evaporated. He wasn't surprised she'd spoken to her parents about his adoption; after all, he'd mentioned it to them himself and told them about losing his mum in the accident. But he'd specifically told Emily that he didn't want her asking around for help to trace his biological mother, even before he'd discovered that Patricia was dead, and yet she'd still gone ahead. It was yet more proof that people let you down in the end and did the things they thought were best, even after they'd pretended to listen to what you wanted. He hadn't trusted himself to respond. Thank God Maddie had called him over when she did.

Emily had tried phoning, but he hadn't picked up and he'd left all her messages unread. He didn't know what to say to her yet, but he wasn't going to act like an idiot and ignore her forever. He wanted a clean break, a way of saying *Thanks for your help, but we don't need to meet again*. Part of him wanted to tell her that he felt like she'd betrayed him, but an even bigger part didn't want her to know she'd been able to affect him that much, because he didn't even like admitting it to himself.

Rufus kept looking at him with disdain too. It had been three days since he'd last seen Gary Barlow and it was clear that was far too long to be acceptable. He'd had yet another message from Viv asking when he was coming over, and playing happy families was something he definitely couldn't face.

'Let's go for a walk.' Jude walked over and took Rufus's lead off the hook by the front door just as an envelope was pushed beneath it. By the time he'd opened the door, whoever had delivered the letter was gone.

He didn't recognise the handwriting on the envelope and, as he pulled the letter out, he realised just how much he was hoping it might be from Emily. But it wasn't.

Dear Jude

I'm so sorry about last night. I've got this horrible habit of jumping into a situation with my big feet before I think it through. I've also got a thing about trying to fix other people's problems, whether they want my help or not. A lot of women suffer from the same complaint, especially those of us who are mothers. I know Patsy does, but this particular faux pas was all down to me.

Patsy mentioned having met you, the fact you were adopted and where you were born. I knew who your biological mother was straight away, because I was there on the day you were born. I should have found a better way of telling you all that rather than just blurting it out and I'm so sorry if it caused you any embarrassment or pain. I'd like to have the chance to apologise properly and to tell you what I know about the circumstances of your birth, if you want to hear them. I'll be in Mehenick's Bakery for the next hour or so, if you want to meet for a chat, or my email address is gwenjonesdancingmidwife@gmail.com

If you don't want to meet, I completely understand and I hope you can accept my apology. If not, please don't hold it against Patsy or Emily. They really were just trying to help before my big mouth ruined it all.

Gwen

Jude stared at the letter until the words started to blur, an argument he remembered his parents having shortly before his mother's death suddenly flashing into his mind.

'Stop trying to resolve all of that boy's problems for him before he even has a chance to try for himself.' His father had sounded exasperated, his voice far louder than it needed to be.

'I'm his mother, Charles. I can't help it. I just want to make everything okay for him.'

Jude wasn't sure he'd ever thought of those words since, but they were there, lodged in his head, and Gwen's letter had just unlocked the memory. His mother had wanted to fix his problems, just like Gwen had said so many mothers did. Suddenly, the urge to know if that was what had driven his biological mother to make the choices she had was almost overwhelming. And no matter how angry he was about having his trust betrayed, if Gwen held any of the answers to that particular riddle, he didn't want to miss the opportunity to find out.

* * *

Gwen was sitting at a table facing the door when Jude walked into Mehenick's, as if she'd known he was going to turn up. But then she probably had. He doubted there were many people who would refuse the opportunity to discover information about their past, when they had no other way of knowing it.

'Hi. Can I get you another drink, or something to eat?' Jude greeted Gwen with the question, suddenly feeling weirdly nervous, aware that it was a delay technique to avoid what he was really here for.

'No, let me get you something. It's the least I can do after last night. I've got all the subtlety of a brick sometimes.' Gwen gave him an apologetic smile, and some of the awkwardness he'd been feeling evaporated.

'It's okay, I think I was more shocked than anything.'

'That's my fault too. I was just so excited to meet you and to tell you what I knew. I didn't even stop to think whether you wanted to hear it. So you've got to let me get you a coffee, and a slice of eggnog cheesecake. It's new on Jago's menu this year and apparently it's delicious.'

'You really don't have to, I—'

'Oh yes I do.' She cut him off. 'What can I get you? A latte, a hot chocolate or something else?'

'Just a tea will be fine, thanks.' Gwen clearly wasn't going to take no for an answer, so he might as well give in to it. Within a couple of minutes she was back at the table.

'Millie's going to bring the order over.' Gwen gestured towards the young girl standing at the counter. 'I can't believe she's old enough to have a part-time job now. It only seems like yesterday that I delivered her.'

'Is there anyone in Cornwall you didn't deliver?' Jude smiled as she pretended to think about it.

'Put it this way, there are an awful lot of women I could recognise without having to look at their faces.' That was the line that broke the ice between them, and after that, Jude felt far less apprehensive about what Gwen might tell him. She'd obviously seen and heard it all over the years, and she clearly thought the information she was about to pass on would help him, and he was more certain than ever that he wanted to hear it.

'What do you remember about the day I was born?'

'I rarely forget anyone I've helped through labour, and I certainly never forgot Trisha. That's what she asked us to call her, because she hated being called Patricia.' Gwen paused for a moment. 'Did you know that?'

'No, I didn't.'

'Maybe you should tell me what you know before I start.'

'I know her name, that I was born on her twentieth birthday and that she died just after my first birthday.'

'I'm so sorry.' Gwen's eyes had gone glassy. 'I didn't know before last night that she'd died, otherwise I'd never have been so blasé about it.'

'It's okay, there's just been a lot to process over the last week, but I want to know what you remember about Trisha.'

'She was so young without any real support, except from a female cousin, about the same age as her, and their former social worker. Trisha told me that she and her cousin had both been in care, but they were sharing a flat by the time she got pregnant with you. I'd met Jill before. She was their social worker until they turned eighteen. She'd kept in touch with both girls and she was clearly fond of them. The main thing I remember from the day you were born is...' She paused for a moment and touched Jude's hand. 'Are you sure you're happy for me to keep going?'

'Absolutely. I doubt there's anything you could tell me that would be worse than the scenarios I've already imagined.'

'Oh, there was nothing bad that day.' Gwen shook her head. 'Like you said, it was Trisha's birthday the day you were born and I remember her telling Jill that there was only one gift she wanted. She asked her to promise to find you a mother who made you her number one priority, because her own mother had never done that for her.'

'That's exactly what I got. My mother was wonderful.' The emotion lodged in Jude's throat like a golf ball and caught him by surprise. After all this time, he wasn't used to it hitting him so hard, but the last few days had shaken everything he thought he knew about himself.

'I'm so glad.' Gwen let go of a long breath. 'Jill didn't have control over who adopted you, but she promised Trisha she'd do whatever she could and I'm so happy it worked out that way.'

'Me too, but it makes me wonder if anyone was looking out for Trisha. She was only twenty-one when she died.' It was a strange sensation, feeling so protective of his biological mother, but it didn't feel like he was talking about a maternal figure. It felt as if he was talking about someone younger than him, someone vulnerable, who'd been just a day out of her teens when he was born. Even though he'd never known her, he couldn't deny he cared about this stranger who'd given birth to him. He hated the thought of what she'd been through and how the aftermath of his adoption might have affected her.

'I remember Trisha and her cousin talking about getting jobs as holiday reps in Spain, once she was over the birth. I got the feeling it was going to be their fresh start and a chance to get away from all the issues in their family.'

'I'm glad she was looking forward to a better future, even if it ended up getting cut horribly short.' There was an ache in his chest for the young woman who'd never got a chance to follow her dreams, but there was a crumb of comfort in the fact she'd had some and had felt they were within her grasp.

Gwen put her hand over his. 'I didn't know Trisha well, we were only together on the day you were born, but I found it impossible to forget her. Like I said, she was young, but her situation was unique in many ways. Most girls of that age chose not to go ahead with their pregnancies, and those who did usually became single parents. I admire anyone who brings up children alone; it's the hardest job in the world, and I've got no doubt she'd have done brilliantly, as so many women do. But Trisha was adamant she wanted more for you than she could give. She wanted you to have everything, and I'm sure she'd have been proud of you. If you want to know more than I can tell you, I'm still in touch with a friend who used to work with Jill, and I'm sure he'll have her contact details. If he puts you in touch with her, she'll probably be able to tell you a lot more. Jill might even know how to find Trisha's cousin.'

'Thanks, but I think all of this is enough for now.' Jude slowly withdrew his hand. He needed to process what Gwen had told him and he didn't want to do that in the company of someone he barely knew, as thankful as he was for the information she'd given him. 'But I really am grateful for what you've told me.'

'If you change your mind at any point, you know how to get in touch with me. I'm so glad the information has been helpful for you, but I'm still sorry I didn't handle it better.'

'It's okay, Gwen, you really don't need to keep apologising. I was never upset with you. I was just disappointed that Emily spoke to you about it after I'd told her it wasn't what I wanted. She had no right to do that.'

'She didn't.' Gwen fixed him with a level look. 'I thought you knew that. All she did was talk to Patsy about it, to try and work out the best way of helping you so that you could find a way of finishing your novel. Patsy used to be a counsellor, and I guess Em thought she might have some insight. It was Patsy who asked me if there was a way of finding anything out, if you decided that's what you wanted, and I think we both just got a bit carried away when I realised that I was one of the midwives who was there when you were born. None of this was down to Emily and, at the risk of overstepping the mark one more time, there's something else I feel I need to say.'

'Okay.' Jude suddenly felt as if he was in the headteacher's office, and his mind was already all over the place, trying to work out if Emily owed him an apology or if it was the other way around.

'It's obvious you like Emily and that she feels the same way, so just don't blow it.' Gwen patted his hand one more time before getting up and leaving without another word. It had been the perfect mic drop moment and she'd given Jude more to think about than he'd ever thought possible. Now he really wanted to talk to someone about it. The problem was, there was only one person he wanted to talk to. But he had a horrible feeling he'd already left it too late to follow Gwen's advice and that his chances of not blowing it were long gone.

17

Emily had tried calling Jude to apologise for what had happened at the bookshop and, when he hadn't answered, she'd messaged him instead. She'd felt awful about Gwen blurting out that she knew his biological mother, which had probably made him feel as if Emily had betrayed him. She hadn't even known that her mother had mentioned it to Gwen, but she didn't blame Jude for not answering her calls. He'd expressly told her he didn't want to go looking for his birth mother unless he was sure she wanted to hear from him, and she'd witnessed how hard the news of Patricia's death had hit him.

Since meeting Jude, she'd come to realise that he found it uncomfortable when anyone's focus was on him. Every time someone at the bookshop had made a comment about how talented he was, or how well his career was going, he'd turn it into some kind of joke, or play it off as lucky. It was obvious he didn't like talking about himself, so the idea of her parents and their friends all talking about him would have been really disconcerting. Emily still wanted the chance to explain, and to tell him that she hadn't gone against his wishes and got Gwen involved. It had just been Patsy trying her hardest to help, and getting it almost as wrong as her daughter. Emily had to set herself a limit though. Three messages of apology and that was it. If he didn't reply after that, she needed to accept he didn't want to hear from her again. She couldn't make sense of why the idea of that bothered her as much as it did, so she didn't even try.

The day after the bookshop event, she took herself off to the studio in Truro to do another recording, something she'd scheduled in weeks ago. She'd hoped it would be a distraction, but it wasn't. She wasn't sure she could even have recalled the plot of the novel she'd been narrating if someone had asked her, because her mind had been elsewhere the whole time. Emily had checked her phone as soon as she'd come out of the studio, but there'd been no response from Jude to her third and final text. When she pulled up to her parents' house, the first thing she did was check her phone again, but there was still no response. Her fingers twitched with the desire to send another message, not just because she wanted him to reply, but because there was a sense of growing injustice rising up inside her. She hadn't gone behind Jude's back; he'd told her mother himself that he was adopted. The only thing she'd told Patsy that Jude hadn't already shared with her was where he'd been born. That was hardly the crime of the century.

'Please stop looking at me like that, you're making me feel miserable.' Gary Barlow fixed her with an exquisitely sad look in his eyes the moment she walked in the door. He wanted to see Rufus, she didn't need to speak dog to work that out. But it wasn't going to happen, and she didn't need him making her feel guilty on top of everything else.

'Seems like you're already pretty miserable to me.' Emily's father called out to her from the lounge, and she walked through to where her parents were cuddled up on the sofa together, underneath a heated throw.

'It's just been a frustrating day. I kept messing up the recording, so I ended up having to pay for some extra studio time. This book is for an author I've never worked with before and she approached me direct, so the rate is more than I usually get. But it will end up being less than normal if I keep having to pay for extra studio time, and if I make a hash of it she won't want to use me again.' Emily flopped heavily into one of the armchairs opposite her parents, the twinkling lights on the Christmas tree seeming to mock her with their jollity.

'I'm sorry you've had a tough day, Em, but we both know the real reason you're out of sorts. It's because I interfered and spoke to Gwen.' Emily's mother bit her lip, her eyes filling with tears. 'I feel terrible about it and I just wish you'd give me Jude's number so I can call him to explain. I'd walk down to Puffin's Rest myself and knock on the door if I could. I can't stand the thought that me being such a busybody has come between you.'

'Oh, Mum, it hasn't.' Emily shook her head. She hated seeing her mum upset and she wasn't going to let Patsy feel guilty about something that would probably have happened anyway. Jude had already gone cold on her after the kiss; what happened at the bookshop had just put the final nail in the coffin. 'It wasn't the best idea for Gwen to just blurt out that she knew Jude's biological mother, but he was already shutting down on me. I don't know, maybe he's got what he needed for the book and he was just ready to move on. Either way, he'd already stopped wanting to meet up before last night.'

'Then more fool him.' Emily's father sighed at the exact same moment her phone pinged with a text message. It was from Jude.

> I'm sorry. I've been acting like an idiot. It's not an excuse but so many things have happened in the last few days and I just needed some time to process it all, but I shouldn't have shut you out. Without you, I'd still be wondering about so much of my past, not even realising how much it was affecting me. I hope you can forgive me for being a giant pain in the arse. Rufus is on his last legs with misery about not seeing Gary Barlow. Please will you both come out with us tomorrow, otherwise I don't think he'll ever acknowledge my existence again xx

Emily looked at the phone, unable to stop the corners of her mouth from curving upwards in response. Maybe she should have been cool and offhand, but she wasn't into playing games and the two kisses on the message from Jude was definitely a first. She decided to keep her reply light-hearted all the same. She didn't want to go in with heavy sentiment and send him running for the hills again.

> Gary Barlow and I would love to come for a walk. He is currently wallowing in a similar amount of misery to Rufus, which simply cannot continue. As such, I am willing to overlook your tendency to act like a massive pain in the arse… What time and where should we meet? xx

'I take it Jude has finally got in touch?' Her mother really didn't miss a trick.

'How did you know?'

'The look on your face, my darling girl. It gives you away every time.' Her mother laughed as another text pinged through from Jude.

A Cornish Winter's Kiss

> Can I pick you up from your parents' house at eleven? I thought we could have some lunch and go for a walk on the headland at Port Tremellien. I need to pick something up from my father's place on the way back, and I thought the dogs might appreciate somewhere new to sniff out all the disgusting things they seem to love xx

Emily typed a short response.

> Sounds perfect. See you then xx

Sitting back in the armchair, she tried to convince herself that Jude's message hadn't changed her mood as drastically as it had. She wasn't sure she liked the idea of anyone having that much control over how she felt. But as Sophia had written in her last book, sometimes emotions had minds of their own.

* * *

Jude had felt like he was back at school and about to take an exam when he was on the drive over to Lowenna Close. It had been a relief to get a jokey text back from Emily, but seeing her face to face again suddenly felt awkward. He'd made their kiss the focus of his tangled emotions on the day he'd discovered that Trisha had died instead of allowing himself to acknowledge how the news had made him feel. It had been the same when Gwen had casually announced that she'd known Trisha. Instead of admitting how apprehensive he felt about what that might uncover, he'd directed the blame at Emily.

'You always push people away when they get too close. It's like you're frightened of coming to rely on them.' That was what Marty had told him after he'd called to see how the event at

Cecil's Adventures had gone. He'd found himself telling Marty a lot more than he'd planned, and admitting that he hadn't responded to any of Emily's messages.

'To be fair, it hasn't always gone that well for me when I've let myself rely on someone.' Jude's reply to his editor had been met with a snort of derision.

'I've had your back for almost ten years, Jude, and I still do, but it's about time you opened yourself up to the possibility of finding someone to share your life with. I sleep with a mouthguard to stop me grinding my teeth, although I have to say working with you is probably one of the main reasons I developed the habit. Either way, unless waking up next to someone who drools on their pillow is your idea of sexy, I don't think I can be your life partner.'

'I've already got Rufus for that.'

'Exactly.' They'd both laughed, but then Marty had cleared his throat. 'Seriously, Jude, the edits to the next book are one thing, but the rest of your life is quite another. Stop closing yourself off from everything you could be experiencing. Life is about more than work.'

'I hope that's some advice you're taking for yourself.' Jude had wished in that moment that he and Marty were face to face so that he could have given his old friend a hug and thanked him for his support.

'I have my moments.' Marty had hesitated for a moment. 'And I might get a whole lot more of them if you'd finally finish that bloody book and cut my stress levels in half, so I don't have to grind my teeth quite as much!'

They'd ended the call still laughing, but Marty's words about Jude pushing people away before he could come to rely on them had lodged in his head. It was a pattern he could see, but changing that would be a huge risk and he still wasn't sure he could take it. At least he understood now how someone like DCI McGuigan might find the motivation to change and finally learn to trust someone. Suddenly finishing the book didn't seem quite so impossible as a result. He could see a way forward for his novel, but he still didn't know what direction his friendship with Emily would take. The only thing he knew for certain was that he didn't want it to end, and that made it feel like there was a lot at stake as he drove over to pick her up.

Emily emerged from the front door when he pulled to a halt on the drive, Gary Barlow shooting out past her and turning in circles, barking as loudly as he could and chasing his own tail.

'As you can see, someone is a little bit excited.' Emily grinned as she opened the car door, bending down to look inside. 'I've got no idea how he knew it was you and Rufus, but he obviously does.'

The dog bounded past her as she spoke, jumping over the passenger seat and leaping into the back of the car where Rufus had been stretched out on a blanket, the pair of them breaking into high-pitched howling at the sight of one another.

'Blimey, they sound even worse than me and my sister when we do karaoke after lunch on Christmas Day.' Emily pulled a face.

'That's something I'd like to see.' Jude realised he meant it. Christmas had been something he'd avoided as much as possible for years, and until very recently the thought of a family Christmas would have felt as alien to him as life on Mars. Yet suddenly he could imagine it, wrapped in the heart of Emily's family, who seemed to have a myriad of festive traditions, all of them fairly simple, but with the sole aim of spending time together. If he wasn't careful, he was going to start wishing for his life to be like the plot of a Sophia Wainwright novel. He might have had a series of revelations about his life recently, but starting to confuse reality with romance novels would definitely be taking things a step too far.

'Do you think you can put up with Rufus and Gary Barlow giving you and your sister a run for your money on the drive to Port Tremellien?' Jude looked at Emily, marvelling at how the dimples in her cheeks appeared from nowhere when she smiled, and the way that seeing them always made him want to smile too.

'We might have to turn up the radio to drown them out. Although I should warn you, if they're playing Christmas songs, I'm going to be joining in, and you might end up wishing you'd stuck to listening to the doggy duo.'

'I'll risk it.' As Jude switched on the radio, he told himself the only risk he was talking about was Emily starting a singalong; even if he could still hear Marty's voice in his head, urging him to risk a whole lot more.

* * *

Spending a few hours in Port Tremellien had been just what Emily needed. It was one of those calm, clear winter days, with a bright blue sky, that would have belied the time of year if it hadn't also been bitterly cold. Both she and Jude were wearing heavy winter coats, and she also had a scarf, hat and gloves on as they followed the dogs along the headland. Jude told her about his meetup with Gwen and the information she'd given him. He tried to apologise again too, but Emily had stopped him and offered up her own apology. He'd told her it was all forgotten. He still didn't know how Trisha had felt about having him adopted, but knowing she'd wanted the best for him had clearly been of comfort.

'I think that might be enough.' He'd shrugged when he said it, but she wasn't entirely convinced by his attempt to sound casual. 'I've found out more in the last few days than I thought I might ever know. I need to let that sit for a while before I decide if I want Gwen's friend or the intermediary agency to get in touch with Trisha's cousin, or any other relatives I might have on that side.'

'Are you glad you know what you know?' Emily hadn't been able to stop herself from asking the question, despite suspecting she already knew the answer. She'd needed to know for sure if she was going to stop feeling guilty about pushing Jude in that direction.

'I'm really glad.' He'd touched her arm, just briefly, but it had left her wanting more and she'd had to push her hands into the pockets of her coat to stop herself from responding. They'd gone to lunch after that, with two dogs who were suddenly much more well behaved, exhausted by their walk and sitting by Emily's feet in front of a roaring log fire as yet more Christmas songs played in the background. They'd talked about Jude's book, and how DCI McGuigan's storyline might unfold. And had found themselves agreeing on the best way to approach it. Now they were headed back to Port Agnes, with just one more stop along the way.

'This is my dad's place.' Jude turned to look at her as they pulled into the sweeping gravel driveway of an impressive Georgian house.

'It's beautiful.' Emily had suspected it might be grand from what Jude had told her about his father, but what she hadn't expected was the huge Christmas tree in the front garden, with a whole family of rattan reindeer outlined in white fairy lights. It didn't look like the home of the man who Jude had described as cold and distant, and he must have seen the look of surprise on her face.

'It is, but if you're wondering about all the decorations, they're down to Viv. She likes to make Christmas special for the grandchildren.'

'I bet it's an amazing place to spend Christmas.'

'I hope they enjoy it, but I can't say I've ever enjoyed a Christmas here since Mum died.'

'Not even after your dad and Viv got together, and you had your stepsister to spend it with?'

'Viv's great, and so are Fiona and her family, but Dad's still always around.' Jude sighed. 'I don't know if it's just because he reminds me of all the bad times after Mum died, especially once Sandra came into our lives, or whether it's just that he and I are worlds apart, but it's like I've forgotten how to be myself around him. If I'm honest, I think I forgot how to be myself around anyone for a long time. Probably because I spent most of it wishing I was someone else.'

'Jude, I don't think you realise how great—' Emily's response was cut off as someone rapped on the window of the car, and she almost jumped out of her skin.

'Are you coming in, darling?'

'It's my stepmother,' Jude said by way of explanation, and he lowered the window on Emily's side. 'Hi, Viv, this is my friend, Emily. I was just about to knock to pick up that box of Mum's stuff you wanted me to take. I can come and grab it, but we won't stop. We've got both the dogs in the car and they're soaking wet from a run on the beach.'

It wasn't true – the dogs had long since dried out by the fire – but it didn't sound like Viv would have been concerned even if they'd come straight off the sand. 'I'd never worry about that sort of thing. Come on in and I'll make a nice hot toddy, or some ginger beer for you, Jude, if you're driving.'

'We'd love to, Viv, but Em's got to get back for a family thing.' It sounded like the kind of vague response you might give if you were making up a lie on the spot, which was exactly what Jude had done. Even so, Emily couldn't deny the warm glow that came from him using the shortened version of her name for the first time.

'That's such a shame.' Viv sounded genuinely disappointed, but then she turned to look at Emily, a broad smile on her face. 'Hopefully we'll get to meet you properly some other time. I know Charles would have loved to, but he's in Truro, doing his Christmas shopping. Heaven help us all!'

Viv's laugh was every bit as genuine as her smile, and Emily found herself wishing they could go inside.

'If he's anything like my dad, you'll have to get your poker face ready so it doesn't give away your disappointment. He bought me a tea cosy last year in the shape of a black sheep, because I once said I thought they were cuter than white ones.'

'I think black sheep are often the best type too, even if they are sometimes misunderstood.' Viv sounded serious for a moment and Emily couldn't help wondering if the statement was aimed at Jude, but then she grinned. 'Although if Charles gets me a tea cosy for Christmas, he'll be wearing it as a hat until June.'

'I wouldn't put it past him.' Jude rolled his eyes. 'Shall I come in and grab the box?'

'It's actually an enormous suitcase, with lots of boxes and bags inside.' Viv pushed her glasses up her nose as she spoke. 'I haven't been through it, but I was sorting stuff out after the leak and I realised it had lots of Ros's things inside. I wanted to keep it safe, so I moved it out of the loft into one of the bedrooms. You can decide what you want to keep and then we can put it back up in the loft once the repairs to the roof are finished, or in one of the bedrooms. I just wanted you to have the chance to go through it first.'

'Thank you, Viv, that was really kind of you. It's lucky Sandra never found it, or it would have ended up in landfill years ago.'

'Let's hope that's where Sandra is instead, eh, darling?' Viv dropped a perfect wink, and Emily decided that she loved Jude's stepmum.

'We should be so lucky, Viv. Right, I'll come and grab the suitcase so that I can get Emily home in time for her family thing.' Jude got out of the car and was back within a couple of minutes, heaving an oversized suitcase into the boot, before getting back inside.

'Viv seems lovely,' Emily said as she waved goodbye to the woman now standing outside the front door of Jude's family home, furiously blowing kisses at them.

'She is. I just wish Dad had met her first instead of Sandra and then maybe I... Oh, I don't know, maybe things might have been different.'

'Some people would say it's never too late to change them.' Emily stole a glance in his direction, just in time to spot him shaking his head.

'And sometimes you just have to accept that the moment has passed.' The silence hung between them for an uncomfortable moment, and then Jude leant forward to turn up the radio. 'Come on then, let's hear some more of your best karaoke, and if you're really lucky, I might even join in.'

* * *

It had surprised Emily when Jude had invited her to his place for dinner and she wasn't sure he'd expected her to say yes. But her parents were going out to a Christmas get-together with some friends and she'd said as long as she could bring Gary Barlow, she'd love to have dinner with him.

'Thank God you invited me over, otherwise it would have been beans on toast in front of re-runs of the *Gavin and Stacey* Christmas specials. Not that I don't love them, but I'm starting to think it's a bit embarrassing that I know all the lines off by heart. It suggests I might not have much of a social life.' Emily wrinkled her nose. 'Anyway, after tomorrow, Charlotte and her family will be coming down, then I'll be on full-time auntie duty.'

'I can offer you a takeaway and a rummage through a suitcase full of old stuff.' Jude gave her a wry smile, but his words took her by surprise for a second time.

'You want me to look through your mum's stuff?' She been certain he'd want to do that by himself.

'I do.' He held her gaze, and the butterflies she'd had on the night of the bookshop event were back with a vengeance.

'Why?'

'Because you have a way of making me look at things from a different angle. I think you're a lot less jaded than I am, and I need that. Otherwise I'm just going to end up chucking out everything that's in the case, and there's a chance I might regret that later on if I do.'

'I think I'll take that as a compliment.'

'You should, because it was meant that way.' Jude smiled again and she wished she didn't find him so attractive. She liked this, being his friend and someone he could lean on for support, because she had a feeling there weren't many people he felt that way about. The trouble was, she couldn't just switch off the part of her that was whispering in her ear how much better it would be if there was more than friendship between them. She needed him to stop looking at her if she was going to silence that voice, but there was only one excuse she could think of to put a bit of space between them.

'What do you fancy for dinner? I don't mind going to pick it up.' Emily would have been halfway out of the door already if she could have been.

'I don't want you to have to go out. There must be some places that deliver, but if not, I can go. Let me check online.' Within a couple of minutes they'd reviewed their options and made a choice. They'd gone for Indian food, and Emily had deliberately ordered the kind of dishes she'd never have gone for if this had been a date. The knowledge that she'd demolished a garlic naan should be enough to stop her from doing anything stupid like trying to kiss him again. He'd made it clear, the first time around, that he thought it was a mistake and he was almost certainly right, but that didn't stop her wanting to do it again every time she looked at him.

'It's going to be a while; about ninety minutes they said. I'll feed the dogs and get us some drinks, and then shall we open the suitcase?'

'Sounds like a plan.' It was strange how natural this felt, as if this kind of everyday domestic bliss was their norm. She felt so comfortable with Jude in some ways and yet so jittery in others, but it was scary how easy it was to envisage this as a part of her life. She had no idea if Jude would still want to be friends when they got back to London and his book was finished, but it was already hard to imagine not seeing him any more.

Ten minutes later, they were on the sofa side by side, with the suitcase open on the floor to one side of the coffee table in front of them. The first thing Jude pulled out was a bag of baby clothes, with a tiny pair of shoes on top of the pile.

'Do you think these were mine?' Jude held them up and Emily leant forward.

'There's a label attached to one of them.' She read the words out loud. 'Jude's first shoes, aged eleven months.'

'I can't believe these great big feet ever fitted into anything that tiny.' Jude grinned. 'Or that Mum kept them. Although maybe I should have guessed.'

'There's a note on all the clothes she kept.' Emily turned over the label on one of the Babygros, reading it out loud again. 'Jude's coming home outfit. Best day ever.'

'I wish I could tell her how lucky I felt to have her as my mum. I took it for granted back then, because I never even contemplated that she'd be taken away from me.' Jude took hold of the Babygro. 'I'm an idiot, aren't I?'

'Of course not. How could you have known what was going to happen?'

'No, I mean I'm an idiot for doubting that love was a thing. How could I have the arrogance to believe that the love I had for Mum, and that she clearly had for me, isn't something other people feel?'

'I thought you said romantic love was different.' Emily couldn't believe she was playing devil's advocate, but she needed to know what Jude really meant.

'I always knew that being a mother was my mum's biggest wish, because she told me, but I never really thought about just how much it meant to her until I started looking at all of this. What I didn't find out until Dad was with Sandra was that it was him who couldn't have biological children. She screamed it at him once during an argument about me, something about at least there was no chance of her ending up with another one of his screaming brats, seeing as he was firing blanks.' Jude shook his head. 'She was such a horrible person. What he saw in her after being married to Mum I'll never know, but this has reminded me that Mum chose Dad, and stayed with him even after they discovered he wouldn't be able to give her the one thing she wanted most. She must have loved him, and it blows all my theories about love being a transaction out of the water.'

'It kind of does. Here's to one hell of a week of revelations for you.' Emily chinked her glass against his, trying not to read too much into the implications of Jude's change of heart, as he lifted a thick scrapbook onto the table. 'I remember this from when I was little. She saved all sorts of things in here, everything from spelling tests to my swimming certificates.'

'That's so lovely. Do you mind if I have a look through this photo album?' Emily asked, picking one up from the suitcase.

'Go for it.' For a few minutes they sat in companionable silence, with just the odd exclamation on her part about the photographs. Jude had been a beautiful child and even in the earliest baby photos she'd have been able to tell it was him. She was staring at a photo of him, when he was about six, with his two front teeth missing, when Jude suddenly spoke.

'The scrapbook doesn't stop.'

'What do you mean?' Emily furrowed her brow.

'There are memories in here from after Mum died. The first thing after her death is my Year Seven school report from secondary school, but it goes right up to an offer letter from the university I went to. That must mean Dad put them in there.' He shook his head, seeming to dismiss the idea. 'Unless Viv found all of this stuff in his office at some point and decided to add it to the book. One thing I know for sure is that Sandra didn't do it.'

'Do you really think Viv would do that?'

'I bet she's got ten of these for Fiona and, like you said, she's a lovely person. So if she thought I'd appreciate it, I think she'd do it. It certainly makes more sense than my father having done it.'

'You should talk to him; you might be surprised.' Emily was getting close to overstepping the mark again, but Jude had asked her to go through the suitcase with him, because she made him look at things differently. 'What have you got to lose?'

'Do you think it's always worth taking a risk, even if there's a chance of being disappointed? Or getting hurt?' He was looking at her again, and she was trying to work out what she was supposed to say, but she couldn't. So she just had to be honest.

'Yes, I do, because you could be disappointed, or get hurt, but the risk could also pay off in the best possible way. Things with your dad might get better than they've been in years.'

'I'm not talking about my dad, I'm talking about us.' Jude was still looking at her, and all the things she'd told herself about not making a move went out of her head. The garlic naan that was supposed to remind her that kissing him again was a stupid idea probably hadn't even made it to the oven yet.

'I'm willing to take a risk if you are.' Emily held her breath, wondering just how quickly she could scoop Gary Barlow up and run out into the night if Jude told her she'd got the wrong end of the stick. But when he moved towards her, she couldn't have stopped herself from leaning into him if her life had depended on it. This time, nothing interrupted the kiss, and she didn't want it to stop. Her hands were in his hair, and then suddenly they were moving down to the buttons of his shirt.

'We don't have to rush any of this.' Jude put his hand over hers for a moment, and it crossed her mind that he might be trying to stop things again, until he made it clear how he felt. 'I mean, I want to. *God*, I want to, but I want to be sure that you do too.'

'I couldn't be more certain, but I think we should stop talking now that we've cleared that up.' There were other things she'd far rather do with her lips, and she pulled his face towards hers again, kissing him in a way that would leave him in no doubt that she meant what she'd said. He was right that there was a risk to what they were doing, but some risks were worth taking and she was certain this was one of them.

18

Jude had woken up early. He wasn't used to sharing a bed with someone, but opening his eyes to see Emily lying next to him had felt so right, like she was meant to be there. He watched her for a couple of moments, her eyelids flickering slightly as she dreamt about something. He was almost tempted to wake her, to ask what she'd been dreaming about. She'd taught him so much about himself in such a short space of time and now he wanted to know all there was to know about her. It wasn't a feeling he'd ever experienced before.

Jude didn't really want to wake her, though. Instead, he slid out from beneath the covers as quietly as he could. Going through to the open-plan living area of the apartment, he smiled at the sight of the two dogs curled up against one another, just as he and Emily had been. The bags from the takeaway delivery were on the kitchen counter. They'd both been ravenous by the time it arrived, and Jude had wondered if it might feel awkward, going back to talking and enjoying a meal together after they'd taken things to the next level.

He'd known there was no use pretending this was just sex, the kind of casual encounter he'd had in the past. With Emily, there were deep feelings tangled up with it too. But it hadn't made things awkward; it had felt good to extend the intimacy as they went through the rest of the suitcase, with a movie they'd both seen before playing in the background. They'd gone back to bed after that, taking things a bit slower second time around, and it still hadn't been awkward, even when she'd fallen asleep in his arms. Usually, he couldn't wait to have his own space back. It felt suffocating for someone else to be around, but he didn't feel that way about Emily. And he already missed her presence, despite the fact that she was only in the next room. There was no denying it was a massive risk, allowing himself to feel things he'd never felt before, but he was starting to like the sense of not being fully in control. It made him feel alive in a way he hadn't felt for a very long time.

'Come on then, you two, let's go for a quick walk before breakfast.' Jude had cleaned his teeth and taken a pair of jeans and a sweatshirt out of the tumble dryer so that he could take the dogs out. Not having a proper garden was one of the only downsides of Puffin's Rest, and it had quickly been established on Gary Barlow's first visit that the little Border terrier was unwilling to have a wee in the courtyard. It was grass or nothing for him.

Jude was glad he'd put on his heavy coat. The weather had dropped another couple of degrees and there was a bitter wind coming straight off the sea, making the Christmas lights strung between the lampposts around the harbour swing up and over like skipping ropes. The dogs seemed even keener than he was to finish the walk, and within ten minutes they were back inside Puffin's Rest. He fed them and put the kettle on, before picking up the scrapbook again, turning to the pages towards the back and looking at the mementoes that had been added there. He hadn't noticed the previous night that one of the learner plates he'd joyfully cut off his car on the day he'd passed his test had been pasted into the book. He'd been delighted that day, knowing it gave him his ticket to freedom and that he could escape the tension of his so-called family home whenever liked. Most of his friends couldn't wait to get home from boarding school for the holidays, but the thought had always filled Jude with dread. It seemed impossible to believe that Charles had been sentimental enough to save one of the L-plates, but the only way to find out was to ask him. Picking up his phone, Jude typed out a message to his father.

> Just wondering if you're free for a chat at some point today?

Jude didn't add any kisses because they didn't have a demonstrative relationship in person, let alone over text. The reply came back almost immediately.

> Of course. Where and when do you want to meet? I'm free all day.

His father's response had caught him off guard. He'd been planning to call and hadn't even considered the possibility of Charles suggesting they meet up, but maybe this was a conversation they needed to have face to face.

> I'll drive over to the house if that's okay? Mid afternoon?

As soon as he pressed send he could see his father was typing a reply.

> Okay. See you then.

It was hardly a gushing response, but somehow it still felt

significant. It had been surprisingly easy to arrange the meet-up, and his father hadn't even tried to put him off. So often in the past, Charles would have sent a reply saying how busy he was in a clear attempt to fob off his only son. But not this time, and suddenly the idea that his father might have been the one adding things to the scrapbook didn't seem quite so ridiculous.

* * *

Emily had woken up to the scent of freshly brewed coffee and what smelt like golden syrup. She tidied up her hair as best she could by raking her hands through it, and came out of the bedroom wearing the same clothes she'd discarded the night before.

'Morning.' Her voice was croaky, and Jude looked over and smiled. He was standing close to the oven, looking about ten thousand times more attractive than she felt.

'Morning. Are you hungry? I'm making waffles.' He laughed at the look of surprise she was sure must have crossed her face. 'I found a waffle maker in one of the cupboards the day I got here, and I bought all the stuff to make some. Of course I never got around to it, until now.'

'Sounds great. I just need to clean my teeth.' Jude had given her a new toothbrush the night before. When she'd teased him about whether he always kept a spare just in case, he'd reassured her he was nowhere near that slick. He'd bought a four-pack of new toothbrushes when he'd booked the trip to Cornwall and had packed them all. She'd been stupidly pleased to hear this wasn't just his go-to move, and that the night before had been every bit as out of the ordinary for him as it had been for her. Heading to the bathroom now, she just hoped she didn't look as rough as she suspected she might. There was no mirror in the bedroom, but the lighting in the bathroom didn't pull any punches.

'Everything okay?' Jude asked as she came back out, already setting down a plate of waffles on the table.

'Hmm, although I thought for a moment that Rod Stewart had broken into your bathroom when I caught sight of my reflection.' Emily tried to flatten down the hair on the top of her head. 'Look at the state of me.'

'You look great.' Jude's mouth twitched. 'If anything, I'd say it was more David Bowie than Rod Stewart.'

'You're not helping!' She stuck out her tongue, but laughter was bubbling up inside her. It was so nice to feel close enough to Jude for them to be able to joke like this. He might be teasing her, but she didn't think for a moment there was a genuine dig intended in anything he was saying.

'Let me get you a coffee to make it up to you.' As Jude turned back towards the kitchen worktop, a text message flashed up on Emily's phone. It was from Charlotte.

> Sounds like you had a good time last night from what Mum said. Fancy not coming home, you dirty stop out! We'll be at Mum and Dad's in time for dinner, and we're expecting to meet Jude. Hope you've been practising for the karaoke and Just Dance. I'm taking you down this year! xxxx

Emily pulled a face, but it had nothing to do with not wanting to see her sister. Her parents had really liked Jude when they'd met him, so she should have known her mother would read far too much into her staying at his place the night before. Emily knew her mum wanted to see her happy, but Pasty had a habit of expecting all of her daughters' relationships to turn into a happily ever after. Maybe it was because she'd married her first ever boyfriend. Either way, it was no wonder Emily had grown up to believe in fairytale romances too. But this was reality, and it was very early days. She wasn't even sure she could call this a relationship yet.

'Is something the matter?' Jude gave her a questioning look.

'No. Just my parents and sister expecting me to try and press-gang you into coming over this evening, but I'm sure that's the last thing you want to do.'

'I'd really like that.' Judging by the expression on Jude's face, his words surprised him almost as much as they did her. 'That's if you don't mind me accepting the offer.'

'No. I'd really like that too.' She'd promised herself that she wouldn't play any games and if being honest was the wrong move, this clearly wasn't meant to go any further.

'Great. I'm going over to see Dad this afternoon to ask him about the scrapbook, but I can come over after I've been back to let the dog out.'

'Bring Rufus with you, the kids will love him. Although I should warn you, my sister might give you the third degree. DCI McGuigan has nothing on her interrogation skills.'

'I'll make sure I'm prepared.' Jude smiled, clearly not worried about facing her sister. And he didn't need to be; Charlotte was going to love him. Emily just hoped none of them got too carried away with where this might be going; she had enough of a battle on her hands making sure she didn't do that herself.

19

Jude hadn't felt able to just walk into his father's house in decades. Even when he'd come back from boarding school, he'd always waited to be let into the house, unless his father had been the one to pick him up. It should have felt like his home too, but Sandra had made sure it never did.

'You can't just stroll in here like you own the place. You don't live here, you live at Membory Grange. You're a visitor here and all visitors need to knock.' Sandra had made sure his father was out of earshot when she'd set out the rules, but Jude wasn't sure it would have made all that much difference if Charles had overheard. Whatever the truth, it was a very long time since Austol House had felt like home. Although not everyone seemed to understand that.

'Jude, why on earth do you always insist on knocking!' Viv enveloped him in her arms. She smelt of cinnamon and nutmeg, like a Christmas cookie come to life. 'I tell you every time just to use your key, but you never do.'

'I'm not even sure where it is.'

'I'll have to get you another one cut then.' She wagged a finger at him as she pulled away. 'Your dad's in the drawing room if you want to go and find him. I'm just keeping an eye on the mince pies I've got in the oven, but I'll bring some down for you both once they're done.'

'Cooking up a storm as always.' Jude smiled, another memory flitting into his head. 'I remember you doing that at Membory Grange. Those peppermint brownies you used to make were what made it feel like Christmas.'

'Oh, sweetheart.' Viv embraced him again, holding him tightly for a moment. When she pulled away for a second time, it was clear she was close to tears. 'I haven't made those in forever. I used to crush up candy canes and stir them in to make the peppermint favour.'

'I remember, and I also remember that you always saved some of the candy canes for me.' Jude took a deep breath, wondering if it was finally time to take another risk, one that he probably should have taken years ago, and tell Viv how he felt about her. 'I'm so glad Dad married you. I just wish he'd waited for you after Mum died, instead of...'

He couldn't finish the sentence, but he didn't have to. 'And I'm so glad I got to be a part of your family, Jude. I think somehow I always knew, deep down, that you were going to be a part of mine. You were my favourite student at Membory Grange, even though my job depended on me pretending not to have one.'

'Thank you.' He squeezed her hand, wanting to say so much more; to tell her that he wouldn't have survived those years without her, and that she'd been the best thing about coming back to Austol House since she'd married his father. But small steps were okay for now, and the things they'd said to each other were enough for one day.

'I suppose I ought to go and find Dad.'

'Okay, darling, and I'd better run before I burn the mince pies. I've got so much baking to do before Fiona and the family get here. They're like a plague of locusts, you'd think they never got fed!'

'No one can resist your baking.' Jude smiled before turning away to head down the hallway. The drawing room had always been his father's domain. It was such a stereotypically masculine space, looking like it had been lifted out of an old-fashioned gentleman's club. Two of the walls were panelled mahogany, with the others painted dark red. There was a large fireplace flanked by two chocolate-brown leather chairs, and soft-lit table lamps were dotted around the room to stop it being quite as dark as it would have been otherwise. It hadn't been to his mother's taste – although Ros's style had been reflected in the rest of the house – and it wasn't to Viv's either, but it was clearly his father's sanctuary and the one room that had remained constant throughout all three of his marriages.

'Hi, Dad.' Jude had stood outside the door for a few seconds before pushing it open, contemplating whether or not to knock. But if his father was irritated that he'd come straight in, he was doing a good job of hiding it.

'Jude, good to see you.' There was a warmth in his father's tone he wasn't sure he'd ever heard before, but he was beginning to wonder if it was because he'd never listened out for it. 'Can I get you a drink?'

'Thanks, but I'm driving.' Jude watched as his father poured two fingers of whisky into a cut-glass tumbler. 'Anyway, I've got a feeling Viv will be down in a little while with mince pies and if it's anything like the old days at Membory Grange, there'll be a vat of hot chocolate too.'

'I'm glad she was there for you during the boarding school years. I should have been and I wasn't.' If Jude hadn't known better, he'd have sworn his father had the hallway bugged, but that wasn't Charles's style. He didn't offer up meaningless platitudes because he thought that was what was expected of him. There were aspects of Charles's parenting that were governed by a sense of duty, but he'd never been hampered by other people's expectations of what being a father should look like. This was all new territory and Jude wasn't entirely sure how to handle it.

'It's in the past, it doesn't matter and—'

Charles cut his son off. 'It does matter, and this is a conversation we should have had a long time ago.'

'So why now?' Jude hadn't had the opportunity to ask his father about the scrapbook yet, and he couldn't help wondering what had made Charles so eager to talk.

'It'll be twenty-five years this Christmas since we lost her.' His father gave a shuddering sigh. 'I've thought about your mother every single day since then, but never more so than just lately. When Viv told me that we should give you the suitcase, I didn't want to. I wanted to hold on to it myself, because it was all I had left of your mother. But she made me realise what an idiot I've been all these years, not sharing all those memories with you and keeping them locked away in the attic instead. It's just one of many things I've handled badly. I let your mother down by not stepping up the way she'd have wanted me to when she died, but worst of all I let you down. It's taken me all these years to face up to it, but I need you to know that I'm sorry.'

A part of Jude wanted to reassure his father that it wasn't true, but if things really were really going to change between them, he needed to be honest too. And he needed the answers to some difficult questions. 'Why did you send me away? I'd just lost

Mum and then you brought Sandra into our lives, and it seemed like you couldn't wait to get rid of me. It felt like I'd lost you too.'

'I messed everything up.' His father's expression was pained, the regret in his eyes unmistakable. 'I missed your mother so much, and I desperately wanted to fill that gap. I knew I could never replace her, so subconsciously I think I sought out someone who couldn't have been more different if I'd searched the whole world.'

'That still doesn't explain why you sent me away.' Jude's voice was quiet and he suddenly felt like that young boy again, desperate to try and understand what he'd done wrong, and even more desperate to find a way to be allowed home again.

'Every room in this house reminded me of your mother, apart from this one. She always hated this room, and it became the only place I could stand to be, because I didn't miss her quite so overwhelmingly when I was here. I knew you didn't have anywhere in the house that felt that way for you. So when Sandra suggested that boarding school would give you a fresh start, I convinced myself she was right and that somehow you'd miss your mother less without the constant reminders. Viv helped me realise how stupid that was, but I honestly thought I was doing it for the best and once I saw how spiteful Sandra was towards you, I didn't want to bring you home to that either.'

'I still don't understand why you didn't send her away instead.'

'I should have done, but I was so scared of being on my own and having to really face up to losing your mum. I met Sandra so quickly, but I never really moved on or processed what happened. I almost enjoyed the fact that she was so difficult to live with; it gave me something else to think about, something to focus on other than the great gaping hole that losing Ros had left in my life. But I should never have dragged you into all of that,

Jude, and I'm sorrier than you'll ever know. I don't expect you to forgive me, but I want you to know that it wasn't because I didn't want you here with me. I'd have given anything to have you and your mum back home where you belonged, but without her I genuinely thought you were better off without me too.'

His father's voice was thick with emotion. They'd never had a conversation like this before, not even close.

'I missed Mum, but I missed you too.' Jude took a deep breath. Being honest was hard, but he'd promised himself he was going to give it a go. 'I still do.'

'Me too. I know we can never make up for lost time, but Viv has been telling me for years that I should lay all my cards on the table. It's taken me all this time of watching her with Fiona to finally admit all the mistakes I made, and I just want the chance to try and undo the ones that I can. I kept that suitcase of stuff up in the attic for years, all the time I was with Sandra, and even since I married Viv. I'd go up there sometimes just to look at it, or to add to the scrapbook and photo albums your mum had kept for you since you were born. It was as if I could still share with her what our boy was doing, but when Viv found the case, and I admitted you didn't know most of the contents even existed, she was angrier than I've ever seen her before. I thought I was saving you pain by not exposing you to memories that might be difficult to relive, just like I thought I was protecting us both by not talking to you about your mum after she died. But Viv told me in no uncertain terms that it was the stupidest thing she'd ever heard, and that by keeping your mum's things from you I was robbing you of so much. She said you were the one I should have been talking to about how proud I am of all the things you've achieved.'

'So it *was* you who added those things to the scrapbook?'

'Yes, and I've kept every press cutting about your career, and a copy of each of your books in every format and translation they've been published in.' Charles opened the door of a mahogany cabinet that was pushed up against one of the walls. 'They're all in here and I wish every day that your mum could have lived to see what you've achieved, despite all the mistakes I've made.'

'I've done my own share of messing things up.' Jude wanted to reach out to his father, but years of distance between them couldn't be bridged in a single day. His father's honesty meant more to him than he could convey, but it couldn't wave a magic wand and suddenly make everything easy between them. This was a huge step in the right direction, but it was going to take time to undo the mistakes of the last twenty-five years, for both of them.

'From where I'm standing you haven't messed anything up, Jude. But I know it hurts Viv when you push her away, and I think it probably hurts you too. I understand why you do it, and that's my fault too, but I don't want you to miss out on anything else because of me. I've taken enough from you.' Charles gave another shuddering sigh. 'Let yourself be a proper part of this family. I'm living testament of how much good that can do you.'

'I think I'd like that.' There it was again – unfiltered honesty. Jude was admitting things out loud that for years he hadn't even admitted to himself, for fear of getting hurt. Yet here he was, being vulnerable and open with the one person he'd spent his life being most guarded around in order to protect himself from the pain of rejection. He'd never in a million years have imagined having this conversation with his father, and he didn't think Charles would ever have said the things he had if it hadn't been for Viv. But the truth was his stepmother wasn't the only miracle worker. If he hadn't met Emily, he'd almost certainly never have been ready to listen to what his father had to say, and it was just one more thing he had to thank her for.

* * *

Emily adored the chaos of the run-up to Christmas when all the family were together. Once Charlotte, Jake and the children descended upon the household it was a whirlwind of activity. By the time Jude arrived, she'd already played three games of Guess Who with Bronte and had been a makeshift horse for the twins, ferrying them up and down the hallway while she was urged to giddy up each time.

She hadn't been sure what Jude would think of spending the day with them all. He'd admitted that he'd avoided spending time at his father's house and hadn't built the kind of relationship he could have done with his stepsister's children as a result. Yet within five minutes of arriving at the house, he'd already been roped into becoming the second horse and racing up the hallway with Ellis on his back, against Emily and Arthur. The dogs had both decided to take refuge in the conservatory, no doubt keen to avoid becoming stand-in horses.

'I like him already.' Charlotte had cornered Emily, speaking in low tones, when Jude had finally conceded defeat in the last race. 'He's a good sport, he's great with the kids and he makes you laugh more than I've seen you laugh in a long time. Not to mention the fact that he's quite wonderful to look at, even galloping along the floor on all fours.'

As Charlotte had laughed, Emily wished she could play it down and tell her sister she was making too much of it. But her stupid romantic soul seemed determined to side with her sister, whispering in every lull in conversation that Jude was exactly what she'd always wanted.

'Will you do Just Dance with me again?' Bronte was hanging off Jude's arm now, looking up at him with puppy-dog eyes and pleading for just one more dance off on the video game that was her new obsession. He really had taken being a good sport to a whole new level.

'No, Jude will not dance with you again. You said that if we let you play for a third time you would absolutely, cross your heart, pinky promise to not ask again.' Jake had got the impression of his daughter spot on, complete with actions. 'So, young lady, a deal's a deal. It's time to go up to bed.'

'But I'm not a baby, I don't want to go to bed at the same time as the twins.'

'Ellis and Arthur have already been in bed for an hour, darling, and if you don't do what your father says, one of the elves might tell Father Christmas.' Charlotte's tone may have sounded matter-of-fact, but there wasn't even a hint of a smile on her face.

'Can you take me up now, Daddy?' Bronte all but threw herself into her father's arms in her haste to get to bed. There was no way she wanted to risk a demotion to the naughty list this late in the game.

'Okay, darling, but say thank you to Jude and Auntie Em for playing with you.'

'Thank you, Joooood.' Bronte hung out the single syllable of his name as she marched over to give him a hug goodnight before turning to her aunt and doing the same thing. She had a powerful squeeze for such a tiny girl, and it was one of Emily's favourite things in the world. 'Night night, Auntie Em, can you bring Jooooood to play again, please?'

'Maybe he could come on Christmas Day?' It was Patsy who made the suggestion, making Bronte shriek in delight.

'Yay!'

'Jude's spending Christmas with his family, and I think one dose of the chaos in this house is probably enough for anyone.'

'I love the chaos.' Jude sounded as though he genuinely meant it. 'And if the offer is open on Boxing Day, I'd love to come back and see if I can finally beat you at Just Dance, Bronte.'

'You can try.' Bronte grinned, suddenly sounding more like sixteen than six, making them all laugh.

'It's probably just as well you're not coming on Christmas Day, Jude.' Charlotte pulled a face. 'Because apparently Em is cooking the dinner. So you might have to come and visit us all in St Piran's Hospital on Boxing Day.'

Emily threw a cushion at her sister's departing back as Charlotte burst out laughing again, going with Jake to put their daughter to bed.

'Can I help you put some of this away?' Jude turned towards Emily, in the middle of a lounge that now looked as though it had been ransacked by looters.

'Don't you dare, you're a guest.' Emily's father moved to stand up from his armchair, but his face twisted in pain. Richard was suffering his third bout of sciatica in the past year and it was part of the reason why Emily had put her foot down and insisted he wouldn't be cooking dinner this year.

'I thought throwing myself in to games night made me an honorary part of the family? I'm sure that's what I signed up to.' Jude was already busying himself with putting the cushions back where there belonged on the sofa.

'Anyway, Dad, Charlotte will be reporting you and Mum to the elves too if you don't do as you're told and take it a bit easy.' Emily blew her father a kiss. 'You can both sit here and take it easy while me and Jude get this place straight, and then I'll make us all another drink.'

'Yes, ma'am.' Her father gave a mock salute, but the relief on his face was obvious as he relaxed back into the chair. Not that anywhere was particularly comfortable at the moment, but it was certainly better than him rushing around the way he usually did.

It only took a few minutes for Emily and Jude to clear away the games and get the lounge looking almost back to normal. Afterwards, he followed her through to the kitchen, offering to help her get the drinks, and it was the first time they'd been alone since he'd arrived.

'Thank you for tonight.' She turned to face him.

'I was about to say the same to you. I had such a great evening.' Jude smiled in a way that lit him up from the inside out. 'This was the kind of family I used to dream of having when I was at boarding school. I used to fantasise about something happening to make Sandra disappear, and my father finding someone who'd give us the kind of life I only ever saw in the movies, with loads of kids around and lots of fun.'

'I'm so sorry you never had that.' Emily couldn't stop herself from reaching out to touch his face.

'For a really long time I felt sorry for myself too, but I don't think I'd have appreciated a night like tonight anywhere near as much if I hadn't been through all of that.' Jude had a way of looking at her that made it feel as if the rest of the world had disappeared. 'I don't know what you've done to me, Emily Anderson, but I like it a lot.'

'I like it a lot too.' She lifted her face up towards his and kissed him, not the way she would have kissed him if she hadn't been in her parents' kitchen, with a very good chance of one of her family bursting in at any moment. But the kind of kiss that made her feel connected to Jude in a way that went beyond the purely physical. It was hard to break away, but eventually she forced herself to take a step backwards.

'I was thinking about you all afternoon. How did it go with your dad?'

'Really well, better than I could ever have imagined.' Jude shook his head, as if he still couldn't quite believe it, and by the time he'd finished recounting the conversation with his father, Emily was struggling with her own emotions.

'It sounds like Viv finally made your dad realise that bottling up his feelings to try and protect you was the worst thing he could have done.'

'It seems all the Cavendish men need someone to help them realise what's right in front of their faces. Although now you've forced me to admit I have feelings, you've only got yourself to blame if I start writing poetry comparing you to stars in the midnight sky, or buying you giant teddy bears clutching red satin hearts.' He laughed and Emily gave an exaggerated shrug.

'I think I can live with the consequences, but if you get me a plastic rose, or a pillow with your face printed on it, I'm taking out a restraining order.'

'Maybe I'll just kiss you again to be on the safe side.' Almost as soon as Jude pressed his lips against hers, Charlotte charged through the door of the kitchen.

'Can you two stop slobbering all over each other for five minutes? Some of us are dying of thirst in there.' Charlotte's laughter was still ringing around the kitchen when she disappeared back down the hallway, her delight at taking the mickey out of her little sister exactly the same as it had been when they were kids.

'Are you still enjoying the chaos of family life?' Emily gave Jude a rueful grin, and he nodded.

'I think I could definitely get used to it.' As Jude took hold of her hand, Emily reminded herself to be careful. It was so easy to picture Jude as a permanent fixture, but his life had been flipped upside down since they'd got to Cornwall. Everything that happened between them might be down to the shock of discovering so much about his past in such a short time. For all Emily knew, this could just be a form of distraction, so that he didn't have to process it all at once. She had to hold on to the possibility that when the dust settled, he'd decide he still didn't really believe in the idea of love. All Emily could do was pray that he didn't go back to thinking that way, because it was already too late to protect her heart from getting broken if he did.

20

On the morning of Christmas Eve, the sky was a strange mix of dove-grey clouds and streaks of pink that hung around long after sunrise.

'Do you think it might snow?' Emily turned to Jude as they climbed the coastal path towards the cliffs that looked down over Port Agnes. She couldn't keep the note of hopefulness out of her voice. She knew the kids would love it if there was snow, but she wanted it too. She wanted that magical Christmas moment featured in so many of the romance novels she adored, but which in truth so rarely happened, especially on the west coast of Cornwall.

'The sky does look like it's promising something. Can you imagine what it would be like in Puffin's Rest, looking out of those full-length windows as the world gets slowly blanketed by soft white snow?'

'Oh, Jude, I don't know what I've done to you, but I think I might have made my favourite crime writer into a romance author instead.' She shook her head in mock concern, and he raised his eyebrows.

'Your favourite crime writer? I know you've read the McGuigan books, but I didn't think it was your genre?'

'It wasn't, but when we met, I wanted to understand you. That's why I started to read the rest of your books too, because there's one thing I've learned about authors since I started working with so many of them.'

'Is it that we're all mad?' He was deadpan, but she couldn't help laughing.

'Well, maybe a bit, but in a good way. That wasn't what I was getting at though. I was going to say that the more authors I've worked with, the more I've realised you all reveal a part of who you are in every book you write.'

'Should it concern me what you've discovered about me?'

'Not at all.' Emily adopted a deliberately neutral expression, looking ahead of them to where Rufus and Gary Barlow were racing one another up the path.

'Can I at least ask what your conclusion was about me?'

'When I read the first book, we'd only met once. I could tell from the story that you were a complicated person, but I also knew I'd like you, if you let me get to know you.' Emily reached for his hand. 'And thankfully you did.'

'I'm not sure I let you.' Jude hesitated for a moment before continuing. 'You found your own way into my life, and I'm really glad you did. As for what you've done to me... I'm not sure that I'll ever make it as a romance writer, but you have changed me.'

'For the better?' Emily's teasing tone was back.

'I hope so.'

'And what makes you think you won't just change back again, the moment you get home to London?' Emily kept her tone light, but his answer mattered far more than she was letting on. She had strong feelings for Jude and they were deepening all the time. If this new version of him only existed in the here and now she wanted to know.

'Because I don't want to let you down.' Jude kissed her before she could respond. She'd wanted to tell him this wasn't about her and that her attempts to convince him that love existed had been for his sake, not hers, but she couldn't think straight when he was kissing her. Before Emily could even try to pull away and get her head together enough to explain that to him, her phone started to ring.

'Sorry, it's Dad, I better get this.' Answering the call, she expected to hear her father's usual upbeat tone, but he sounded breathless and panicked.

'Em, your mum's had a fall. She's okay I think, just a bit bruised, but I can't get her up. It's my back.'

'I'm on my way. I'll be there in five minutes, ten at the most.'

'Okay, sweetheart, I'm sorry.'

'Don't be sorry, just please don't hurt yourself trying to help Mum. Wait until I get there. I'll see you soon.' Ending the call, Emily looked at Jude, his face already a picture of concern.

'What's happened?'

'Mum's had a fall and Dad can't help her up, his back's too bad. Charlotte and Jake have taken the kids to the soft play in Port Tremellien. I need to get back home.'

'I'll come with you.' Jude was already turning back towards the harbour, whistling to get the dogs' attention.

'You don't have to.'

'I know I don't have to, but I want to. And the last thing your mum and dad need is you hurting yourself trying to help out on your own.'

'Thank you.' Some of the tension in Emily's spine eased. She wasn't used to having someone to lean on and it scared her a bit, but right now she wanted to lean on Jude, and for once in her life she wasn't going to overthink it.

* * *

Patsy was still lying on the kitchen floor when Jude and Emily got to Lowenna Close. 'I feel like such a fool. I knocked the dog's bowl with my foot and then slipped in the water. It's only my ego that's hurt really, but I can't seem to get myself back up and it nearly finished Richard trying.' She looked up at Jude. 'Sorry, I bet this is the last way you wanted to spend Christmas Eve, hauling some old girl off the floor.' Jude smiled, relieved that Emily's mother still had her sense of humour and that the fall wasn't as bad as he'd feared.

'Your wonderful daughter has spent the last two months trying to teach me how to write about romance and, from what I remember, fairytale romances always involve rescuing beautiful damsels in distress.'

'There you were, expecting Sleeping Beauty, and instead you got Flat-Out Patsy.' She laughed again and this time Richard joined in, but not even that completely lifted the pained expression from his face.

'The big question is, what's the best way to get Flat-Out Patsy off the floor?' Emily looked to her father for an answer.

'You can't just haul her up, there's too much of a risk of injury. That's why I suggested calling the paramedics, but your mother won't hear of it.' Richard shook his head, and Jude could see how tired he was. It was the same kind of look his father had worn in the forty-eight hours after his mother's skiing accident, when she'd been in a coma and Jude had desperately hoped she might somehow cling to life. With the benefit of hindsight, he could imagine the toll it had taken on his father to feel so powerless when someone he loved was gravely ill. Patsy was coping with her illness the best way she could, but there was no denying that Richard had taken on a new role in their relationship and that caring for someone you loved could be completely exhausting. It was written all over his face. The least Jude could do was offer what little help he was able to.

'I know how to do it.' The certainty in Jude's tone must have taken Emily by surprise, because her head shot up in response. She clearly hadn't expected him to know anything about first aid. 'We need to move two of the chairs from the kitchen table and put one by your head, Patsy, and the other by your feet.'

'Are you going to try and levitate me? If so, I hope you know a magic spell. I'm heavier than I look.' Patsy grimaced. 'And I look quite heavy!'

'No levitation involved, I promise. I did some first aid training when I was still at school as part of the Duke of Edinburgh scheme.' Jude looked at Emily, another wave of surprise washing over her face. 'I know that probably makes me sound like a total nerd, but after Mum's accident I wanted to be prepared if I was ever around when someone got hurt. I remember people out on the ski slope trying to help Mum when she had her accident and I just wanted to be able to do the same thing.'

'She'd have been so proud of you and I'm very thankful you're here.' Patsy blew him a kiss, but she'd been on the floor for far too long already and he just wanted to get her up safely.

'I hope she would, but she'd have wanted to make sure I wasn't all talk and no action. Do you think you're ready?' When Patsy nodded, Jude talked her through the process of getting up off the floor safely. It involved helping her into a kneeling position, and then getting her to support her weight with her arms braced on the chair in front of her, and finally using that as leverage to help Patsy into the chair behind her. It meant that

Jude wouldn't have to lift her off the floor, even though he could probably have done so relatively easily. He wanted Richard and Emily to see that it was something they could do in the future, if they had to, and that it was the best way of avoiding accidentally hurting Patsy in the process.

'Thank you so much, Jude. Do you fancy moving in?' Patsy smiled and patted his cheek once she was comfortably in the chair. 'We could do with you around full time.'

'You'd soon get sick of me.' Despite everything that had happened lately, there was still a part of Jude that suspected it was true. He couldn't help wondering if Emily might eventually feel that way too. Having spent so long convinced he was unlovable, it was impossible to undo that mindset overnight. The words that Sandra had said to him about no one wanting him were deeply ingrained and the impact they'd had on him couldn't just be washed away. He'd never wanted a long-term relationship before, so it had never mattered to him this much whether someone would want him around for the long haul. But right now this wasn't about him, it was about making sure Patsy was okay and he didn't plan on going anywhere until he was certain she was. 'Are you happy staying here or would you like us to help you through to the lounge?'

'Oh yes please, Jude.' Patsy patted his hand this time. 'Otherwise I'll be in the way out here when Emily starts doing the preparation for tomorrow's dinner, and Richard was going to put *It's a Wonderful Life* on for us, before we all watch *The Muppet Christmas Carol* together later on.'

'We'll get you both sorted so you can put your feet up,' Emily said, worry still etched on her face despite the fact her mum was now safely off the floor, with just a couple of bruises to show for her fall. Jude wasn't sure what he could do to help reassure her, but he wanted to be there for whatever she needed.

It took less than ten minutes to get Patsy and Richard settled in the lounge. Emily had helped her father into a winged-back chair where he could sit more upright, with a rolled-up towel behind the small of his back to help alleviate his sciatica. Jude had supported Patsy as she'd walked to the sofa, before putting their film on and making sure there was a bowl of Christmas chocolates within easy reach for both of them.

'I'm going to make us all a cup of tea. I think we've earnt it after all the drama.' Emily looked worn out and Jude could tell how much she worried about her parents.

'I'll give you a hand.' He followed her through to the kitchen and Emily breathed out slowly.

'I'm scared all this is going to kill Dad. He won't admit he needs help and I know neither of them will want a stranger coming in, but he's exhausted and he needs to have some time to himself, when he doesn't have to worry about what might happen to Mum if he meets up with one of his friends for a drink. He hasn't done that for ages, and if the Parkinson's keeps progressing, it's only going to get worse.'

'Have you spoken to Charlotte about it?' Jude wished he could say something to help, but he couldn't pretend there was an easy solution to any of this.

'No, but I'm going to have to. She can't relocate to help out, not with her accountancy clients being in Exeter and Jake's job meaning he's away so much. Not to mention the fact that she's got three young kids.' Emily bit her lip. 'I'm going to have to move back home.'

'You'd come back here permanently?' Jude understood why she was thinking that way, and he hoped he was a good enough person to have made the same decision in similar circumstances. But he didn't want Emily to stay in Cornwall; he wanted her to be in London with him.

'I don't think I've got any choice.' She massaged her temples as she spoke. 'I'm only renting my place in London and technically I can work from anywhere, as long as I have access to a studio.'

'I suppose that's the benefit of jobs like ours. It makes relocating really easy.' Jude waited for her to look at him and ask if he'd be willing to stay too. For a moment he wasn't even sure what his answer would be, but the longer the silence went on, the more he knew he *would* have been willing to stay in Port Agnes, if she asked him to. Except she didn't. She was still massaging her temples, a pained expression on her face. So it was Jude who broke the silence in the end.

'Are you sure you don't want to think about it for a bit longer and see what happens after your mum's operation?'

'Dad's already been doing this for so long. I need to be here to support him, because I'll never forgive myself if anything happens to him. I'll have to give notice on my flat and think about finding a more permanent solution to studio space. I might have to drop some authors, depending on how often Mum needs me. My head feels like it's all over the place.' Emily's words were coming out quickly, and she didn't leave any space for Jude to answer. It was probably just as well, because he wasn't sure he'd have been able to respond appropriately. He wanted to tell her that this didn't need to come between them unless they let it, but the last thing she needed was Jude making demands on her time on top of everything else. Emily had been straight with him from the start about how big a part love played in her life, and right now her love for her parents was centre stage, just as it should be.

She hadn't even responded when he'd hinted that staying in Cornwall could be an option for him too, and he couldn't really blame her. It was a crazy idea. He'd have laughed if anyone had told him two months ago that he'd be in this position, and yet here he was, in love with Emily. But Jude knew better than anyone that just because you loved someone, it didn't necessarily mean they wanted you around. He'd allowed himself to forget that for a moment, and he only had himself to blame for the pain he knew was just around the corner.

* * *

Emily was certain that staying with her parents was the right thing to do, but that didn't make the decision any easier. When she'd thought about what next year might look like, she'd pictured spending huge swathes of it with Jude. Spring in the city, with lunch dates in bookshop cafés, and evenings spent walking along the river, hand in hand, as the days grew longer and brighter. Okay, so maybe she was romanticising it, the way she always did. In reality, there'd be plenty of rainy days when the whole world felt grey, and they'd probably have some dates that didn't go well, maybe even some heated arguments. But she wanted all of that with Jude; the good, the bad, and the ugly bits of a relationship. She might be a romantic, but she wasn't naïve enough to believe that any relationship was all sunshine and lollipops. They could all be hard work at times, but she wanted what her parents had. She wanted someone who was willing to stay by her side if she couldn't get up off the floor, and who was happy to sit next to her and watch an old movie they'd both seen twenty times before, just because they were together.

Emily wanted to build a family and create traditions, making the kind of memories that could carry them through the bad days. She might not have known Jude for long, but she'd seen him, the *real* him, these past few weeks and they had potential to go the distance. No one could know for certain that they'd last forever. Not even when they were standing up in front of all their friends promising to be together until death tore them apart, otherwise there'd be no such thing as divorce. All she'd wanted was the chance to see where things went with Jude and to discover whether her hunch about them was right. His whole life was in London and it was crazy to think he might be willing to uproot that for her. They could try to make a go of things on a long-distance basis, seeing each other when they could. But she had no idea how long her parents would need her for, or how much of her time would be taken up by supporting them.

Despite all of that, part of her wasn't prepared to give up on Jude. Romcoms might suggest that chance meetings happened all the time, and that finding love really was that easy, but real life wasn't like that. Meeting someone you connected with the way she had with Jude didn't happen every day. Emily knew that, because it had never happened to her before. She wasn't just going to let him go without talking it through and telling him that the decision to stay in Cornwall was the hardest one she'd ever had to make, because of him. It was a big statement to make after such a short time of knowing him, and Jude might think she was crazy to get so far ahead of herself, but she had to take a chance and she needed to do it soon.

Jude had been quiet in the hour or so since she'd told him she was planning to stay in Port Agnes. Although he'd barely had a chance to get a word in edgeways when they were in the kitchen, she'd been so busy thinking out loud and trying to convince herself that everything would be okay if she moved back to Cornwall. She hadn't really wanted any suggestions from him about what she should do, and he didn't seem to want to give her any either.

They'd sat with her parents in the lounge and he'd barely said a word, despite her parents talking all the way through the film they'd claimed they wanted to watch. He'd already said he needed to head off after he'd taken Rufus and Gary Barlow for another walk, because the first one had been cut short, and about halfway through the film he suddenly stood up.

'I'm going to take the dogs out now, before it starts getting dark.'

'I can come with you if you like?' Emily looked up at him, but Jude shook his head, and it was as if she could feel him withdrawing.

'You stay here with your mum and dad, make sure Patsy doesn't get herself into any more mischief.' Jude's tone was light, and Emily's mother reached up and took hold of his hand as he moved past her chair.

'Life is no fun unless there's a bit of mischief, Jude, remember that!'

'I will, Patsy, don't worry about that.' The dogs followed Jude out in a flurry of excited barking and tail wagging, leaving the house feeling strangely quiet once they were gone, and a sense of loneliness swept over Emily, despite the fact that she wasn't alone.

* * *

She was out in the kitchen making more tea when Jude and the dogs came back into the garden. She'd been about to tap on the window and suggest that they sat out in the garden together for a bit so she could tell him she didn't want things to just come to a full stop between them, but then she realised he was talking on the phone. As he got closer to the house and leant up against the wall next to the kitchen window, Emily could hear what he was saying.

'I know what I need to do to make the final changes now,

Marty. I've got it all clear in my head.' There was a brief pause as he listened to Marty's reply.

'Yes, don't worry, I'll get the edits in on time. I'm going to drive back tomorrow evening, after Christmas dinner at my father's place. The roads should be pretty quiet.' There was another pause before he continued.

'Yes, Emily was great, but I've got what I need and I don't think me staying down here any longer will be helpful.'

She closed her eyes for a moment, trying to think of some way the conversation she'd overheard could mean something different to how it sounded. But there wasn't one. Jude had got what he needed from her and now he was going back to London, without even keeping the promise he'd made to Bronte about coming back to see them all again on Boxing Day. She wondered if he was even intending to tell her, or whether he planned to just not show up. But then he pushed open the door from the garden and she realised she was about to find out.

'Good walk?' Her words sounded accusatory, but if Jude noticed, he wasn't showing it.

'Yes, but I think you were right about the snow coming. It's bitterly cold.'

It was on the tip of her tongue to tell him he'd better get on the road to London sooner rather than later in that case, but somehow she held it in. She already felt like a complete idiot for falling so hard for him, and she was determined not to let Jude see the full extent of her foolishness.

'The kids will love that.'

'I think you're amazing.' His words took her by complete surprise, and she shook her head. This wasn't how she'd expected the conversation to go, and he didn't get to say things like that when he'd already decided that he'd taken all he needed from her. But he wasn't finished yet. 'I knew you were special, but when you said you were staying here to look after your mum and dad, I realised just how incredible you are. You've helped me so much, and I don't think I'd ever have finished the book without you.'

'But now you're ready to do it?' She fought to keep her voice steady, and he nodded slowly.

'I spoke to Marty while I was out and I've decided to head back to London tomorrow night to get stuck into the edits.' He hesitated for a moment, as if he was expecting her to respond, but she had no idea what to say to him. The idea she'd had of asking him to stick around suddenly seemed even more crazy, and she couldn't bring herself to say it out loud. So it was left to Jude to continue. 'With everything you've got going on, I'm sure the last thing you want is me hanging around.'

When she finally found her voice, her tone was so tight it made her throat feel sore. 'I suppose it makes sense for you to go sooner rather than later.'

'Yeah.' Jude had that look again, as if he was about to say something else, but then he just shook his head. 'I'll go and say goodbye to your parents, and then me and Rufus will get out of your hair.'

'Okay, great.' Emily turned back to the sink, blinking back the tears that were burning her eyes. She wasn't going to let him see just how much she wanted him to stay. She'd been a fool for love once too often already. It was time to take a leaf out of Jude's book and try to shut off her feelings, before they swallowed her whole.

21

Emily was really glad she'd offered to cook Christmas dinner. She couldn't be expected to join in with all the fun and games that made up an Anderson family Christmas while she was elbow deep in potato peelings. It also meant she wasn't able to check her phone every five seconds to see whether there were any new messages from Jude. He'd texted to wish her a happy Christmas and she'd responded in kind, keeping things short and sweet. But it hadn't been any different to the kind of message she'd have sent a friend, and not even a particularly close one at that.

She'd been about ten minutes from serving the dinner up when Jasmine had called.

'Happy Christmas, Em, I'm on my third glass of champagne so this is shaping up to be a good one!'

'That's great. Happy Christmas, Jas.' Emily put the call on speakerphone while she stirred the gravy, and she thought she'd done a good job of sounding far more upbeat than she felt.

'Okay, what's wrong?' Her best friend had always known her

far too well, but she didn't want to get into this on Christmas Day, and she didn't want to bring Jasmine down either.

'Nothing, I'm fine. I'm just on Christmas dinner duty and it's stressing me out a bit.'

'Well, that's a load of crap.' Charlotte's voice behind Emily made her jump, and her face flushed red.

'Do you mind? I'm having a private conversation with Jasmine.'

'You don't mind, do you, Jas?' Charlotte moved closer to the phone.

'Absolutely not, I just want to know what the hell is going on. It's Christmas Day and Em sounds like she's spent the day filling in her tax return.'

'She's miserable because she's decided to stay in Cornwall to look after Mum and Dad, and a certain handsome author is going back to London tonight.' Charlotte sounded exasperated and Emily was already regretting confiding in her sister, but it was too late now.

'You're staying in Cornwall?' Jasmine sounded horrified.

'I've got to, Mum and Dad need me.'

'You don't have to. I love you for offering, but I don't want you to have to put your life on hold, and I don't think they will either.' Charlotte sighed. 'She won't even let me speak to them about the option of having some paid help. I'm not denying Dad needs a break, but I'm sure this isn't the only solution.'

'I want to stay in Cornwall. It's where I need to be right now, and nothing either of you can say will change my mind.' Emily stirred the gravy so vigorously that a big puddle of it splashed over the side of the pan and almost put the gas burner out.

'Then why the hell do you sound so miserable?' Jasmine had clearly decided that Charlotte was right.

'I...' Emily had never been able to lie to her best friend or her sister, and they were already on her back, so she might as well tell them the truth. 'I did think that maybe Jude and I had something special. But when I told him I was staying, his first reaction was to leave even sooner than he'd originally planned.'

'Don't you think that might be because by staying in Port Agnes you're essentially putting an end to your relationship? He's probably gutted.' Jasmine's response made Charlotte shriek in agreement.

'That's what I said!' Emily's sister wasn't done with sharing her opinion yet either. 'Do you know what's worse, Jas? She hasn't even told him that she wants to try and make this work. He probably thinks she's not interested in him if she's staying. But if he could see her face now, looking like a slapped arse, he'd know how miserable she really is.'

'For God's sake, Em, why don't you just tell him?' Jas and Charlotte were ganging up on her now, but she wasn't backing down.

'Because he already thinks I'm a hopeless romantic and I'm not going to make a fool of myself by admitting how much these last couple of months have meant to me, if they didn't mean anything to him, apart from a way to finish his book.' Emily sighed. 'Maybe he was right in the first place and all of this stuff is just in my head.'

'What are we going to do with her, Jas?' Charlotte still sounded exasperated, but neither of them seem to understand why she wasn't willing to open herself up to any more hurt than she was already feeling. Maybe Jude had taught her just as much as she'd taught him.

'Do you think we need to stage an intervention? The queen of romance saying she no longer believes in it?' Jasmine made it sound like the end of the world.

'Maybe I've finally grown up.' Emily picked up her phone. 'I must have done, because I'm cooking Christmas dinner and I'm refusing to chase after another man who's proven he's not that into me. And weren't you the one who told me never to do that again, Jas?'

'I can't argue with that I suppose.' Jasmine finally seemed to have got the message, but Charlotte still wasn't ready to give up.

'Yeah, but if you saw them together, you'd realise how much he likes her too. One of them just needs to have the guts to admit it.'

'Well, it's not going to be me.' Emily shot her sister a look. 'Bye, Jas, have a great day, I'll call you tomorrow.'

Ending the call, she turned to her sister. 'I know you're only trying to help and I love you for it, but I'm not going to go running after Jude. Maybe he was right all along and I was chasing after something that doesn't even exist. Either way, I'm not doing it any more, not even for him.'

Emily turned her back on her sister, giving the gravy one final stir. Next time she got involved with someone, she wasn't going to be the one doing all the running. If she was going to be a romantic fool, she might as well hold out for someone who was willing to fight for her, even if that meant losing Jude.

* * *

Jude was playing a seemingly never-ending game of Monopoly with his nephew and niece, but somehow he was still enjoying it. That would never have happened if Emily hadn't opened his eyes to all the things he was missing. His thoughts had kept drifting back to her all day. He didn't want them to, but they did. She'd turned his whole world upside down and now she was walking out of it. He wanted to be angry about it, but in truth he was just sad. It turned out he wasn't doing as well at keeping that to himself as he'd thought he was, but maybe it shouldn't have been a surprise that his stepmother was the first one to spot it.

'It's been so lovely to have you here today, Jude.' Viv had come outside to find him when he'd gone into the garden with Rufus to make sure the dog didn't chase the ducks that lived on the lake at the back of his father's house.

'I've had a really good time. I should have done this years ago.' Jude might not have felt able to be honest with Emily, but he'd been determined not to revert back to the person he'd been before he met her, and he'd wanted Viv to know how grateful he was to her.

'Today should be proof that it's never too late to make a change to your life.' Viv had squeezed his hand.

'Why do I think I'm about to get a lecture.'

'Not a lecture, Jude, just a nudge. This girl you've been working with means something to you, doesn't she?'

'I thought so, but she's decided to stay in Cornwall and when I suggested that I stay on for a while too, she wasn't interested.'

'You suggested it?' Viv had shaken her head. 'Why didn't you just come out and ask her?'

'I did.'

'No, you didn't.' Squeezing his hand again, Viv had forced him to look at her. 'You're an amazing person, Jude, but sometimes you can be a closed book and you might have to spell it out for Emily in order for her to realise how much she means to you. What's the worst that can happen?'

Jude hadn't replied, even though he knew only too well what the worst thing was. Emily could reject him, and he'd had enough of that to last a lifetime. But when Jude didn't answer, Viv had sighed heavily.

'You've been through a lot, sweetheart, things that should never have happened to you, but nothing can undo that. What you've got to remember is that you need to keep looking forward, not back. Don't let your past take your future away from you too. It's taken enough already. Life is short; losing Fiona's dad taught me that. Don't miss out on what could be important because of pride. If you try and fail, that's still a hell of a lot better than not trying.'

Viv had planted a kiss on his cheek without waiting for him to answer and disappeared back inside, leaving him alone with his thoughts. He'd told himself she didn't really understand, but ever since the conversation with Viv, he couldn't stop thinking about how much he wanted to talk to Emily. Even as he sat here now, playing Monopoly with the children, he just wanted to tell her how much the things she'd taught him had changed his Christmas for the better. But it wasn't just his Christmas she'd changed. Emily had changed how he thought about so many things, and suddenly he realised that Viv was right; he had to tell her. It didn't matter if she didn't want to take things any further. She deserved to know how much impact she'd had on his life, and he wanted to tell her today. Right now. It couldn't wait.

'I think I'm going to have to concede the game.' He smiled at Grace and Hector. 'But I think I owe you both a penalty payment for losing so spectacularly.' Jude pulled two twenty-pound notes out of his wallet and handed one to each of the children.

'Thank you, Uncle Jude!' the children chorused in union and threw themselves towards him for a hug.

'Thanks for playing Monopoly with me, and I'm going to keep practising so I can try to beat you next time.' Jude hugged them tightly for a moment, shocked at how emotional he suddenly felt about saying goodbye to them.

'Are you off already?' Viv came into the room just as he let the children go. 'I was going to come in and see if you needed me to take over.'

'I've just paid off these two Monopoly champions, because they were thrashing me and there was no coming back from it.' Jude smiled. 'I've conceded the game and I'm going to take your advice and talk to Emily. After all, like you said, I've got nothing to lose, because it'll be over anyway if I don't try.'

'I've got a feeling that unlike Monopoly, you're going to win this one.' Viv kissed him on both cheeks this time. 'Good luck, sweetheart, and remember that whatever happens, you are loved.'

'I know.' Giving his stepmother a hug, he breathed out, because he'd finally realised it was true. He knew now that no matter how Emily reacted to what he was about to tell her, he'd be okay because he had people who loved him, and that was something he'd probably never have realised without her.

* * *

When Charlotte started setting up the karaoke machine, Emily's heart sank. The last thing she felt like doing was singing. She just wanted the day to be over so that she could go upstairs and wallow in the misery she was feeling. It was exhausting trying to hide it and painting on a smile, but the last thing she wanted was for her parents to think it had something to do with her decision to stay in Cornwall. In a way it did, but she shouldn't have to choose between them and Jude. If the two of them were supposed to be together, they'd have found a way of working through it, but instead he'd taken the first opportunity to run back to London. She'd been convinced their connection had gone way beyond that, and it had left her wondering if real life was always going to fall short when she'd spent so long filling her head with stories like Sophia's.

'Can you stop being so miserable and pick a song?' Charlotte thrust the list of options in Emily's direction. They'd had the karaoke machine since they were both still living at home full time, and the most recent songs were from the 2010s as a result, but they stretched right back to the 1960s.

'You could always do "Heaven Knows I'm Miserable Now" by The Smiths. You're in the right sort of mood for it.' Charlotte poked out her tongue. 'Either way, you've got to do something. It's tradition. We've sung karaoke every Christmas Day for the last fifteen years.'

'Maybe it's time to break with tradition.' Emily pushed the songbook back towards her sister. They stared at each other for a moment, neither of them willing to back down, and then the doorbell rang.

'That's probably Gary and Louise.' Emily's father moved to stand up. 'I told them to pop in for a drink. I thought they might be lonely with James out in Thailand for Christmas.'

'Don't get up, Richard, I'll go to the door.' Jake was already halfway out of the room when he made the offer, probably pleased of the chance to get away from his wife and her sister bickering about karaoke. Gary and Louise had been Emily's parents' neighbours for the last ten years, and they had an eighteen-year-old son who was currently travelling the world on a gap year. It was typical of Emily's dad to worry about them missing their son. When the lounge door opened again, Emily expected to see the two of them following Jake into the room, and she caught her breath when she realised it was Jude.

'What are you doing here?' She couldn't stop herself from blurting out the question, the sharpness of it obvious even to her own ears.

'I heard it was karaoke time.' He exchanged a glance with Charlotte's husband. 'And I didn't want to miss out. That's if I'm not gatecrashing?'

'Of course you aren't, son.' Her dad sounded as delighted as he looked, and her mother was beaming too. It was just Emily who felt as though she'd somehow dropped into a parallel dimension.

'You're going to sing karaoke?' She widened her eyes. It had been enough of a shock when he'd been willing to take on Bronte at Just Dance, but she'd have bet every penny she owned that Jude would rather run naked around Port Agnes than sing karaoke in her parents' front room.

'If you've got the right song.'

'If it's pre-2010 then we've probably got it.' Charlotte handed him the songbook. 'Check it out, it's in alphabetical order of song title.'

Jude flicked through the pages until he found what he was looking for. 'Right, I'm going to give song number 293 a go. It was one of my mum's favourites, but that's not the only reason I'm singing it.'

Jude took a deep breath as the first strains of Abba's 'Take A Chance On Me' filled the room. He kept his eyes firmly fixed on the TV as the lyrics appeared, but if he was nervous about making a fool of himself, he was hiding it well. Maybe it was because he could carry a tune; it was nothing like the butchering that Emily and Charlotte usually gave to whatever songs they ended up picking. The only time Jude took his eyes off the screen was when he sang the title line of the song. The first time he looked at Emily, she stared back at him, her mouth dropping open, wondering if she'd wake up any moment and realise this was one of those weird dreams she sometimes had when she'd eaten too much cheese or chocolate. But by the third time he did it, Jude was grinning, and she found herself laughing. He was making a complete idiot of himself, in the best kind of way, but even better was the fact that he didn't seem to care.

'I think we all got the not-so-hidden message in that song.' Charlotte was laughing too as she took the microphone off Jude when he finally finished. 'Would you like to sing something in response, sis?'

'I think I'd rather have a chat with Jude without an audience.' Emily stood up and held out her hand to him.

'Spoilsport!' Charlotte called after her, but there wasn't a force on earth that could have persuaded Emily to have the conversation she needed to have with Jude in front of her family.

'I thought you were going back to London?' They'd barely reached the quiet of the kitchen before she blurted out the question.

'So did I, but then I realised I couldn't leave without making it absolutely clear how I feel about you.' Jude was holding her gaze, and she wanted to treat this moment with the seriousness it deserved, but every time she thought about him belting out those lyrics she wanted to laugh.

'So you decided to sing an Abba song?'

'I was planning to come and tell you that I want to do whatever it takes to make this work, or at least to give it our best shot. But when I got in my car, I had a text message from your sister.'

'How did she get your number?'

'Apparently she got it off your phone.'

'I should have known she was up to something when she asked to borrow it to take a photo of the twins. She said her battery was dead.'

'She's a resourceful woman and she's also a straight shooter. She told me you were moping around, and that we were both as bad as each other for not being honest about what we wanted. She also said I should come here and tell you exactly how I felt, because you'd decided you were done with being the one to put yourself on the line and taking the risk of getting hurt.'

'That's not what I said to her.' Emily tried to give him a nonchalant look, but what Charlotte had told him was spot on, even if she hadn't said it to her sister in quite that way. It was time to stop pretending. She'd always said she didn't want to play games, and her attempts to do so had just left her feeling miserable.

'If you meant what you said or, more accurately, sung' – she couldn't suppress another smile at the thought of his karaoke performance – 'then yes, I want to take a chance on you.'

'Oh, believe me, I meant it. I don't publicly humiliate myself for just anyone, you know.' Jude pulled her into his arms. 'I should have said all of this to you as soon as you told me you were staying, but I'm still getting used to talking about the way I feel. I've been pretending not to feel anything much at all for so long, and I'm not going to be able to break that habit overnight, but I promise I'll get there. I know we've got stuff to sort out about how the logistics of all this are going to work too, but you took a man who didn't even believe in love and showed me I was wrong in the most convincing way possible, by making me fall in love with you.'

A slow smile crept across Emily's face. Her feelings for Jude had been something she hadn't been able to control, and there'd been so many moments when she'd been sure he felt the same, but then he'd close down again and pull away. She'd been almost certain he'd never admit to himself that they could have something special, let alone share that belief with her. Now here he was, putting everything on the line and taking a huge risk by telling her how he felt. Emily knew she'd be taking a leap of faith by getting involved with Jude. The thought of being with him thrilled her, but it terrified her too, because he had the power to break her heart. Despite that, there was still no doubt in her mind that he was worth it. As complex and infuriating as he could sometimes be, Emily had never felt as strongly as this about anyone before. She loved Jude, and now it was her turn to be honest.

'I had to make you fall in love with me, because if it had only been me falling for you, I'd have proven you right, and then you'd never have been able to finish your book.' Emily looked up at him. 'And Gary Barlow would never have forgiven me if he didn't get to hang out with Rufus again.'

'See, I told you love was all about transactions, and now I know you only want me for my dog.' Jude smiled, and she gave an elaborate shrug.

'Does that change how you feel about me?'

'Not one little bit. You're stuck with me now, Em, and you've only got yourself to blame.' Jude smiled again, and she couldn't wait another second to kiss him. She had no idea how many romance novels she'd read in her lifetime, but it must have been hundreds. It didn't matter how many it had been, or that she and Jude hadn't worked out the details; she was still utterly convinced that not one of those stories had an ending more perfect than this.

* * *

MORE FROM JO BARTLETT

Another book from Jo Bartlett, *Together Again at the Cornish Country Hospital*, is available to order now here:
https://mybook.to/TogetherCornishBackAd

ACKNOWLEDGEMENTS

As always, I want to start by thanking my wonderful readers. I'm so grateful to you for choosing my books and I will never take that for granted. It means so much to receive your messages of support and they really help keep me going when I'm struggling with a plot line, or another deadline is looming. Thank you all so much.

I had so much fun writing this story, drawing on my own experiences of sometimes struggling with the romance element of my books. If it wasn't for my brilliant editor, Emily Ruston, pushing me to draw those touching moments out, there'd be far fewer heartfelt scenes. I am so grateful for Emily's input and her support since I joined Boldwood Books in 2021, and I couldn't think of anyone I'd rather dedicate this novel to.

I really enjoyed indulging my love for all things Cornish and Christmassy in this story too, and I gave the protagonist a job I find fascinating as an audio book narrator. I hugely admire the talent it takes to bring stories to life through audio, and I was lucky enough to be able to consult with my own brilliant narrator, Emma Powell, to ask her some questions about her job.

This is the point where I begin to thank all the other people who help spread the words about my books, especially the book bloggers and the incredibly loyal social media supporters. I wanted to take this chance to thank as many people as possible again and, as such, my thanks go to Rachel Gilbey, Meena Kumari, Wendy Neels, Grace Power, Avril McCauley, Kay Love,

Trish Ashe, Jean Norris, Bex Hiley, Shreena Morjaria, Pamela Spearing, Lorraine Joad, Joanne Edwards, Karen Callis, Tea Books, Jo Bowman, Jane Ward, Elizabeth Marhsall, Laura McKay, Michelle Marriott, Katerine Jane, Barbara Myers, Dawn Warren, Ann Vernon, Ann Stewart, Nicola Thorp, Karen Jean Wright, Lesley Brett, Adrienne Allan, Sarah Lizziebeth, Margaret Hardman, Vikki Thompson, Mark Brock, Suzanne Cowen, Debbie Marie, Sleigh, Melissa Khajehgeer, Sarah Steel, Laura Snaith, Sally Starley, Lizzie Philpot, Kerry Coltham, May Miller, Gillian Ives, Carrie Cox, Elspeth Pyper, Tracey Joyce, Lauren Hewitt, Julie Foster, Sharon Booth, Ros Carling, Deirdre Palmer, Maureen Bell, Caroline Day, Karen Miller, Tanya Godsell, Kate O'Neill, Janet Wolstenholme, Lin West, Audrey Galloway, Helen Phifer, Johanne Thompson, Beverley Hopper, Tegan Martyn, Anne Williams, Karen from My Reading Corner, Jane Hunt, Karen Hollis, @thishannahreads, Isabella Tartaruga, @Ginger_bookgeek, Scott aka Book Convos, Pamela from @bookslifeandeverything, Mandy Eatwell, Jo from @jaffareadstoo, Elaine from Splashes into Books, Connie Hill, @karen_loves_reading, @wendyreadsbooks, @bookishlaurenh, Jenn from @thecomfychair2, @jen_loves_reading, Ian Wilfred, @Annarella, @BookishJottings, @Jo_bee, Kirsty Oughton, @kelmason, @TheWollyGeek, Barbara Wilkie, @bookslifethings, @Tiziana_L, @mum_and_me_reads, Just Katherine, @bookworm86, Sarah Miles aka Beauty Addict, Captured on Film, Leanne Bookstagram, @subtlebookish, Laura Marie Prince, @RayoReads, @sarah.k.reads, @twoladiesandabook, Vegan Book Blogger, @readwithjackalope, @mysanctuary, @thelarlbookworm, @theloopyknot. @kirsty_reviews_books, @burrowintoabook and @staceywh_17. Huge apologies if I've left anyone off the list, but I'm so thankful to everyone who takes the time to review or share my books and I promise to continue adding names to the list!

My thanks as ever go to the team at Boldwood Books, especially my amazing editor, Emily, my copy editor, Jennifer Kay Davies, and proofreader, Rachel Sargeant, who all help shape this story into something I can be proud of. I also want to thank my good friend Jennie Dunn for her final checks on the novel.

I'm also hugely grateful to the rest of the team at Boldwood Books, who are now too numerous to list, but special mention must go to my marketing lead, Marcela Torres, and the Directors of Sales and Marketing, Nia Beynon and Wendy Neale, as well as to the inimitable Amanda Ridout, for having the foresight to create such an amazing company to be published by.

As ever, I can't sign off without thanking my writing tribe, The Write Romantics, including my fellow Boldies Helen Rolfe, Jessica Redland, and Alex Weston, and to all the other authors I am lucky enough to call friends, especially Gemma Rogers, who is another fellow Boldie.

Finally, as ever, my most heartfelt thank you goes to my wonderful family, who make every Christmas magical, no matter where we spend it.

ABOUT THE AUTHOR

Jo Bartlett is the bestselling author of over nineteen women's fiction titles. She fits her writing in between her two day jobs as an educational consultant and university lecturer and lives with her family and three dogs on the Kent coast.

Sign up to Jo Bartlett's mailing list for a free short story.

Follow Jo on social media here:

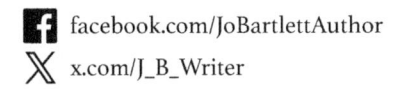

facebook.com/JoBartlettAuthor
x.com/J_B_Writer

ALSO BY JO BARTLETT

The Cornish Midwife Series

The Cornish Midwife

A Summer Wedding For The Cornish Midwife

A Winter's Wish For The Cornish Midwife

A Spring Surprise For The Cornish Midwife

A Leap of Faith For The Cornish Midwife

Mistletoe and Magic for the Cornish Midwife

A Change of Heart for the Cornish Midwife

Happy Ever After for the Cornish Midwife

Seabreeze Farm

Welcome to Seabreeze Farm

Finding Family at Seabreeze Farm

One Last Summer at Seabreeze Farm

Cornish Country Hospital Series

Welcome to the Cornish Country Hospital

Finding Friends at the Cornish Country Hospital

A Found Family at the Cornish Country Hospital

Lessons in Love at the Cornish Country Hospital

Together Again at the Cornish Country Hospital

Standalone Novels

Second Changes at Cherry Tree Cottage

A Cornish Summer's Kiss

Meet Me in Central Park

The Girl She Left Behind

A Mother's Last Wish

A Cornish Winter's Kiss

BECOME A MEMBER OF

THE SHELF CARE CLUB

The home of Boldwood's book club reads.

Find uplifting reads, sunny escapes, cosy romances, family dramas and more!

Sign up to the newsletter
https://bit.ly/theshelfcareclub

Boldwood

Boldwood Books is an award-winning fiction publishing company seeking out the best stories from around the world.

Find out more at www.boldwoodbooks.com

Join our reader community for brilliant books, competitions and offers!

Follow us
@BoldwoodBooks
@TheBoldBookClub

Sign up to our weekly deals newsletter

https://bit.ly/BoldwoodBNewsletter

Printed in Dunstable, United Kingdom